精闢分類 ╳ 漸進練習 ╳ 寫作模板

用超強英文寫作技法，

幫你深度解密，文情並茂，場場高分！

Preface 前言

　　無數的英文老師告訴學生：「國際化的世界，你當然也一定要當個有國際觀的人。而要當個有國際觀的人，語言表達能力絕對是你不可或缺的武器！」課堂教學不斷著重語言的輸入（Input），但卻忽略語言在輸出（Output）的這一環，這樣的狀況實在不太好。因為，擁有高強的英文寫作實力不只能幫助你考試奪得高分，更能讓你面對各類人馬都能清楚表達自己的想法，無論是在職場上或交朋友的時候，都可以一路順暢、走到哪裡大門都為你敞開！

　　升大教學近 20 年，所面對的學生皆是處於英語養成最重要的階段，有英檢（中級或中高級）複試作文的需求，有學測指考 28 分作文的壓力（其中 8 分為翻譯題）。但我深深了解不只是學生，就連普羅大眾的你面對一個作文題目的那一瞬間，很可能都會煩惱該如何下筆才對。

　　因此，我在這本書中以十二堂課、十二大主題的方式，特別為了對英文寫作一竅不通的人貼心設計了寫到哪裡套到哪裡的模板概念，讓寫起作文常常苦思許久不知道如何下筆、甚至連要寫出一個完整的句子都有困難的人也能填一填、套一套，就完成一篇文句優美的英文寫作，從此你不但面對英文考試信心大增，在英文使用者面前也能勇敢地表達意思。本書當然也不是讓你隨手填就算了這樣而已，針對每一個主題整理了最好用的單字、最畫龍點睛的片語，並讓你從最基本的翻譯式造句開始練習起，紮實地鞏固你的英文實力。此外，我也針對每一篇範文，從一個經驗豐富的閱卷老師的角度來分析優缺點，並替大家整理出絕對要避免的錯誤、詳細介紹每個標點符號的用法，讓你的作文沒有死角。我就是希望可以用這本麻雀雖小五臟俱全的書，讓大家再也不覺得英文寫作很可怕，而且遇到怎樣的題目，都知道如何克服難關。

　　我在讀過暢銷書《最後十四堂星期二的課》後，感動之餘也希望能夠效法書中的教授，提供讀者一生受用的課程，讓讀者擁有一生受用的作文實力，不用再花大錢去上其他的作文課。我的課程也許沒辦法像書中的老教授一樣意義深遠，但希望大家上完這 12 堂寫作課之後，不論遇到任何寫作主題都能靈活地表達自己。我希望你能每天花一點點時間填填看、練習寫寫看，或是讀幾篇精選的範文，這樣你很快就會有英文語感，寫作文的時候也不會再一直像女神卡卡 Lady Gaga一樣卡在那裡（笑）。所以，來聽聽看我的十二堂英文作文課吧！學完這十二堂課，世界就握在你的手中！

本書使用方式

密技1 精準分門別類，掌握技巧就從學習架構開始

依照英文寫作的各大方向，編製出 12 種分類，包括在「敘述說明文」中便收錄「經驗敘述」、「地方敘述」，及「人物敘述」；在「看圖寫作文」中囊括「圖表分析」、「連環圖片」，以及「描寫照片」等，旨在幫助讀者正確架構各種寫作類型的眉角，避免寫出尷尬拗口的句法，直接從零開始突破！

密技2 循序漸進練習，穩紮穩打成就強大寫作實力

為了幫助讀者快速進入學習狀態，每一個單元皆從「思路第一站」開始，提供該主題寫作要點，接續便逐一展開實用單字和句型解析，而後進入正式的模擬練習，從各兩篇初階及高階範文開始，再引入填充式作文練習，最後以高階句子填空題結束，所有練習題皆附參考解答，不知不覺就成為超強英文寫作高手！

密技3 採用模板練習，輔以單字及句型替換用法

每篇練習皆以前面曾出現的句型釋義作為基礎，透過單字補充，幫助讀者靈活運用各大萬用句型，掌握起承轉合，下筆絕對如有神！除此之外，藉由特定的模板練習，讀者還能從範文中學習不同句型使用的方法，讓英文寫作除了有高度彈性，還能畫龍點睛，精準到位又完整豐富！

Contents 目錄

Chapter 4 看圖寫作文

 Chapter 5 書信聲明文

Chapter 1
打開地圖前的注意事項

Part 1 ▶ 英文寫作常犯錯誤
Part 2 ▶ 標點符號

Part 1 | 英文寫作常犯錯誤

 思路第一站

✏️ 下筆前問問自己 ❶：動詞的被動與主動

錯誤	Suddenly, a strong wind was blowed and a big caterpillar was fell into the lunchbox.
正解	Suddenly, a strong wind **blew** and a big caterpillar fell into the lunchbox.
錯誤	The way it ate was attracted my attention.
正解	The way it ate **attracted** my attention.

　　使用動詞的時候要仔細想想這個句子的主詞是什麼，到底是誰在做這個動作。例如在第一個例子中的毛毛蟲 caterpillar，雖然它掉到便當盒裡基本上也不是自己願意的，但做出「掉進去」這個動作的主詞還是它，所以不應使用被動式。

　　如果這裡是說毛毛蟲被丟進便當盒，那「丟」這個動作就真的不是毛毛蟲自己做的了，這時就要用被動式：A big caterpillar was thrown into the lunchbox.

✏️ 下筆前想一想 ❷：除非很確定怎麼用，不然不要濫用倒裝句。

> 例句：**It was not until** his apartment was filled with smoke that James knew there　was a fire.

> 例句：**No sooner had Mia read** the note from Daniel than she burst out crying.

　　這些都是很漂亮的倒裝句。不過牽一髮動全身，動詞時態和句型的組合都會被影響，沒有完全搞清楚怎麼用的話就不要用，避免被扣分。說James saw that his apartment was filled with smoke, and knew that there was a fire. 和 Mia read the note from Daniel, and burst out crying immediately. 感覺雖然沒那麼帥氣，但減少了一些出錯的機會。

✏️ **下筆前想一想 ❸：單複數、動詞時態……再檢查一次，小錯誤無所 遁形！**

複數變化、動詞時態、a跟an等，很容易一不小心就忽略掉了。另外， 也要特別注意不規則的複數和不規則的動詞變化，如：

錯誤	doggys and kittys
正解	doggies and kitties
錯誤	He teached me English.
正解	He taught me English.

✏️ **下筆前想一想 ❹：盡量不要用 but, and 和 because 當一句的開頭 或單獨成句。**

錯誤	Whenever I am reminded of this tragic experience, I can't help bursting into tears. Because I realize that my puppy would never come back.
正解	Whenever I am reminded of this tragic experience, I can't help bursting into tears, because I realize that my puppy would never come back.
錯誤	I am very hungry. But there's no food.
正解	I am very hungry, but there's no food.
錯誤	Maria washed the dishes. And Natasha fed the cat.
正解	Maria washed the dishes, and Natasha fed the cat.

✏️ **下筆前想一想 ❺：the next day 和 tomorrow 的差別：在講過去的事 的時候，不要用tomorrow。**

錯誤	When I was a little boy, I brought a puppy home and hid it under my bed. However, my mom found out **tomorrow** and kicked it out of the house.
正解	When I was a little boy, I brought a puppy home and hid it under my bed. However, my mom found out **the next day** and kicked it out of the house.

在這段話裡面，雖然狗被踢出家門時的確是狗被撿回家當天的「明天」，但絕對不是你寫下這篇作文當天的「明天」。如果你是在2012年8月1號寫下這篇作文，你作文中的「tomorrow」就會是2012年8月2號，而不是多年前你還在念國小時的某一天。這種時候用the next day或the following day「下一天／第二天」就可以了。

✏️ **下筆前想一想 ⑥**：相似形容詞的區分：**excited/exciting, bored/boring, delighted/delighted, confusing/confused** 等。

錯誤	Thank you for your gift! I'm so **delightful**!
正解	Thank your for your gift! I'm so **delighted**!

delightful是用來形容一件事情，說這件事情很令人開心，而delighted則是形容人的心情。這裡講的是這個人的心情（覺得很開心），所以用delighted。I'm so delightful! 雖然文法上無誤，但會變成在說「我真是個令人開心的人！」，這樣稍嫌自我感覺良好，且和收到禮物這件事無關。

錯誤	This is such a **bored** book.
正解	This is such a **boring** book.

boring用來形容一件事情，說這件事情令人覺得很無聊，而bored則是形容人的心情，形容這個人覺得很無聊。這裡是在講這本書令人覺得很無聊，所以用 boring。若使用bored，表示這本書有情緒，而且它還覺得很無聊，一般而言應該不會遇到這樣有個性的一本書。

✏️ **下筆前想一想 ⑦**：平行對等結構

錯誤	This serious problem came from the technological inventions, such as TV programs, video games and **using computers**.
正解	This serious problem came from the technological inventions, such as TV programs, video games and **computers**.
錯誤	As far as I am concerned, an ideal idol should possess confidence, special talents and **be a humorist**.
正解	As far as I am concerned, an ideal idol should possess confidence, special talents and **a sense of humor**.

第一個例子同時列舉三種科技發明：電視節目、影像遊戲和電腦，應該統一用「名詞」（相同詞性且對等）比較好。第二個例子的意思是一位理想的偶像應該具備自信、特殊才華以及幽默感，同樣地，統一用名詞使得結構看起來整齊一致。

上述的錯誤句不見得文法真的有錯，但同時列舉好幾件事、好幾樣東西的時候，全部統一詞性會讓文章漂亮許多。

✏️ 下筆前想一想 ❽：not only A but also B 的句型中，A和B必須要是相同結構。

錯誤	I think that he is similar to Harry Potter. **Not only because of** his appearance **but also** his courage.
正解	① I think that he is similar to Harry Potter because of not only his appearance but also his courage. ② I think that he is similar to Harry Potter **not only for** his appearance **but also for** his courage.

和❼的狀況類似，要用常見的not only A but also B句型的時候，A與B兩者的詞性或結構必須相同。❼的狀況就算詞性不同，也不見得一定是錯的，但在這裡若詞性結構不同，文法就不對了，要特別小心。

✏️ 下筆前想一想 ❾：注意句子的主詞，後面的動詞都要配合它。

錯誤	**Keeping a pet** can not only **cultivate** my sense of responsibility but also **accompany me**.
正解	A pet can not only **help me cultivate** my sense of responsibility but also **accompany me**.

錯誤的例句說「養寵物不但能培養我的責任感，還能陪伴我。」但「養寵物」是一件事，它不能陪伴你，陪伴你的是寵物才對。如果改成以「寵物」為主詞，就不會有這個問題了。

✏️ 下筆前想一想 ❿：very 是用來加強形容詞和副詞的，不能拿來加強動詞。

錯誤	The reason I **very admire** him is his strong will to win.
正解	The reason I **admire him very much** is his strong will to win.
錯誤	Kenny **very likes** it.
正解	Kenny **likes it very much**.

切記！中文可以說「很羨慕」、「很喜歡」，但英文則沒辦法。

下筆前想一想 ⑪：which, that 的限定與非限定用法

錯誤	When I feel tired, I wash my face **which** makes me feel better.
正解	When I feel tired, I wash my face, **which** makes me feel better.

其實這兩句文法上都沒有問題，只是第一句的意思會是「我累的時候，我就洗那讓我感覺比較好的臉」。言下之意就是我還有別的臉，而且洗起來感覺不太好。理論上我是不會有「別的臉」的，所以不會用這一句。

第二句的意思就是「我累的時候，我就洗我的臉，洗臉這件事讓我感覺比較好。」這樣就沒有問題了。

在寫這樣的句子時，可以先讀一遍句子，問問自己這個修飾語到底是用來形容什麼的？像上面這個狀況，如果修飾語（makes me feel better「讓我感覺比較好」）是用來形容臉，那就不需要逗號（限定用法）。如果是用來形容洗臉這整件事，那就要加個逗號（非限定用法）。

下筆前想一想 ⑫：句子的主詞、動詞時態要統一，不要跳來跳去的。

只要在寫的時候多留意、多檢查，注意同一句裡面不要有一堆不一樣的時態和不一樣的主詞，應該就不會發生這樣的狀況了。

錯誤	I went to the night market and have great fun.
正解	I went to the night market and had great fun.

下筆前想一想 ⑬：斷句（Fragment）的錯誤

即寫出未完成的句子。有些句子雖有主詞及動詞，卻無法獨立成為一個完整的句子。此時，可結合兩個斷句，或是修正原來斷句成為一個完整的子句。

錯誤	I was late to school. Because I stayed up late last night.
正解	I was late to school because I stayed up late last night.
錯誤	I grew up in Tainan. A small town with beautiful scenery.
正解	I grew up in Tainan, a small town with beautiful scenery.

下筆前想一想 ⑭：連寫句（Run-on Sentence）的錯誤

寫作應避免直接連接兩個主要子句，卻未使用任何連接詞。要修正此錯誤，可用句號（.）分開兩個子句，使其成為兩個獨立的主要子句，或用分號（;）來連接兩個子句。但是如果兩個子句太長，則不建議使用分號連結。

錯誤	Some students are studying English some are chatting with their classmates.
正解	Some students are studying English; some are chatting with their classmates.
錯誤	The sales are dropping seriously we need to do something about it.
正解	The sales are dropping seriously. We need to do something about it.

下筆前想一想 ⑮：逗點謬誤（Comma Splice）

寫作應避免用逗號連接兩個完整的獨立子句。修正此錯誤時，可依照句意，加上對等連接詞、從屬連接詞，或是其他轉折語來連接兩個子句。將逗點改成分號也可以。

錯誤	A home is not just a home, it's more than that.
正解	A home is not just a home; it's more than that.

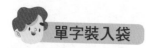 單字裝入袋

◆ 常見拙劣破題句：

❶ 自相矛盾：

Although I don't have any pets, I believe no one can live without pets.
雖然我沒有寵物，但我認為沒有人可以沒有寵物。

❷ 連自己都搞不清楚自己的論點：

Sometimes I think money can buy everything, but sometimes I don't think so. 有時候我覺得錢可以買到一切，但有時候我又不覺得。

❸ 毫無意義地向讀者解釋題目單字的意思：

What's the meaning of a house? A house is a building.
房子的意思是什麼呢？房子就是一棟建築。

❹ 對題目提出抗議：

Frankly speaking, I don't keep any pet, so I don't know how to write this composition.
老實說，我沒有寵物，所以我不知道這作文該怎麼寫。

◆ 常見拙劣結論句：

❶ 連自己都不知道自己的論點好不好：

Do you think my idea is good?
你覺得我的想法好嗎？

❷ 以老套的方式反問讀者：

My favorite is xxx. How about you?
我最喜歡的是×××。你呢？

❸ 對自己的論點沒有信心：

To tell the truth, I don't expect everyone will agree with me.
說真的，我不預期大家都會同意我說的話。

❹ 指出自己的文章不完整：

I still have many things to say, so tell you next time.
我還有很多其他的事情要說，所以下次告訴你吧。

Part 2 | 標點符號

 使用標點符號有哪些要注意的地方？

❶ 每句最後都一定要有標點符號。

❷ 很多英文標點符號用法和中文的不一樣，要注意不要搞混。

❸ 一定要把標點符號標清楚，句點、逗點要分清楚，分號、冒號要分清楚，破折號、連字號要分清楚，別讓閱卷老師因為眼花看錯而白扣你分數。

❹ 除了雙引號之外，標點符號不可出現在文章左邊開端的地方。無論空間剩餘多少，標點符號都一定要想辦法塞在句子的右邊。

❺ 剛開始練習寫作時，盡量少用破折號、分號、冒號、刪節號等等比較難使用的標點，避免用錯被扣分。

 英文寫作常用的標點符號

英文寫作常用的標點符號有十二種。不需要把它們的名字記起來，但一定要認得它們的長相！它們是：

❶	Period	句號（.）
❷	Comma	逗號（,）
❸	Semicolon	分號（;）
❹	Colon	冒號（:）
❺	Apostrophe	上標點（'）
❻	Quotation marks	引號（" "）
❼	Hyphen	連字號（-）
❽	Dash	破折號（—）

❾	Exclamation mark	驚嘆號（！）
❿	Question mark	問號（？）
⓫	Parentheses	括號（( )）
⓬	Triple	刪節號（...）

 ## 句號「.」的運用

❶ 用在直敘句和祈使句的句尾：

> 例：Necessity is the mother of invention.（直敘句）
> 需要為發明之母。
>
> Put on your coat before going out.（祈使句）
> 出門前要穿上你的外套。

❷ 較長而複雜的句子，最後收尾時當然也要用：

> 例：I forgot to wash the dishes yesterday, but it was all right because someone else washed them for me.
> 我昨天忘記洗盤子，但沒關係，因為有別人幫我洗了。
>
> I wish you would just tell me what it is that's making you so mad, because I won't be happy until I get an answer.
> 我希望你可以跟我講到底是什麼讓你那麼生氣，因為我得不到答案的話絕不會高興的。

❸ 用來標示單字或片語的縮寫：

> 例：

Monday→Mon.（星期一）	January→Jan.（一月）
Before Christ→B.C.（西元前）	Anno Domini→A.D.（西元年）
Street→St.（街）	Doctor→Dr.（醫生）

逗號「,」的運用

❶ 用來隔離由and, but, or, so, for, nor等連接的兩個獨立子句：

例：He is always absent-minded, but never fails to pass exams.
他總是心不在焉，但從沒考試不及格過。

I really wanted to go surfing, but my mother insisted that I stay at home. 我真的很想去衝浪，可是我媽媽堅持要我待在家裡。

❷ 在句中插入獨立的分詞片語時，句子前後要加逗點：

例：He is, so to speak, a walking dictionary.
他可以說是本活字典。

She is, of course, richer than I am.
她當然比我有錢。

❸ 獨立分詞片語放在句首時，則在片語後加逗點：

例：To be honest, I don't think you should try this.
老實說，我不認為你應該試這個。

Judging from his face, he is probably around fourteen years old.
從他的臉來看，他大概十四歲左右。

❹ 句子中的同位語前後要加逗點，而若是在句尾的同位語則在前面加逗點就好：

例：Mr. Fan, a friend of mine, came to visit me last night.
范先生，我的一位朋友，昨天晚上來拜訪我。

The latest album of Jay, a pop singer in Taiwan, has been released recently. 台灣流行歌手Jay的最新專輯最近已上市。

❺ 在句首直接稱呼人或打招呼時，後面通常使用逗點：

例：Boys, cheer up!
男孩們，開心起來！

Hey, I'm over here!
嘿，我在這裡！

❻ 附加問句前加逗點，以和主要子句隔開：

例：Let's go swimming, shall we?
我們去游泳吧，要嗎？

You love me, don't you?
你愛我，不是嗎？

❼ 在疑問句中要對方做出選擇，在提供選項前使用逗點：

例：Which do you prefer, tennis or badminton?
你喜歡哪種，網球還是羽球？

When should we leave, today or tomorrow?
我們該哪天走，今天還明天？

❽ 口語或感嘆語後使用逗點：

例：Well, I guess you're right.
嗯，我想你是對的啦。

Oops, I'm lost again.
糟糕，我又迷路了。

❾ 書信中，稱呼語或結尾語後使用逗點：

例：Sincerely, James
詹姆士敬上

Yours, Amy
愛咪敬上

❿ 一系列等級相同的字或子句可用逗點分開：

例：We sang, danced and chatted all night.
我們整晚唱歌、跳舞、聊天。

We have to postpone the meeting because John is sick, Jane's flight is delayed and Judy has mysteriously disappeared.
我們必須延後開會，因為約翰病了，珍妮的飛機誤點，茱蒂又莫名其妙地消失了。

⓫ 以逗點由小而大分隔地方和時間：

例：I live at No. 155, 3rd Sec, Roosevelt Rd., Taipei, Taiwan.
　　我住在台灣台北市羅斯福路3段155號。

例：I was born on February 26, 1980.
　　我在1980年2月26日出生。

 分號「;」的運用

❶ 分號常用於隔開兩個相關的主要子句，或是放在轉折語之間來連結兩個主要子句（若是三個以上，那就要用逗點而不用分號）。它可以代替 **and, or, but, because**這樣的連接詞。

例：He is very diligent; she is very lazy. = He is very diligent but she is very lazy. 他很認真（但）她很懶。

　　I regretted having dinner at that restaurant; the food there was awful.
　　= I regretted having dinner at that restaurant because the food there was awful. 我真後悔去那間餐廳吃飯（因為）那裡的菜真難吃。

❷ 兩個獨立子句若用下列的連接副詞來連接：**besides**（此外）、**consequently**（因此）、**nevertheless**（然而）、**otherwise**（否則）、**still**（仍然）、**then**（那麼）、**therefore**（因此）、**thus**（因此），那就在這些連接副詞前用分號，後面用逗點。

例：He did not pass the examination; therefore, he was unhappy.
　　他考試沒過；所以心情不好。

　　She worked and worked from morning till night; consequently, she felt sick. 她從早到晚工作又工作；因此，她病了。

　　I really want to go with you; however, I have to finish my assignment.
　　我真的很想跟你去；可是我必須完成我的作業。

　　We plan to take a trip to Germany; however, it's canceled because of the bad weather.
　　我們計劃到德國旅遊；可是因為壞天氣而取消了。

分號「;」的運用

❶ 在舉例或是表明理由時，可以用冒號來表達「就是……」的意思。

例：The students who join the competition share the same goal: they want to win the championship.
參加競賽的同學都有一個相同的目標：贏得冠軍。

The squad consists of five people: James, Mia, Sean, Jasmine, and Max. 這個小隊共有五個人：詹姆、米雅、尚、賈斯敏和麥斯。

❷ 用於信箋開頭的客套語，會比使用逗點更莊重正式。

例：Dear Sir:
親愛的先生：

Dear Sirs:
親愛的先生們：

❸ 用來分隔「時」與「分」。

例：3:45 P.M.
下午三點四十五分

2:00 A.M.
凌晨兩點整

 省略符號「'」的運用

❶ 表示字母的省略。

例：I won't be home tomorrow. = I will not be home tomorrow.
我明天不會在家。

You shouldn't kick your dog. = You should not kick your dog.
你不應該踢你的狗。

❷ 表示數字的省略。

例：Thursday, June 1, '89. = Thursday, June 1, 1989.
1989年6月1日星期四。

I was born in the'90s. = I was born in the 1990s.
我在90年代生的。

❸ 平時替名詞加複數時，不需要加省略符號，而直接加s就好，但表示字母、單字、數字的複數時就要。

例：There are five s's in "sleeplessness."

在sleeplessness（睡不著的狀態）這個字裡面有五個s。

Our teacher told us not to use so many so's.

我們的老師告訴我們不要用那麼多次「so」這個字。

Her 7's and 9's look alike.

她的7和9都寫得好像。

❹ 用來當名詞的所有格使用。如果名詞的字尾不是[s] 或 [z]，就用「's」來表示所有格。如果是[s] 或 [z]，那就直接加上「'」。要注意的是，如果前面的名詞是專有名詞（人名等），而且還是單音節，那就要加「's」。

例：my mother's earrings

我母親的耳環

my friends' opinions

我朋友們的意見

Chris's house

克里斯家

❺ 職業或人物等後面，可使用's，再把其後面的名詞省略，以表示其服務的場所。

例：I'm going to the dentist's today. = I'm going to the dentist's office today. 我今天要去牙醫診所。

I think my dad is probably at my uncle's. = I think my dad is probably at my uncle's house.

我想我爸大概在我叔叔家。

 分號「" "」的運用

❶ 用在引用句的前後。

例："I don't like her," she explained, "because she is far too proud."

「我不喜歡她，」她解釋，「因為她實在太驕傲了。」

My teacher always says, "Where there is a will, there is a way."

老師總是說：「有志者，事竟成。」

❷ 如果引用句本身是敘述句，但整個句子是問句，那就必須先用引號，再用問號。如果引用句本身是問句，則必須先用問號，再用引號。

> 例：Did he say, "I am going to college next year"?
> 他有說「我明年要去上大學」嗎？
>
> Did he say, "Are you going to college next year?"
> 他有沒有說「你明年要去上大學嗎？」

❸ 引用句中另有引用句時，用單引號表示。但要注意：美式英文中，雙引號在外，單引號在內，英式英文中則恰好相反。

> 例：She said, "I quite agree with the saying 'To love and to be loved is the greatest happiness on earth'."
> 她說：「我很同意這句說法『愛與被愛是世界上最快樂的事』。」
>
> I thought, "Wow, did he really say 'I'm the most handsome guy ever'?"
> 我心想：「哇，他真的說了『我是有史以來最帥的男子』這種話嗎？」

連字符號「-」的運用

❶ 分數用英文表示的時候，分子與分母之間要用連字符號。

> 例：one-fourth 四分之一
>
> five-ninths 九分之五

❷ 21到99之間的數字用英文表示時，十位數與個位數之間要用連字符號。

> 例：twenty-one 二十一
>
> ninety-eight 九十八

❸ 名詞與字首字合用時，使用連字符號：

> 例：Anti-American 反美的
>
> non-drinker 不飲酒的人

❹ 用兩個或以上單字複合而成的單字，也可以使用連字符號。

> 例：passer-by 行人
>
> father-in-law 岳父

a heart-to-heart talk　一場交心的談話

a strong-willed fighter　一名意志堅強的鬥士

 破折號「—」的運用

❶ 用來表示一句話說到一半，主題突然轉變，或整句中斷。

例：I believe that we should try to—oh wait, where did he go?
　　我覺得我們應該試著——喔，等一下，他去哪裡了？

　　I thought we would be fine, but—
　　我以為我們不會有事，可是——

❷ 兩個破折號互相配合，可以代替圓括弧使用，特別是一次要舉很多個例子的時候。

例：Your friends—Emma, Karen and Lisa—all told me to say hi.
　　你的朋友艾瑪、凱倫和莉莎都要我跟你打個招呼。

　　These presents—the book, the doll, and the puppy—are all from your aunt.
　　這些禮物，書、娃娃和小狗，都是你阿姨給的。

❸ 可以代替逗點來介紹特別重要，需要強調的事物。

例：This book will teach you one important thing—how to speak in public.
　　這本書將教你一件重要的事——如何在公開場合說話。

　　She has only one interest—food.
　　她只對一件事有興趣——食物。

 驚嘆號「!」的運用

❶ 在感嘆句的結尾使用。

例：What a beautiful a lady she is!
　　她是位多美麗的女士啊！

　　What a wonderful experience!
　　多棒的經驗啊！

❷ 表達命令語氣時也可以使用。

例：Go home now!
現在就回家！

Finish your dinner!
把你的晚餐吃完！

 問號「?」的運用

❶ 用在直接問句之後。

例：Do you find English difficult?
你覺得英文難嗎？

Would you please do me a favor?
你可以幫我一個忙嗎？

❷ 用在附加問句之後。

例：You don't have a pet, do you?
你沒有寵物，對嗎？

I can't turn back now, can I?
我不能回頭了，對吧？

❸ 用在選擇疑問句之後：

例：Which do you like better, coffee or tea?
你喜歡哪個，咖啡還是茶？

What do you want for dinner, noodles or rice?
你晚餐要吃什麼，飯還是麵？

 括號「( )」的運用

❶ 括號可以用來在句中補充一些其他的資訊。一般而言，如果是拿掉以後對句子的文法不會有任何影響的東西，都可以放在括號裡面。

例：For the last five years (some say longer), the house on the hill has been haunted.
最近這五年（有人說還要更久），這間山丘上的房子一直在鬧鬼。

We read "Hansel and Gretel" (one of my favorite stories) this semester in class.
我們這學期在課堂上讀了「糖果屋」（我最喜歡的故事之一）。

❷ 在搞不清楚你想要講的名詞確切的數量到底是多少時，可以用括號把複數的s括起來。

例：If anyone has any information about the person(s) who committed this crime, please call the police.
如果有人知道關於犯了這個罪的人（們）的資訊，請打電話到警察局。

In the following section of the exam, circle the grammatical error(s) in each of the sentences.
在這個測驗接下來的部份，把每句內的文法錯誤（可能不只一個）圈起來。

 刪節號「...」的運用

❶ 用以表示引用句中省略的文字。如刪節號用在句尾，另加原句句尾的標點符號。

例：Stephen King once said, "Fiction writers...don't understand very much about what they do."
史蒂芬金曾說：「小說家……不太懂他們到底在做什麼。」這裡就表示史蒂芬金講的這句話，在fiction writers和don't understand之間還有一些別的字，但引用的人可能覺得太長或是不適用，就把那些字拿掉，用刪節號代替。

❷ 刪節號也可以拿來表示講話時語氣中的停頓、或是被打斷的地方。

例："Well, I...uh...don't know," she said.
「嗯，我……呃……不知道。」她說。

"I think we should..." she said, but didn't get to finish because she saw a giant spider and ran out screaming.
「我覺得我們應該……」她說，但她沒說完，因為她看到一隻巨大的蜘蛛，就尖叫著跑出去了。

Chapter 2
敘述說明文

Part 1 | 經驗敘述

 思路第一站

✎下筆前問問自己 ①：到底是怎樣的經驗？

What? Who? When? Where? Why? How? 牢記這雖然老套但偏偏就是這麼好用的5W1H，不但可以充實文章的內容，更能讓讀者清楚瞭解狀況。讓我們以題目 An Unforgettable Day（難忘的一天）為例：

• What? 什麼事？

要是你不說清楚，讀者可搞不清楚你難忘的一天到底做了什麼。在這裡就可以說 My most unforgettable day is the day I moved to a new house.（我最難忘的一天就是我搬到新房子的那一天。）

• Who? 誰？

例如 I moved to the new house with my parents and my brother.（我和我的父母和哥哥一起搬到新房子。）

• When? 什麼時候？

例如 It was when I was ten years old.（那時我十歲。）

• Where? 在哪裡？

例如 Our new home was at the north of our old home.（我們的新家在舊家的北邊。）

• Why? 為什麼？

例如 We had to move because my father found a new job.（我們必須搬家，因為我爸找到新工作。）

這麼一來，讀者便可以感覺到這件事當時如何發生、為什麼會發生、

如何完成的，整件事的來龍去脈便很清楚。有了這樣清楚的畫面，在讀者心中就一定會加分。

下筆前問問自己②：到底是怎樣的經驗？

光是只有「什麼時候、做了什麼」等等的事實，只會讓文章看起來有如課本一樣。這時候就要回想發生這個經驗時的情形。有什麼特別的地方？為什麼這件事就是比其他事值得一寫？

例如，你可以說 Because we were moving to another city, I had to say goodbye to my friends. I thought I would never see them again, and it made me very sad. It was raining very hard that day, and we hugged and cried in the rain. （因為我們要搬去另一個城市，我得跟我的朋友說再見。我覺得我再也見不到他們了，這讓我很傷心。當天雨下得很大，我們在雨中抱著哭。）

這麼一來，漸漸就有畫面了。

下筆前問問自己③：到底是怎樣的經驗？

講完發生了什麼事之後就直接結束會太突然，也沒有一個結論。這時就可以加上你的心得感想。這件事讓你感覺如何？發生了這件事後，你的人生有什麼改變？有讓你從此對某些事情改觀嗎？同樣的經驗你還想要再體驗一次嗎？例如，你可以說 After that experience, I learned to cherish my friends even more. No matter old friends or new, I enjoyed every moment with them, because I can never know when they might be taken from me. （經過這次經驗，我學會更珍惜我的朋友。無論是舊朋友還是新朋友，我享受和他們在一起的每一刻，因為我永遠不會知道他們究竟何時必須與我分離。）

就算題目只叫你描述事情，閱卷老師看到只有敘事而沒有感情的文章，還是會覺得有些機械化，無法感同身受。所以用自己的感想收尾，可以讓文章更完整也更生動。

單字裝入袋

　　只要在這些形容詞後面加上「experience」即可清楚表達作文中要描述的是什麼樣的經驗。例如wonderful experience「很棒的經驗」、terrifying experience「很嚇人的經驗」。

◆ 表達時間的連接詞

❶	當……之時	when / while / as
❷	一……就……	as soon as
❸	有一天	one day
❹	前幾天	the other day
❺	翌日；第二天	on the next day / on the following day
❻	在那一瞬間	at that moment
❼	當場	on the spot
❽	不久	soon
❾	然後	then
❿	稍後；後來	later / afterwards
⓫	在那之後	after that
⓬	立刻	immediately
⓭	突然間	all at once / all of a sudden
⓮	同時	meanwhile / in the meantime
⓯	從現在起	from now on
⓰	從那時起	from then on / since then
⓱	過去	in the past
⓲	到目前為止	so far
⓳	目前	at present / for the present / for the time being
⓴	最後	at last / in the end
㉑	（不久的）將來	in the (near) future
㉒	未來的某一天	someday

◆ 表達正面經驗的形容詞

❶	很棒的	wonderful
❷	好玩的	interesting
❸	有趣的	amusing
❹	愉快的	pleasant
❺	浪漫的	romantic
❻	珍貴的	valuable
❼	具有啟發性的	inspiring

◆ 表達負面經驗的形容詞

❶	難過的	sad
❷	糟糕的	horrible
❸	嚇人的	terrifying
❹	苦澀的	bitter
❺	糟糕的	terrible
❻	倒楣的	unfortunate
❼	丟臉的	embarrassing
❽	不愉快的	unpleasant
❾	令人氣餒的	discouraging
❿	令人精神受創的	traumatic
⓫	令人毛骨悚然的	hair-raising

◆ 正面負面皆可

❶	難忘的	unforgettable
❷	值得紀念的	memorable
❸	奇特的	peculiar
❹	特別的	unusual
❺	驚心動魄的	thrilling

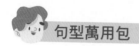 **句型萬用包**

　　開始下筆寫作前，總要想好一篇作文要如何開頭、承接、結尾。快來把以下的句型套色的部份當作模板，然後在黑色畫底線的部份依照自己的內容放入適合的單字（想不出填什麼的話，也可以參考前面「實用單字」的部份找尋靈感）。這樣就能輕鬆完成考場必備的超實用金句、一口氣加好幾分！

・第一部分：文章開頭先背這些句型！

❶ 我永遠不會忘記發生在我身上這個很（形容詞）的經驗。當時我還是（身份／年紀／形容詞）。

I will never forget the unforgettable / valuable / memorable experience that happened to me when I was a child / a senior high school student / a teenager.

---

❷ 我喜歡回想我過去的經驗，就算它們可能會讓我難過也一樣。不能否認地，在人生的旅程中，我們經歷很多事。我有個難忘的經驗發生在我（時期／階段）的時候。沒有什麼事比這更難忘了。

I am fond of thinking about my past experiences, even if they may make me sad. It is an undeniable fact that in the journey of life, we may encounter many events. One of my unforgettable experiences happened in my childhood / high school days. Nothing is more unforgettable than this.

---

❸ 無論我何時想起這個（形容詞）的經驗，我還是會覺得（形容詞）而且忍不住要 _____ 。

No matter when I think of this horrible / terrible / touching / sad experience, I still feel excited / embarrassed / frightened / upset and cannot help crying / laughing.

---

❹ 每當我想起這件事時，我不禁覺得（形容詞）。

Whenever I recalled this event, I always felt pleased / excited / regretful / sorrowful /grievous / repentant / all choked up and inundated with a multitude of feelings.

・第二部分：文章開展再記這些句型！

❶ 我還記得它發生在（時間點）的時候。

I can still remember that it happened when I was playing basketball one day/ I was hanging out with my friends one afternoon/ I was having lunch at school.)

❷ 這個（與事件有關之事）一直清楚地印在我的腦海。

The image/ The memory/ The scene has always remained clear in my mind.

❸ 每當我想到這件事，它就會清晰地出現在我心裡，就好像昨天才發生。

Whenever I think about it, the images will vividly come to my mind as if it happened just yesterday.

• **第三部分：文章收尾就用這些句型！**

❶ 這個珍貴的經驗對我有很（形容詞）的影響。

This precious experience has a great / everlasting / strong impact on my life.

❷ 這個珍貴的經驗改變了我對（名詞）的（名詞）。

This precious experience has changed my view on / opinion on / belief in / attitude towards life / my studies / my English learning.

❸ 從這個（形容詞）的經驗我學會如何（對事件的反應）。

From this precious / valuable / strange experience, I learned how to strive for the best / focus on my goals / face the harsh reality / overcome difficulties.

❹ 就是因為這樣，我永遠都會記得這個經驗。

This is the reason why I will always remember the experience.

❺ 如果這件事沒有（發生；出現），我現在應該已經變成一個（形容詞）的人了。

If this had never happened / occurred / taken place , I would have become a completely different / lazy / less happy person.

❺ 我想要再次（動詞）像這樣的事情。

I would like to enjoy / witness / appreciate / participate in something like this again.

❼ 經過那次經驗後，我瞭解到我應該（動詞），並開始對（與事件相關之事）更加留意。

After that experience, I learned that I should be a good son / stop being arrogant / take care of myself, and started paying closer attention to the little details / other people's needs / my parents' words .

 **模擬小示範**

連接超實用的單字和好用的必備模板句型，就能拼出一篇完整的文章囉！

1. An Embarrassing Experience

I will never forget the embarrassing experience that happened to me when I was **a junior high school student**. No matter when I think of this **memorable experience**, I still feel **mortified** and cannot help **blushing**.

I can still remember that it happened when **I was in a school play**, and I got a very important role: Romeo in Romeo and Juliet. The whole school came to watch our performance. I felt ecstatic because I could act in front of such a large audience. I thought I was very handsome and felt very proud. I was so proud that I forgot to watch where I was going, and fell off the stage. The crowd laughed so hard! Even the principal was laughing. **The image of my principal laughing so hard that his glasses fell off** has always remained clear in my mind.

This precious experience has changed my **attitude towards life**. If this had never **happened**, I would have become an **arrogant** person. This is the reason why I will always remember the experience.

一次丟臉的經驗

我永遠不會忘記我還是<u>國中生</u>時發生在我身上的丟臉經驗。無論我什麼時候想起這個<u>難忘的</u>經驗，我總是覺得很<u>窘</u>，忍不住<u>臉紅</u>。

我還記得這件事是在<u>我演出一齣學校的戲劇</u>時發生的。我拿到一個很重要的角色：羅密歐與茱麗葉裡的羅密歐。全校都來看我們的表演，我覺得超興奮，因為我可以在這麼多觀眾前表演。我覺得我超帥，很驕傲。我驕傲到忘記注意我要走去哪裡，結果摔下舞台。全場哄堂大笑，連校長都在笑。<u>校長笑到眼鏡都掉下來的畫面</u>往後一直清晰地留在我心中。

這個珍貴的經驗改變了我<u>對人生的看法</u>。如果它沒有<u>發生</u>，我會變成一個<u>驕傲的</u>人。所以，我永遠不會忘記這個經驗。

2. My Most Unforgettable Experience

I am fond of thinking about my past experiences, even if they may make me sad. It is an undeniable fact that in the journey of life, we may encounter many events. One of my unforgettable experiences happened in **my childhood**. Nothing is more unforgettable than this. I can still remember that it happened when **my father was driving me to my violin lesson**.

The road was muddy, for it had been raining for two days. When we were turning around a big corner, a van ahead of us lost control on the slippery road and collided with a RV head on. The driver was still breathing but was bleeding terribly. My father, a doctor at the ER of the local hospital, immediately joined the rescue.

As the siren of the ambulance gradually faded away, a feeling of sadness enveloped me. Oh Lord! Why do such things have to happen? A precious life disappeared without any warning. Whenever I think of this event, it will vividly come to my mind as if it had happened yesterday. It taught us that every cause has its effects and **every action has a consequence**. I got a lesson from the experience that **life is so short that we should make the best use of the days we are living because we don't know what is going to happen the next moment.**

我最難忘的經驗

我喜歡回想我過去的經驗，就算它們可能會讓我難過也一樣。不能否認的，在人生的旅程中，我們會遇到很多事件。我有個難忘的經驗發生在**我的童年**。沒有什麼事比這更難忘了。我記得這件事發生在**我爸開車載我去上小提琴課**的時候。

路很泥濘，因為已經下了兩天的雨了。正當我們要經過彎過一個大轉角的時候，我們前面的貨車在濕滑的路上失去控制，直直撞上一台休旅車。駕駛還有呼吸，但流很多血。我爸是這一區醫院的急診室醫生，他很快地加入救援的行列。

救護車笛聲漸漸遠離消失後，一種哀傷的感覺籠罩著我。天啊！為什麼這種事一定要發生？一個珍貴的生命就這樣毫無預警地消失了。每當我想起這件事，它就會清晰地出現在我心裡，就好像昨天才發生。這件事告訴我們，**每件事都會帶來影響，每個行為都會造成某個結果**。這個經驗替我上了一課：**生命短暫，我們要好好利用我們有的每一天，因為我們不知道下一刻會發生什麼事**。

 更上一層樓

　　學會使用模板句型寫出一篇漂亮的文章後，還可以怎麼在一些小地方讓文章錦上添花呢？

1. What I Did Last Summer

　　During the last summer vacation I worked part-time at a bookstore. As an assistant to the storekeeper, I had to classify books and put them on the proper shelves. At first, I was not quite sure where to put each book. However, after a few days, I was able to help a customer find the book that he was looking for. I liked this job very much in that I could learn about many books; what was better, during my break time, I could read as many books as possible. Therefore, it seems that I became a knowledgeable person after the part-time job.

　　By working part-time, students can not only earn their own pocket money, but they can also gain some working experience and earn their tuition. In addition, they can acquire a feeling of independence and a sense of responsibility. But a part-time job should by no means affect studies. **<u>And students are not allowed to work at places such as KTVs, night clubs, and saloon bars. In other words, students cannot be too careful when choosing their part-time job.</u>**

去年夏天我做的事

　　去年暑假，我在一家書店打工。我是店主的助手，要把書分類、放到正確的架子上。一開始，我不太確定每本書要放哪裡，但是過了幾天後，我已經可以幫顧客找到他要找的書了。我很喜歡這個工作，因為我可以學關於許多書的知識，更好的是，在我休息的時候我可以想看多少書就看多少書。因此，我在打這個工之後似乎成為一個知識豐富的人了。

　　打工不但可以讓學生自己賺零用錢，也可以讓他們獲得工作經驗、賺學費。而且，他們可以得到一種自主、負責的感覺。但是打工絕對不能影響課業，<u>而且學生不可以在**KTV**、夜店、沙龍酒吧工作。也就是說，學生在選擇打工地點的時候，一定要很小心。</u>

★這篇文章不但說出自己的經驗，也在結尾舉出其他的打工地點作比較，並提出警惕，比起只說明自身經驗的感受更有層次，加強與讀者的互動性。

2. An Experience of Helping Others

I always feel very grateful when other people give me a hand. I came to realize recently, though, that while it's great to receive help from other people, it feels even better to help others. A few days ago on my way to school I happened to pick up a wallet on the street. Inside the wallet were a college student's identity card, a motorcycle license, a monthly ticket, credit cards, a photo sticker as well as a few hundred dollars. As it contained so many important items, I thought the person who lost this wallet would surely be very anxious and worried. After checking it again, I hurried to a police station. After that, I felt relieved. However, I was late for school. A few days later, I received a thank-you note form the owner of the wallet. He sincerely appreciated my deed for saving him a lot of trouble. **The note made my day, and I still keep it in my drawer even now. From this experience, I came to understand that happiness consisted in helping people.**

一個幫助他人的經驗

　　其他人幫助我的時候，我總是覺得很感激。不過我最近開始發現，接受他人幫助固然好，但幫助別人又感覺更棒了。幾天前在上學的路上，我在街上撿到一個錢包。裡面有一張大學生的學生證、一張機車駕照、一張月票、幾張信用卡、一張大頭貼和幾百塊。因為重要的東西這麼多，我想說掉了這個錢包的人一定會很緊張、很擔心。重新檢查過後，我趕到警察局。之後，我覺得如釋重負，但是上課也遲到了。幾天後，我收到一張失主的感謝字條。他真心地感謝我替他省了許多麻煩。這張字條讓我整天開心，我到現在都好好收在抽屜。從這個經驗，我瞭解到快樂就是幫助別人。

★實際舉例形容幫助別人之後自己心情極好的狀況，強調幫助別人是非常快樂的事，開頭與結尾前後呼應，是加強語氣的方法。

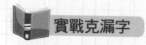

實戰克漏字

◆ 填充翻譯式引導作文

翻譯能翻得好的人,絕對也能寫出順暢的英文作文!直接開始下筆還沒有把握的話,先從把中文翻譯成英文開始做起吧!每篇文章都有中文可以參考,請照著中文填入單字片語,這樣就可以很快熟悉文章的結構、瞭解到句型如何實際運用在文章裡了。套上顏色的地方,都有套用前面的模板句型喔!

> **題目 ①：** An Embarrassing Experience

> **提示:** 先描述你最丟臉的一次經驗,描述整件事情的經過。
> 後描述你現在對這個經驗的看法。

I will never forget the 1 _____ experience that I had in Los Angeles last summer. No matter when I think of this 2 _____ experience, I still feel 3 _____ and cannot help 4 _____.

我永遠不會忘記我去年夏天到美國洛杉磯時發生的丟臉的經驗。無論我何時想起這個糟糕的經驗,我都覺得很後悔,忍不住要搖頭。

I can still remember that it happened when 5 _____ and was feeling tired and hungry. So I went to the McDonald's in the airport, standing 6 _____ to order my 7 _____. At the very moment, a tall and strong foreigner 8 _____ my toes.

我記得這件事發生在我剛下飛機,覺得又累又餓的時候。我到機場的麥當勞排隊等著點餐。就在那時,排在我前面的一個高大的外國人踩到了我的腳趾頭。

Maybe he didn't realize 9 _____, but it 10 _____ to me. I used some 11 _____ in Chinese to 12 _____ him continuously. Suddenly, he 13 _____ and said: "Sorry!" to me in Chinese. I was so 14 _____ that I had no time to 15 _____. 16 _____ has always remained clear in my mind.

他可能沒發現他做的好事,不過我痛得不得了。我用中文裡一些不堪

入耳的字眼一直咒罵著他。突然，他轉過頭來，用中文對我說了聲：「對不起。」當時我實在是嚇了一跳，以致我根本來不及想辦法回應。他難過的臉一直鮮明地留在我心裡。

If I could turn back time, I think I 17 _____ "It's ok." to him. I was so 18 _____ at the moment that I forgot one important thing, "19 _____."

如果我可以回到那個時候，我想我應該會跟他說：「沒關係。」那時的我實在是太不理智，以致於我忘記了一件重要的事情：「人非聖賢，孰能無過？原諒才是聖賢之道！」

And I 20 _____ too easily, which not only made myself unhappy, but also made others 21 _____. From this 22 _____ experience, I learned how to 23 _____. I also learned that the old saying "Don't make bad remarks behind people's back" is really true!

而我也太容易生氣，不但自己不高興，也讓別人不舒服。從這個珍貴的經驗，我學到如何作個更冷靜的人。我也學到了俗話「不要在別人的背後說壞話」說得真對！

• 填空引導式參考解答

❶ embarrassing	❾ what he had done	⑰ would have said
❷ terrible	❿ couldn't be more painful	⑱ irrational
❸ regretful	⓫ words unfit for innocent ears	⑲ To err is human, to forgive, divine
❹ shaking my head	⓬ curse at	⑳ got angry
❺ I got off the plane	⓭ turned	㉑ uncomfortable
❻ in line	⓮ astonished	㉒ valuable
❼ meal	⓯ think of a reply	㉓ be a calmer person
❽ stepped on	⓰ His sad face	

題目 ①： Cooperation

提示： 在生活中與人接觸時，有許多事我們無法獨立完成，因此常有很多合作互動的關係。文分兩段，第一段請試論「合作」的優點或重要性。第二段請舉例說明。可以是你親身或是聽說的狀況，或是你認為社會上什麼事情是需要眾人合作才可以達到效果。

    I will never forget the 1 _____ experience that happened to me when I was a 2 _____ . It taught me that cooperation 3 _____ leads to success.

    Outstanding abilities may 4 _____ personal achievement, but teamwork can 5 _____ a better chance to 6 _____ competitors. With the 7 _____ of cooperation, work can be done 8 _____, and 9 _____ can be avoided more easily.

    我永遠不會忘記在我是高中生時發生的難忘的經驗。它教我合作絕對是成功之道。傑出的能力也許會造成個人的成就，但是團隊合作保證有更多超越競爭者的勝算。有適當份量的合作關係，工作才能更有效率地被完成，不可修復的傷害才更容易避免。

    Last semester, our history teacher 10 _____ us a group report after the 11 _____ exams. Since I 12 _____ my great knowledge of history, I told 13 _____ members of my team that I would do the whole job myself, including everything from 14 _____ the 15 _____ to 16 _____ out the 17 _____ .

    上學期，歷史老師指派我們在期中考後交一篇分組報告。因為我對我歷史的豐富知識充滿信心，所以我告訴其他組員，我可以一手包辦從蒐集資料到打報告的全部工作。

    I was doing fine for 18 _____, but I soon began to regret my 19 _____. I was totally 20 _____ by the heavy 21 _____ and got terribly frustrated.

    剛開始幾天我做的還不錯，但是我很快地開始後悔當初的自吹自擂。我完全被龐大的工作量壓的喘不過氣，然後開始感到挫折。

So, I had to 22 _____ my teammates 23 _____ help. Our paper 24 _____ be an excellent I of work, and was finished well 25 _____ schedule.

所以我必須打電話向我的組員求救。我們的報告結果是一件很棒的作品，並且遠遠在期限之前就完工了。

This precious experience has changed my attitude towards 27 _____. Now, I know that cooperation is 28 _____ the best way to success. This is the reason why I will always remember the experience.

這個經驗改變了我對人生的態度。我現在知道合作確實是成功的最佳方式。這就是為什麼我永遠都會記得這個經驗。

• 填空引導式參考解答

❶ memorable	⓫ midterm	㉑ overwhelmed
❷ high school student	⓬ am proud of	㉒ workload
❸ definitely	⓭ the other	㉓ ask
❹ result in	⓮ collecting	㉔ for
❺ guarantee	⓯ data	㉕ turned out to
❻ overtake	⓰ typing	㉖ piece
❼ right amount	⓱ report	㉗ ahead of
❽ in a more efficient way	⓲ the first few days	㉘ life
❾ unrepairable damage	⓳ boasting	㉙ indeed
❿ assigned	⓴ overwhelmed	

 高階填空題

　　把文章的句型和結構都練熟了，已經有信心可以不用參考範文自己寫一篇了嗎？從這裡開始，你可以依照自己的狀況，套用模板句型練習寫作。請從以下的題目中選一個，現在就開始寫吧！

題目 ①： A Sad / Happy Experience

　　I will never forget the _____ experience that happened to me when I was a _____. Whenever I recalled this event, I always felt _____.

　　I remember that it happened when I was _____ _____ _____ _____.

　　The _____ ____ has has always remained clear in my mind.

　　Would that this had not _____ _____ _____ _____, I would have become a _____ _____ person. This precious experience has changed my _____ _____ _____. This is the reason why I will always remember the experience.

• 自由發揮的參考解答範本：

1. A Sad Experience

I will never forget the sad experience that happened to me when I was a little boy. Whenever I recalled this event, I always felt terrible and couldn't help shedding bitter tears.

I remember that it happened when I was playing in front of my home with my puppy. She was a very sweet and naughty puppy, and we had lots of fun together every day. I threw a ball at her and told her to fetch it and bring it to me. As she barked happily and ran towards the ball, a speeding truck appeared out of nowhere and crushed my puppy right in front of my eyes. The frightening image has always remained clear in my mind.

Would that this had not happened, I would have become a careless, less loving person. This precious experience has changed my perspective on life and taught me that I need to cherish life and those around me more, because we never know what would happen next. Now, I do my best to enjoy and savor every moment I have with those around me. This is the reason why I will always remember the experience.

I am fond of thinking about my past experiences, even if they may make me sad. It is an undeniable fact that in the journey of life, we may encounter many events. One of my unforgettable experiences happened in _____ _____ _____. Nothing i s more unforgettable than this. I can still remember that it happened when _____ _____.

Whenever I think of this event, it will vividly come to my mind as if it had happened yesterday. It taught us that _____ _____ _____ _____. I got a lesson from the experience that _____ _____ _____ _____.

• **自由發揮的參考解答範本：**

2. A Scary Experience

I am fond of thinking about my past experiences, even if they may make me sad. It is an undeniable fact that in the journey of life, we may encounter many events. One of my unforgettable experiences happened in my high school days. Nothing is more unforgettable than this. I can still remember that it happened when my friends and I went to a classmate's house after school one day. One friend went off to buy some drinks, and the rest of us sat around and chatted happily. Soon, we all felt very tired for some reason and lost consciousness after some time. When we woke up, we were in the hospital. It turned out that there was a gas leak in my classmate's house, and had the friend who went to get drinks not come in later and found us, we could very well be dead!

Whenever I think of this event, it will vividly come to my mind as if it had happened yesterday. It taught us that we can never be too careful when it comes to our own safety. I got a lesson from the experience that we need to be very aware of our surroundings and act quickly as soon as we feel that something is wrong. This is indeed a scary but life-changing experience!

Part 2 | 地方敘述

 思路第一站

下筆前問問自己 ①：說明這個地點的位置！

　　題目中提到的地方在哪裡？如果要去的話，大概要花多久的時間？在第一段中就先讓讀者瞭解這個地方的概況，讓他們更容易想像這個地方到底是什麼樣子。例如，你可以説：I went to Sapporo last summer vacation. It is in the north of Japan, and it took us three hours by airplane to get there. 「我去年暑假去了札幌。它在日本北邊，我們坐了三個小時的飛機到那裡。」

　　這麼寫的話，讀者就算不知道札幌在哪裡，只要看到你給的這些資訊，便能知道你去的地方肯定不會很熱，離台灣也不是那麼遠，還能知道那裡的人大概是講日文的。讀者對你描述的地方有了基本的概念，便能更容易看下去。

　　如果你沒有出過國，你也可以生動地描述你家旁邊的廟宇。例如：To release my pressure from academic studies, I always take a stroll at the nearby temple. 「我經常散步到臨近的廟宇藉以抒發課業壓力。」只要簡短兩三句便能讓讀者了解那座廟宇大概離你家不遠，而且你經常去那邊放鬆心情。

下筆前問問自己 ②：再來說明一下這個地方有哪些特色！

　　光是説這個地方在哪裡還不夠，最好再針對這裡的自然、人文特色加以描述，如該地的氣候、當地著名的景點或自然奇觀以及名產等等，讓讀者對這個地方的狀況更有概念。因為篇幅有限，也不必真的把這個地方的資訊詳細報告給大家知道，只要挑比較具有代表性的幾個點來描寫就好了。例如你可以説：The most notable thing about Kenting is its beautiful beaches, sunny weather and, of course, hot girls in bikinis!「墾丁最顯著的特色就是有漂亮的沙灘、晴朗的天氣，當然還有比基尼辣妹！」這樣讀者的

腦中就可以勾勒出相當生動的一個墾丁的畫面了。

下筆前問問自己 ③：最後當然也要加上感想！

和讀者介紹完這個地方後，一定要加上自己的感覺，不然每個人寫出來的作文不是都會長一樣了嗎？你可以說明你為什麼會來到這個地方、第一印象如何？跟自己想像的一樣嗎？最後也可以說你喜不喜歡這個地方？有機會還要不要再來？加了自己的感想，讀者會對你的文章比較有印象，而不會覺得好像讀了地理課本一樣枯燥乏味。

例如，如果你對這個地方充滿了感情，以後還想再到這個地方來（或是根本不想離開了），就可以在最後一段盡量強調自己覺得這地方有多好：The scenery here may not be spectacular enough to rival the Seven Wonders of the World, but it is still the most beautiful place in the world to me. 「這裡的景色也許沒有壯觀到可以跟世界七大奇蹟相比，但對我來說這還是全世界最美的地方。」

除了強調風景之外，英文功力高強的你還能投入情感，寄情於景，例如：Though Kaohsiung is famous for the countless tourist sites, it is its hospitable citizens that touch me the most. 「雖然高雄有數不盡的旅遊景點，但真正感動我的是高雄人的熱情與好客。」

而如果你實在不喜歡這個地方，希望以後再也不要來了，那麼就在最後一段強調自己對這個地方的不滿：I suppose I can understand why people like this place—there are countless seafood restaurants, and lots of sunshine. However, I'm allergic to seafood and hate being under the sun, so this is not the place for me. I don't think I want to visit this place ever again. 「我想我可以瞭解為什麼人們喜歡這個地方：這裡有無數的海鮮餐廳，陽光普照。但是，我對海鮮過敏，也不喜歡在太陽下，所以這不是我該來的地方。我不覺得我還會想要再來拜訪這裡。」

 單字裝入袋

要學會寫一篇作文前，最重要的是要先有足夠的字彙，以下提供描述地方相關的作文絕對好用的單字！

◆ 形容天氣氣候的單字

❶	豪雨	downpour
❷	暴雨；洪水	deluge
❸	豪雨	torrential rain
❹	暴風雪	blizzards
❺	隨風飄飛的雪	snowdrifts
❻	冰雹	hailstones
❼	冷得刺骨	bitingly cold
❽	炎熱	boiling hot
❾	令人窒息地熱	stifling hot
❿	悶熱	sweltering heat
⑪	悶熱	oppressive heat
⑫	悶熱的天氣	sultry weather
⑬	灼熱的豔陽	scorching sun

◆ 描述天氣的形容詞

❶	寒風刺骨的	nippy
❷	濕冷發黏的	clammy
❸	濕熱的	humid
❹	乾燥的；不毛的	arid
❺	風大的	windy / blustery
❻	微風輕拂的	breezy
❼	無風的	windless
❽	有薄霧的	hazy
❾	多霧的	misty / foggy

⑩	煙霧彌漫的	smoggy
⑪	星星多的	starry

　　寫與旅行有關的作文時，總會提到旅行的方式，而形容景點的景觀更是一大重點。這裡有一些很好用的單字片語，在作文裡使用可以立刻顯示出程度！

◆ 形容旅行景觀的單字

❶	度假者	vacationer
❷	旅行車	travel van
❸	邊開車邊玩的旅行	road trip
❹	站在街邊打手勢攔車、搭便車	to thumb a ride
❺	背包旅行	backpacking
❻	徒步旅行；遠足	(n.) hike
❼	市集 (n.)	marketplace
❽	冒險 (n.)	venture
❾	引人注目的景色風光	dramatic outlook
⑩	奇觀	spectacle
⑪	最佳視角	best viewpoint
⑫	偏遠地區	remote region
⑬	壯麗宏偉的（陸地）景色	sublime landscape
⑭	宏偉、壯觀的景觀 (n.)	grandeur
⑮	圖畫般的；美麗的 (adj.)	picturesque
⑯	荒野 (n.)	wilderness
⑰	遺跡 (n.)	relic
⑱	摩天樓；超高層大樓 (n.)	skyscrapers
⑲	多岩石的海灘	rocky beach
⑳	波濤洶湧	fierce swell and tide
㉑	高高聳立的山脈	soaring mountains
㉒	被雪覆蓋的火山	snowcapped volcanoes

形容一個地方在哪裡、怎麼去，聽起來好像簡單，其實片語最容易用錯。這裡提供一些與距離、方向有關的片語，在描述地方時都很實用喔！

◆ 和距離、方向有關的片語

1. 和「東西南北」有關的說法：（以"south"為例）

　　(1) S + faces south...　　　　　某地點面向南方。

　　(2) S + is in the south of...　　　某地點位於……這個地方的南部區域

　　(3) S + is to the south of..　　　某地點比……這個地方還要更南一點

【例】According to Chinese tradition, a house facing south will be comfortable.

　　（根據中國傳統，面向南方的房子比較適合居住。）

【例】Fongshan is in the south of Kaohsiung. （鳳山位於高雄市的南方。）

【例】Pingtung is to the south of Kaohsiung. （屏東位在高雄以南。）

2. on the left / right side of... 在……的左／右邊

【例】The coffee shop is on the left side of the post office.

　　（咖啡店就在郵局的左邊。）

【例】Go down the street and you'll find the department store on the right.

　　（沿著街走下去，就會看到百貨公司在你的右手邊。）

【例】John waved at me from the other side of the river.

　　（約翰在河的另一邊向我招手。）

3. S + be close to / near... 離……很近

【例】The train station is close to / near my house. It's within walking distance. （火車站離我家很近，走路就可以到。）

4. in the neighborhood 在附近

【例】My father enjoys jogging around the park in the neighborhood.

　　（老爸喜歡繞著附近的公園慢跑。）

5. at the edge of... 在……的邊緣

【例】Some trees stand at the edge of the park. （公園的周圍有幾棵樹。）

6. at the center of... 在……的中心

【例】At the center of the lake, there is a pavilion. （湖心有一座涼亭。）

7. be opposite (to)... 在……的對面

【例】The new bookstore is opposite (to) the bank.
（新開的書店就在銀行的對面。）

8. next to... 在……的隔壁

【例】Next to the department store is a fast food restaurant.
（百貨公司的隔壁是一家速食店。）

9. in the distance 在遠處

【例】After reaching the top of the mountain, we saw a castle in the distance.（到達山頂之後，我們看到遠方有座城堡。）

10. S + be situated + 地方副詞或片語 某地點位於……。
be located
lie /stand /sit

★註：以上的主／被動用法為固定，要特別注意不要弄混了！

【例】The temple is located / situated at the top of the hill.
=The temple stands / lies at the top of the hill.（小廟位於山丘的頂上。）

11. 地方 + is famous / known for... 某地以……而有名。

〔例〕Taipei is famous for its skyscrapers.（台北以其摩天大樓而有名。）

12. 地方 + is a place where + S + V... 某地是個……的地方。
地方 + is a place for +人 + to Vr

【例】A library is the best place for students to look for reference books and studyfor their exams.
（圖書館是學生尋找參考書籍和唸書準備考試的好地方。）

13. 某地 + commands a fine view. 某地的視野不錯。
=The view from + 某地 + is great / beautiful.

【例】The villa commands a fine view. = The view from the villa is beautiful.
（這棟別墅的視野很棒／看得到美景。）

14. to be surrounded by... 被……所環繞。

【例】The house is surrounded by beautiful lakes.
（這棟房子為美麗湖泊所環繞。）

15. in a beautiful / lovely setting 某處的環境很美。

【例】The hotel was in a lovely setting at the head of a peaceful river valley.
（這間飯店座落於一處幽靜的河谷上游，附近的環境很棒。）

開始下筆寫作前，總要想好一篇作文要如何開頭、承接、結尾。快來把以下的句型**套色的部份**當作模板，然後在黑色畫底線的部份依照自己的狀況放入適合的單字（想不出填什麼的話，也可以可參考前面「實用單字」的部份找尋靈感）。這樣就能輕鬆完成考場必備的超實用金句、一口氣加好幾分！

• 第一部分：文章開頭先背這些句型！

❶ 我最喜歡的（名詞）是（地點／場所），它的位置在（形容地方的位置）。

My favorite place / country / vacation spot is the park / Kenting / Egypt, which is not very far from my home / a two-hour drive from my home / in Europe.

---

❷ 我上次去（名詞）是在我（名詞）的時候。

The last time I went to the zoo / Taipei / Hawaii was when I was a little boy / in high school / ten years old.

---

❸（地名）是個多面的（名詞），在這裡你能體驗（名詞）和瞭解（名詞）。

Taipei / New York / Taichung is a city / place / scenic spot of many faces. Here you can experience a relaxed lifestyle / a rich cultural history / a fast-paced lifestyle and understand the value of traditional food / the way farmers live / the beauty and warmth of humanity.

---

❹（地名）是個（名詞）和喜歡（形容詞）氣氛的人的天堂。

Taichung / California / the beach is a paradise for both shoppers / animal-lovers / geeks and people who enjoy a(n) comfortable / calming /exciting atmosphere.

---

❺（過去的時間）的時候，（人）去了（地名），要（動詞）。

Last week / yesterday / last Tuesday my family / I / my friends and I went to Kenting National Park / the zoo / the beach to have some fun / spend our weekend / visit some relatives.

---

❻ 説到（名詞），（地名）總是我最先想到的地方。

When it comes to my favorite place / my secret refuge / good honeymoon spots, my school / my little attic / Hawaii is always the first place that comes to my mind.

❼ （地名）是個我實在不得不（v.+ing）的地方。

Taichung / Penghu / Finland is a place that I really can't help liking / adoring / hating.

• 第二部分：文章開展再記這些句型！

❶ 除了那些（名詞）以外，（地名）也有一些（名詞），譬如說（名詞）。

In addition to all the tall buildings / trees / lakes, Taiwan / Russia / Ilan offers some great scenery / great food / tourist attractions, such as Buffalo chicken wings / the Lake Chateau / ancient temples.

❷ 因為（名詞），在（動詞）很容易就（名詞）。

Due to the confusing pathways / the hordes of people / the terrible traffic jams, it is very easy to get lost / find good hotels / get stuck in the traffic in Taipei / Taoyuan / the forest.

❸ 對（名詞）來說，在（名詞）這個地方不只有（名詞）還有（地名）。

For shopaholics / otaku / nature-lovers, there are not only lots of cute boutiques / exciting rides / lots of cute animals but also really good Italian food / fun activities / lots of trees in Tainan / the national park / the area.

❹ 在（城市、國家名）這個地方，氣候很（形容詞）、居民很（形容詞）、城市很（形容詞）。

In Changhua / Kaohsiung / Tokyo, the climate is humid / dry / warm, the residents are friendly / busy / cold and the city is vibrant / bustling / spectacular.

❺ 每當我去（地名）的時候，我總是覺得（形容詞），因為那實在是個（形容詞）的地方。

When I go to the mall / Taitung / London, I always feel happy / excited / inspired / worried because it is such a strange / lively / relaxing / lovely place.

---

❻ 那裡的（名詞）和（名詞）是一些我覺得（地名）是個很（形容詞）的地方的原因。

The friendly people / pretty scenery / dirty streets and the sandy beaches / straight roads / ugly houses are some of the reasons that I find Kenting / Japan / Australia a very attractive / nice / terrible place.

---

❼ 有人認為（地名）是個（形容詞）的地方，但其實它很（形容詞）。

Some people think that Taiwan / Nantou / Malaysia is a dangerous / hot / ugly place, but it's actually very safe / cold / beautiful.

・第三部分：文章收尾就用這些句型！

❶ 去（地名）對我來說是我心靈的靈藥，能鼓舞我的意志。

To go to the amusement park / the basketball courts / Hualien is, to me, the elixir for my soul as well as stimulation of my will.

---

❷ 很多人都專注在（名詞）上，但他們常常都忘了（地名）也有可能成為（名詞）。

While most people focus their attention on dazzling buildings / fantastic scenic spots / the biggest cities, it is often forgotten that Taiwan / Korea / the local park has the potential to be an international city / a fun place to spend the weekend / a place that soothes the nerves.

---

❸ 如果你想要一趟（形容詞）的旅程，（地名）很值得你一遊。

If you would like to have a exciting / inspiring / relaxing trip, Mt. Ali / Nantou / Istanbul is worth your visiting.

❹（地名），一個（**adj. + n.**），永遠歡迎我們來（動詞）。

Taipei / Chiayi / Boston / Sun Moon Lake, **a** beautiful city / lovely place / traditional town, **always welcomes us to** visit / have fun / call it home.

---

❺ 這是一趟很（形容詞）的旅行，我希望我們可以（動詞）。

It was a great / disastrous / amazing **trip, and I hope we can** (v.) come back to visit again / come here every year / steer clear of places like this in the future.

---

❻ 和（地名）相比，（地名）有更多（名詞）、更多（名詞）和更多（名詞）。

Compared to my home / China / our train station, Taipei / Taiwan / their train station **has more** food / vending machines / gift shops, **more** bookstores / beautiful parks / tall buildings, **and more** people / houses / buses.

---

❼ 我現在有時還是會想到去（地名）的那趟旅程。當我心情不好的時候，我可以用這個快樂的回憶來讓自己開心起來。

I still think about the trip to Canada / Tainan / Japan sometimes, even now. When I feel down, I can use this happy memory to cheer myself up.

---

❽ 我已經是在（v+ing）（地名）的專家了。下次，讓我當你的導遊吧！

I have become quite an expert in finding good boutiques / driving / taking photos in Turkey / London / Nanjing. Next time, let me be your tour guide!

連接超實用的單字和好用的必備模板句型，就能拼出一篇完整的文章囉！這裡就有兩篇例子，並附上翻譯。就照著這個方法來套套看吧！

1. My Favorite Retreat

My favorite **retreat** is **Nan-liao fishing port**, which is **about a hundred meters from my home**. I go there very often, especially when I am stressed out. As long as I am standing by the sea, I feel all the obstacles in life drifting away with the current. The sound of the ocean surf can cleanse my mind from pessimistic thoughts, and I can return to my study with full attention.

I went there again just three days before GSAT (General Scholastic Ability Test), during the late night. Due to the **mild weather**, it was easy to **see a myriad of stars glittering in the sky as if they were putting the spotlight on me**. Enjoying such beautiful scenery and breathing the freshening air, I shed the pressure coming from the GSAT for the time being. At that moment, I felt myself totally integrated with the tranquility of the night. And I also swore to the stars above me, hoping that I would do extremely well in the GSAT. When I go to **Nan-liao fishing port**, I always feel **relaxed** because it is such a **peaceful** place. To go to **Nan-liao fishing port** is, to me, the elixir for my soul as well as stimulation of my will.

我最愛去的僻靜場所

我最愛**去的僻靜場所**是**離我家差不多一百公尺遠**的**南寮漁港**。我常常去那邊，尤其當我感到壓力很大的時候。只要站在近海的地方，就覺得我所有生活中的阻礙都隨著波浪流走了。海浪拍擊的聲音可以洗滌我悲觀的想法，然後我又可以全神貫注的回歸我的課業上。

就在學測考試的前三天深夜，我再次到了那個港口。因為**天氣很溫和**，很容易**看到天上的繁星們閃閃爍爍，好像把光線都聚焦在我身上一樣**。欣賞如斯美景，呼吸著振奮精神的空氣，我真的覺得我把來自學測的壓力暫時拋開了。就在那個時候，我感覺自己完全和平靜的夜色融為一體。而我也對著天空的星星立誓，希望我在學測中可以表現得非常好。每當我去**南寮漁港**，我總是覺得**很放鬆**，因為那實在是個**平靜**的地方。對我來說，到**南寮漁港**不但是我心靈的靈藥，同時也能鼓舞我的意志。

2. Taipei City

<u>**Taipei**</u> is a <u>**city**</u> of many faces. Here you can experience <u>**a typical urban lifestyle**</u> and understand <u>**the traditional value of Chinese culture**</u>.

In addition to <u>**all the skyscrapers and tall office buildings**</u>, <u>**Taipei**</u> still offers <u>**some amazing Greens**</u>, such as <u>**Ta-An Forest Park**</u>, <u>**Taipei Botanical Garden and Yangmingshan National Park**</u>.

As the capital of the ROC, Taipei is the political, financial and fashion center of the island. Taipei 101, though recently surpassed by the Burj Khalifa in Dubai, still holds the position of the landmark of Taipei, attracting thousands of people who want to follow the latest fashion and experience a fashionable lifestyle every day. <u>**The Eslite Bookstore**</u>, <u>**which stays open for 24 hours**</u>, is a paradise for both <u>**booklovers and night owls**</u>. Due to the <u>**excellent public transportation system**</u>, <u>**including the MRT and buses**</u>, it is very easy to <u>**get around**</u> in <u>**Taipei**</u>.

If you would like to have a <u>**fun**</u>, <u>**fast-paced**</u> trip, <u>**Taipei**</u> is worth your visiting. <u>**Taipei**</u>, a <u>**lively**</u> city, always welcomes us to <u>**have fun adventures**</u>.

台北市

<u>台北</u>是個多面的<u>城市</u>，在這裡你能體會<u>典型的都會生活</u>，也能瞭解<u>中國文化中傳統的價值</u>。除了<u>高樓大廈和辦公大樓</u>之外，台北還有<u>令人驚奇的多處綠地</u>，像是<u>大安森林公園</u>、<u>台北植物園還有陽明山國家公園</u>。

做為中華民國的首都，台北同時是政治、金融和流行的中心。「台北一〇一」雖然最近已被杜拜的哈里發塔超越，仍是台北地標，每天吸引了成千上萬想要跟上最新時尚、體驗流行生活的人來到此地。<u>二十四小時營業的誠品書店</u>，是<u>愛書人</u>和<u>夜貓族</u>的天堂。有了<u>由捷運和公車所形成的優良大眾運輸系統</u>，在<u>台北趴趴走</u>一點也不難。

如果你想要來趟<u>有趣</u>、<u>快速</u>的旅程，<u>台北</u>很值得你來訪。<u>台北</u>是個<u>有活力</u>的城市，總是歡迎我們來<u>享受愉快的冒險</u>。

學會使用模板句型寫出一篇漂亮的文章後，還可以怎麼在一些小地方讓文章錦上添花呢？看看其他同學的作品，注意他們有哪些地方值得學習，加入這些特色，讓文章更有變化、更加分！

1. Changhua, a Great Town

Changhua is located in the center of Taiwan. It is a part of the Chianan Plains. Changhua is well-known for its fertile soil and is called "the granary of Taiwan". In the 1700s, Lugang was a major political and economic town. Therefore, there is an old saying "I-Fu, Erh-Lu, San-Mengchia" (Tainan first, Lugang second, and Taipei third), which represents the importance of Changhua.

Furthermore, the Dadu River has rich ecological sources and attracts families to visit on weekends. Changhua has been an important fortress since the Ching Dynasty. It owns rich cultural sites, such as Confucius Temples, Buddhist Temples, Taoist Temples and ancient schools, etc. The buildings have delicate structures and are well-preserved.

彰化，一個很棒的城市

彰化位於台灣中部地區，屬於嘉南平原的一部分。彰化以豐富的沃土聞名，而且被稱為「台灣的糧倉」。在18世紀，鹿港是主要的政治以及經濟重鎮。因此有一句古老諺語「一府二鹿三艋舺」（一是台南，二是鹿港，三是台北），這句話突顯彰化的重要性。

此外，大肚溪擁有豐富的生態資源，所以吸引很多家庭在週末時拜訪這邊。自清朝開始，彰化已經是重要要塞。這裡富有文化古蹟，例如；孔廟、佛寺、道觀和古老學堂……等等。這些建築物架構精緻而且保存良好。

★本文使用了不少較難的字，顯示出程度，但較缺乏感情，所以即使對彰化的描述不少，但因為沒有半點寫作者的心得感想，以至於看起來似乎比較像是地理課本而不像是作文，會令閱卷老師懷疑寫作的人是不是真心覺得彰化是個很棒的城市。

2. The Place I Miss the Most

I used to live in a lovely little town with very few people. I know all of my neighbors, all the storekeepers in all the stores (I loved the lady who owned the ice cream store the most), and every little detail of the town roads. I would watch the perfect pink-and-orange sunset every evening, and gaze at the stars at night. Because there weren't many people to meet, I mostly kept to myself and learned to enjoy solitude.

Now, I live in a bustling city. People are everywhere, and I never felt lonely. I have friends to hang out with, and can always find someone to chat with. It is great—except sometimes, when I want to watch the sunset, I can't because there are too many tall buildings. There is no lovely ice cream store lady here either. Also, when I feel like spending some time by myself, it's impossible. It's times like these that make me miss my little town that I will never have a chance to return to.

我最想念的地方

　　我以前住在一個人很少的小鎮上。我認識我每個鄰居、每家店裡的每個店主（我尤其喜歡冰淇淋店的太太）、和小鎮路上全部的小細節。我每天傍晚都會觀賞完美的粉紅橘色夕陽，晚上凝視星星。因為那裡沒什麼人可以認識，我幾乎都自己一個人，並學會享受孤獨。

　　現在我住在一個喧鬧的城市。到處都是人，我從來不覺得寂寞。我有朋友可以一起玩，而且隨時都找得到人聊天。實在是太棒了，但有時候我想看夕陽時，因為高樓太多，我看不到。這裡也沒有可愛的冰淇淋店太太。還有，當我想要自己一個人時，根本就不可能真的一個人。這種時候我就會想念我的小鎮，那個我再也沒有機會回去的小鎮。

★用兩段來對比兩個不同的地方，可以有效突顯自己想念某個地方的理由，直接把小鎮稱為「我的」（my town）更能讓自己對它的喜愛一目了然。不過開頭和結尾都太倉促，比較沒有完整的感覺。

實戰克漏字

◆ 填充翻譯式引導作文

翻譯能翻得好的人，絕對也能寫出順暢的英文作文！直接開始下筆還沒有把握的話，先從把中文翻譯成英文開始做起吧！每篇文章都有中文可以參考，請照著中文填入單字片語，這樣就可以很快熟悉文章的結構、瞭解到句型如何實際運用在文章裡了。套上顏色的地方，都有套用前面的模板句型喔！

題目 ①： Taichung City

提示： 就你所知，描述出你心目中台中市的樣子，並與自己的家鄉做比較。如果你的家鄉本來就是台中市，則敘述對台中市未來的展望。

Taichung is a paradise for both 1 _____ and people who enjoy a 2 _____ atmosphere. For 3 _____ , there are not only huge 4 _____ but also many European-style 5 _____ stores in Taichung.

台中對於血拼族及喜愛享受輕鬆氣氛的人是個天堂。對血拼族而言，台中不但有很大的百貨公司，也有很多歐式的精品店。

After a long day of shopping, people can 6 _____ in 7 _____ cafes or in teahouses located in 8 _____ Chinese gardens. Besides, the National 9 _____ of Natural Science provides people with an 10 _____ and 11 _____ place to spend their weekends. While most people in Taiwan focus their attention on the 12 _____ between Taipei and Kaohsiung, it is often forgotten that Taichung has the potential to be an international 13 _____ .

在一天的採購之後，人們可以在寬敞的咖啡館或是座落於中式傳統花園中的茶樓中小憩聊八卦。此外，國立自然科學博物館還提供了一個寓教於樂的週末去處。台灣人大都注意台北和高雄之間的競爭，卻常忘了台中其實也同樣具有發展為國際大都會的潛力。

Compared to my 14 _____ , Taichung has more interesting restaurants, more fun places to spend the weekend at, and more convenient means of 15 _____ . Perhaps, if I get a chance in the future, I can live in Taichung!

和我的家鄉相比,台中有更多有趣的餐廳、更多好玩的、可以度過週末的地方,更多便利的交通方式。也許,如果我未來有機會,我可以住在台中!

• 填空引導式參考解答

❶ shopaholics	❻ rest and gossip	⓫ entertaining
❷ relaxing	❼ spacious	⓬ competition
❸ shopaholics	❽ traditional	⓭ metropolis
❹ department stores	❾ Museum	⓮ hometown
❺ boutique	❿ educational	⓯ transportation

提示：請寫一篇文章敘述和自己的家人一同出遊的詳細過程，及你對這次旅行的感想。

Last weekend my family went to Yangmingshan 1 _____ to see the 2 _____. Due to the 3 _____, it is very easy to get into 4 _____ on Yangmingshan. We made our way up the mountain at the speed of a snail. Fortunately, the weather was lovely, the skies were clear, and we had enough snacks in the car to ease our hunger, so the trip itself was fairly 5_____. Though we set out early in the morning, it was late afternoon by the time we reached our Bed and Breakfast. Since the splendid 6 _____ couldn't be viewed in the dark, we retired early and enjoyed the hot spring tubs that they had in each room.

上週末我和家人去陽明山國家公園賞櫻。因為人潮眾多，很容易就會在陽明山上塞車。我們以蝸牛般的速度上山，幸好天氣良好，天空晴朗，而我們在車上有足夠的食物可以填填肚子，因此路程本身也還蠻好玩的。雖然我們早上很早就出發了，但到達民宿時已經快傍晚了。既然黑夜中無法觀賞美妙的景色，我們就提早進房，享受每個房間提供的溫泉浴。

The following day, we woke up at the crack of 7 _____ and set out on one of the 8 _____ recommended by the 9 _____. The view of the cherry trees in full blossom was 10 _____, and we 11 _____ many pictures as we went along. In addition to all the beautiful 12 _____, Yangmingshan offers lots of 13 _____ worth exploring. We for example explored the hiking trail that crosses over the extinct 14 _____ Seven Star Mountain. After we came back, sweating but happy, we had a light meal at the hotel before driving back home. I still think about the trip to Yangmingshan sometimes, even now. When I feel down, I can use this happy memory to cheer myself up. It was a 15_____ trip, and I hope we can 16 _____ Yangmingshan next year.

隔天,我們天亮的時候就出發前往旅遊手冊裡面推薦的步道。盛開的櫻花樹美得令人窒息,我們邊走邊拍了很多照片。除了這麼多漂亮的櫻花外,陽明山還有很多值得探險的小徑。例如我們就沿著越過死火山七星山的步道探險。等到我們回來後,流著汗卻很快樂,我們在旅館簡單地吃了一餐才開車回家。我現在有時還是會想到去陽明山的那趟旅程。當我心情不好的時候,我可以用這個快樂的回憶來讓自己開心起來。這是趟很棒的旅行,我希望我們明年能再舊地重遊。

• 填空引導式參考解答

❶ National Park	❼ dawn	⓭ trails
❷ cherry blossoms	❽ paths	⓮ volcano
❸ huge crowds	❾ guidebook	⓯ wonderful
❹ traffic jams	❿ breathtaking	⓰ revisit
❺ enjoyable	⓫ snapped	
❻ scenery	⓬ cherry blossoms	

高階填空題

　　把文章的句型和結構都練熟了，已經有信心可以不用參考範文自己寫一篇了嗎？從這裡開始，你可以依照自己的狀況，套用模板句型練習寫作。請從以下的題目中選一個，現在就開始寫吧！

> **題目 ①**：The Place which I Want to Visit the Most

_____ is a _____ of many faces. Here you can experience _____ and understand _____. _____ is a paradise for both _____ and people who enjoy a _____ atmosphere. For _____, there are not only _____ but also _____ in _____ _____ _____.

_____ _____ _____ _____ _____ _____ _____ _____ _____. _____, a _____, always welcomes us to _____ _____. _____ _____.

• 自由發揮的參考解答範本：

1. The Place which I Want to Visit the Most

Hawaii, the place which I want to visit the most, is a land of many faces. Here you can experience diving and surfing and understand the laid-back islander lifestyle. Hawaii is a paradise for both honeymooners and people who enjoy a relaxed atmosphere. For tourists, there are not only luscious beaches but also amazing shopping malls in Hawaii.

Hawaii is almost always sunny, but contrary to popular belief, it's never hot. Also contrary to popular belief, Hawaii is not all beaches and flat land. There are many mountains, even volcanoes. It rains sometimes, but the sun comes out again in mere seconds. The people are friendly, and the sunset is spectacular. Hawaii, a state with lots of rainbows and sunshine, always welcomes us to have fun and hang loose. That's why it's the place I want to visit the most.

題目 ②： My Favorite Place in the World

     My favorite _____ is _____, which is _____. The last time I went to _____ was when I was a _____. In _____, the climate is _____, the residents are _____ and the city is _____. Due to _____, it is very easy to _____ in _____ _____.

     _____ ____
_____ _____
_____ _____
_____ _____
_____ _____
_____ _____
_____ _____
_____. To go to _____ is, to me, the elixir for my soul as well as stimulation of my will. If you would like to have a _____ trip, _____ is worth your visiting.

• 自由發揮的參考解答範本：

2. My Favorite Place in the World

My favorite place in the world is my grandparents' house in Hsinchu, which is a one-hour drive from where I live. The last time I went to Hsinchu was when I was a high school student. In Hsinchu, the climate is breezy, the residents are friendly and the city is lively. Due to the strong winds, it is very easy to have your umbrellas damaged in Hsinchu, but it does not make me like the place less, because when I see my grandparents, I forget all my worries!

My grandparents like to take me to get delicious meat ball soup and to take walks in Tsing-Hua University. I love those afternoons I spend with them. To go to my grandparents' house in Hsinchu is, to me, the elixir for my soul as well as stimulation of my will. If you would like to have a calming, relaxing trip, Hsinchu is worth your visiting.

Part 3 | 人物敘述

 思路第一站

下筆前問問自己 ①：想好需描述的人物有哪些特點？

每個人都是獨一無二的，所以無論想要形容的人是誰，一定能想出一些他／她和其他人不一樣的特點。就靠這些特點讓你形容的人栩栩如生地出現在大家面前吧！

假設題目偏向正面，就想一些好的特點。若是不見得一定正面、中庸性質的題目，則朝正面或負面發展都可以，看你覺得哪一個角度方便下手。若能想出三個特點，在結構上來說是很理想的數字。

例：My Idol 我的偶像

My Favorite Teacher 我最喜歡的老師

My Best Friend 我最要好的朋友

這些明顯地就是要你寫出這些人令你喜歡的地方，所以可以舉出優點。

例：My Neighbor 我的鄰居

My Teacher 我的老師

An Unforgettable Person 一個難忘的人

這樣的題目就不一定要寫優點，因為鄰居和老師都不見得是你喜歡的人，而難忘的人可能也是討厭得令你難忘。這時就看你覺得從哪個角度來寫比較容易發揮了。

🖊️ 下筆前問問自己 ②：再舉例並說明影響！

光是舉出這個人的特點還不夠，還需指出這些特點造成什麼影響，或者是舉出實際的例子來證明這個人有這些特點。

例：My friend is a very strong and brave person. 「我朋友是個很強壯、
很勇敢的人。」 這樣還不夠，光是看這句讀者無法知道他到底有
多強壯、多勇敢。

你可以說：Because my friend is a very strong person, people always ask him to carry heavy things for them. 「因為我朋友是個很強壯的人，人們總是請他幫忙搬重物。」

或是：My friend is very brave. All my classmates scream and hide when they see a cockroach in the classroom, but my friend just calmly picks it up and throws it out of the window. 「我朋友很勇敢。我的同學們在教室裡看到蟑螂的時候都慘叫、到處躲，但我朋友都會很平靜地把蟑螂拿起來丟出窗外。」

這樣的話，你所形容的人就變得生動多了，文章內容也可以因此豐富一些。把每個特點和這些特點造成的影響或實際例子按照順序對應排好，文章就可以變得有條理、循序漸進。

🖊️ 下筆前問問自己 ③：加上結論，讓文章更完整！

以上所敘述的這個人的特點，讓你有什麼想法？你想要也擁有這些特點嗎？還是完全不想要呢？你會希望身邊有更多人有這些特點嗎？你會希望這個人繼續保持這些特點，還是最好不要呢？這個人的特點改變了你的人生嗎？將自己的感想寫出來，為文章做個收尾吧。

 單字裝入袋

◆ 描述外表

近視眼	near-sighted	體質	constitution
戴眼鏡	wearing glasses	強健	with strong constitution
身材很高	tall in stature	彪形大漢	burly chap
身材很矮	short in stature	老當益壯	old but vigorous
六呎高	six feet tall	身高	height
胖	heavy / fat	體重	weight
圓胖	chubby	優雅	graceful
矮矮胖胖	chunky	矮小	diminutive
粗壯	stout	瘦小	slight of figure
結實	stocky	豐滿	round out
健壯	robust	豐腴	plump
留短髮	short-haired	鬢髮	hair on the temples
留長髮	long-haired	柳腰	small waist
留平頭	with a crew cut	過胖	obese
留辮子	wearing braids	啤酒肚	big-bellied
運動員的體格	have an atheletic build	臃腫	encumbered
憔悴	wan and sallow	枯瘦	gaunt
骨瘦如柴	all skin and bone	衰弱	emaciated
苗條	slender	柔弱	delicate

硬朗	virile	虛弱	debilitated
結實	solid	有氣無力	feeble
面黃肌瘦	sallow and emaciated	有活力的	vigorous

◆ 描述個性

性急	hot-tempered	外向	extroverted
樂觀	optimistic	內向	introverted
悲觀	pessimistic	好問	inquisitive
體諒	considerate	好爭論	argumentative
小心眼的	narrow-minded	頑固	stubborn
思想開放	open-minded	無私心	fair-minded
圓胖	chubby	優雅	graceful

◆ 描述儀態

儀態	presence	小巧玲瓏	small and exquisite
儀表	appearance	其貌不揚	undistinguished appearance
容貌	looks	面目可憎	repulsive in appearance
舉止	bearing	油頭粉面	heavily made-up
悅目	pleasing to the eye	齜牙咧嘴	look fierce
婀娜	supple and graceful	鬼鬼祟祟	thievish-looking
高雅	graceful	蓬頭垢面	disheveled hair and a dirty face

膚色	complexion	尖嘴猴腮	have a wretched appearance
天國姿色	surpassing beauty	眼睛發亮	bright-eyed

◆ 描述家庭

小家庭	a small family	大家庭	a big family
核心家庭	a nuclear family	小康家庭	a middle-class family

◆ 描述生病狀態

生病	be ill	嘔吐	vomit / throw up
染病	be infected with	奄奄一息	on the verge of death
發病	come down with illness	危在旦夕	one's life is in danger
臥病	be confined to bed	九死一生	a narrow escape from death
垂危	in dire danger	病癒	recover from an illness
絕症	incurable disease	復原	rally from (an illness)
保養	take good care of oneself	康復	recover
療養	recuperate	出院	discharged from the hospital
積勞成疾	fall ill from constant overwork		
妙手回春	effect a miraculous cure and bring the dying back to life		

◆ 描述頭部、眼睛動作

垂頭	hang one's head	偷看	peek
仰頭	raise one's head	瞇著眼睛	narrow one's eyes
向某人拋媚眼	set cap for sb.	眨眼	blink one's eyes
仰望	look up at	展望	look ahead

瞥視	glance at	目擊	witness
睜眼	with one's eyes open	注視	look at
瞪眼	glower at	凝視	gaze at
闔眼	sleep	怒視	glare at
遠眺	look far into the distance	回眸	glance back
凝視	fix one's eyes on	眨眼示意	wink at
左顧右盼	cast glances here and there	豐腴	plump
眾目睽睽	under the watchful eyes of the people	鬢髮	hair on the temples
刮目相看	look at sb. with new eyes	柳腰	small waist
留平頭	with a crew cut	過胖	obese
留辮子	wearing braids	啤酒肚	big-bellied
運動員的體格	have an atheletic build	臃腫	encumbered
憔悴	wan and sallow	枯瘦	gaunt
骨瘦如柴	all skin and bone	衰弱	emaciated
苗條	slender	柔弱	delicate

◆ 描述興趣嗜好

閱讀	reading (such as science fiction, mystery / detective novels, historical novels, romance novels, martial arts novels)
看電影	going to movies (such as comedies, tragedies, disaster movies, romance movies, suspense thrillers, martial arts movies, action movies)
看電視	watching TV programs (such as news, variety shows, informative channels, soap operas, game shows)
打球 玩遊戲	playing (tennis, baseball, basketball, badminton, bowling) playing (chess, poker, bridge, Monopoly)
聽音樂	listen to (classical, pop music, rock music, jazz, rap, heavy metal, opera, musical, symphony, hip-hop)

 **句型萬用包**

　　開始下筆寫作前，總要想好一篇作文要如何開頭、承接、結尾。快來把以下的句型套色的部份當作模板，然後在黑色畫底線的部份依照自己的狀況放入適合的單字（想不出填什麼的話，也可以可參考前面「實用單字」的部份找尋靈感）。這樣就能輕鬆完成考場必備的超實用金句、一口氣加好幾分！

• 第一部分：文章開頭先背這些句型！

❶ 半因（名詞），半因（名詞），（某人）是我最（動詞）的人。

Because of her good looks / her amazing personality / his lovely voice / his guitar skills, **and because of** her passion for art / his athletic build, (someone) is the person I (v.) admire / love / hate most.

---

❷ 如大家所知，（某人）以身為（名詞）聞名。但是，身為（某人）／（名詞），（名詞）才是我真正仰慕他的原因。

As everyone knows, (someone) **is famous as** (n.) a great football star / a talented singer / the proud winner of two Oscars. **However, as** (someone)'s close friend / diehard fan, **I like her more because of** the story behind her success / the sincerity under her appearance.

---

❸ 有句話說得好：（俗語）。我們可以從（名詞）得知這句話的真實性。

Well goes an old saying, "_____". We can tell how true this is from our interactions with our friends / our experiences with our teachers / the people we meet in life.

---

❹ 說到（名詞），（某人）一定是我第一個想到的。

When it comes to artists / basketball players / actors, (someone) **is definitely the first one that comes to my mind.**

---

❺ 我覺得（某人）是（名詞），這已經不是秘密了。

It is no secret that I consider (someone) my best friend / the best artist / my idol.

---

❻ 在全世界我遇過的人中，我認為（人名）是我最（動詞）的人。

Out of all the people I've met in the world, I believe that my mother / my teacher / my friend Brock **is the one that I** love / hate / admire **the most.**

• 第二部分：文章開展再記這些句型！

❶ 我會 ＿＿＿＿＿＿＿＿＿ 有很多原因。首先，＿＿＿＿＿＿＿＿＿。然後，
＿＿＿＿＿＿＿＿＿＿＿＿＿＿＿＿＿＿＿＿＿＿＿。最後（但不
是最不重要的），＿＿＿＿＿＿＿＿＿＿＿＿＿＿＿＿＿。

I (v. +某人) love my mother / don't like her / admire him for many reasons. First
of all, ＿＿＿＿＿＿＿＿＿＿＿. Secondly, ＿＿＿＿＿＿＿＿＿＿＿＿.
Last but not least, ＿＿＿＿＿＿.

---

❷ 在經歷了（名詞）之後，（某人）不但沒有 ＿＿＿＿＿＿，（某人）反而
＿＿＿＿＿＿。

After experiencing such a failure / painful surgeries / multiple setbacks /
serious loss, (someone) didn't give way to the cruel destiny; instead, (someone)
still held a positive / determined attitude towards life / her games / his work.

---

❸ 雖然（某人）很（形容詞），他還是帶著一個（形容詞）的態度來面對其他
人，以及他的工作。

Although (someone) is young and successful / beautiful and talented, he /
she still holds a modest and polite / responsible / professional / genuine and
helpful attitude in dealing with people and his work.

---

❹ （某人）也許看起來（形容詞），但他其實是個很（形容詞）的人。

(someone) may look weak / stupid / mean, but he / she is actually a very strong
/ clever / nice person.

---

❺ （某人）是（名詞）最好的例子。

(someone) is the prime example of a fool / crybaby / model student.

---

❻ 有些人認為（人名）很（形容詞），但我一點都不覺得。

Some people think my neighbor / my sister / my friend Alexis is cute / strong /
stupid, but I don't think so at all.

• 第三部分：文章收尾就用這些句型！

❶ 正因（名詞），（某人）被刻畫、描述為（名詞）。的確，（某人）是（名詞）的絕佳典範。

It is because of his / her amazing performance / great personality / remarkable achievements that (someone) is depicted as a modern hero / the Glory of Taiwan. Indeed, (someone) i is an excellent example for us / teenagers / everyone / students to follow.

---

❷ 我從（某人）身上學到（名詞）。

From (someone) I learned to (v.) work hard to achieve my goals / be a considerate and loving person / be strong and independent.

---

❸ 這就是為什麼我覺得（某人）是我的（名詞）。

This is why I find (someone) my favorite actor / idol / favorite person in the world.

---

❹ 無庸置疑地，（某人）對我（動詞）的方式有很大的影響。我很高興我有機會認識這麼（形容詞）的人。

It is undeniable that (someone) has a huge influence on the way I treat others / view life / strive towards my goals. I'm very glad that I have the chance to get to know such a wonderful / inspiring / amazing person.

---

❺ 我個人認為，（某人）是現代的（已過世的名人名字）。

Personally, I think (someone) is a modern day Mother Teresa / Albert Einstein / Beethoven!

---

❻ 我覺得很（形容詞），世界上有一個像（人名）這麼（形容詞）的人存在。

I'm glad / grateful / angry that a wonderful / amazing / terrible person like my uncle / my professor / my friend Milly exists.

模擬小示範

　　連接超實用的單字和好用的必備模板句型，就能拼出一篇完整的文章囉！這裡就有兩篇例子，並附上翻譯。就照著這個方法來套套看吧！

1. The Person I Admire Most

Because of **her great talent in sports**, and because of **her great perseverance**, <u>Yani Tseng, a golf player</u>, is the person I admire most. As everyone knows, she is famous as **the youngest player to have won five major championships**; however, as **her diehard fan**, I like her more because of **the story behind her success**.

Yani has not always been seen as a good player. She too has lost several important games, and you can imagine how disappointing losing can be for a professional golfer. However, after experiencing **such a failure in her career life**, **Yani** didn't give way to the cruel destiny; instead, she still held **a confident and determined attitude** toward **every game she played**.

Although **Yani is young** and **successful**, she still holds a **modest and polite** attitude in dealing with **her fans and her golf career**. It is because of **her remarkable achievement** that **Yani Tseng** was depicted as **the Glory of Taiwan**. Indeed, she is a perfect example for **us Taiwanese teenagers** to follow.

我最欣賞的人

　　因為她的**運動天賦**，也因為**她的毅力**，我最崇拜的人是**一位高球選手**，曾雅妮。大家都知道，她是**以最小年紀獲得五個獎盃的選手**，但是，身為**她的死忠粉絲，她成功背後的故事**才是我真正喜歡她的原因。

　　雅妮並不是一直都被認為是個厲害的選手。她也輸過幾場重要的比賽，而你可以想像輸球對一個職業高球選手有多令人失望。但在經歷過**職業生涯中的重大打擊**後，**曾雅妮**沒有被殘酷的命運擊倒，相反的，她還是保持著**自信且堅定的態度打每一場比賽**。

　　雖然**曾雅妮年輕有成**，她還是保持**謙虛有禮**的態度對待**球迷及她的工作**。就因為**她的非凡成就**，曾雅妮被刻畫為**台灣之光**。的確，她是**我們台灣青少年**的仿效對象。

1. An Embarrassing Experience

Well goes an old saying, "**A good fence makes good neighbors**." We can tell how true this is from **our experiences of interacting with our next door neighbors**. Although we have been neighbors for many years, Mrs. Li is the last person I'd like to talk to in the world.

I **don't like her** for many reasons. First of all, **she is very snobbish**. She fawns over people who she thinks are rich and powerful but looks down on people who she thinks are poor and worthless.

Secondly, **she likes to gossip and exaggerate about others' affairs**. As a result of her circulating rumors, I've been hurt many times.

I admire **her capability of borrowing** the most. A bottle of soy sauce yesterday, newspapers today, a bicycle tomorrow—but she never returns them. Strangely, she doesn't seem repentant at all. From **Mrs. Li**, I learned to **keep a suitable distance from certain people who I will never get along with**.

我的鄰居

俗話說得好：**籬笆築得牢，鄰居處得好**。這句話的真實性可以從**我們和隔壁鄰居的經驗**了解。雖然我們做鄰居已有多年，我的鄰居李太太是我最不願意與她交談的人。

我**不喜歡她**有很多原因。第一，**她很勢利**。她奉承她認為有錢和有勢力的人，而瞧不起她認為對她沒有價值的人。其次，**她喜歡八卦和對別人的事實誇大其詞**。由於她傳播的謠言，我受到很多次的傷害。

我最佩服的就是**她借東西的本領**。昨天借醬油，今天借報紙，明天借腳踏車，但總是有借無還。奇怪的是，她看起來一點悔意都沒有。從**李太太**身上，我學到**與那些我不可能與之好好相處的人保持距離**。

更上一層樓

學會使用模板句型寫出一篇漂亮的文章後，還可以怎麼在一些小地方讓文章錦上添花呢？看看其他同學的作品，注意他們有哪些地方值得學習，加入這些特色，讓文章更有變化、更加分！

1. A Model Student

As far as I am concerned, a model student should possess three special qualities: a balance between sports and studies, a sense of humor, and willingness to help others.

Firstly, I regard neither a mere wimpy bookworm nor a burly but brainless chap as a model student. I am deeply convinced that a model student should be able to take care of both studies and sports at the same time. I think a person who can master studies and sports simultaneously deserves a lot of praise.

Besides, a model student should have a sense of humor. He needs an interesting personality that enables him to get along with others easily. In this way, a model student can be a lovable character in a group.

The most important thing is that a model student must be willing to help others, especially those in need. He should not only take care of himself well. On the contrary, as a model student, he should try his best to help others to get better. This is what being a model student means; that is, to set a good example for others to follow. Therefore, a model student can not only perform well in his studies and sports but also make a lot of friends because of his good personality.

> **一個模範生**
>
> 　　對我而言，一個模範生應該具有三個特質：在運動與學業間取得平衡、有幽默感、樂於助人。

首先，我認為一個懦弱的書蟲或是一個沒大腦的大漢都不該是模範生。我深信一個模範生應該能同時兼顧學習與運動。我認為，能同時精通學習與運動的人是真正值得讚美的。

此外，模範生應該要有幽默感。他需要有個有趣的性格來讓他能容易與別人相處。如此一來，模範生在一群人之中就能也成為一個受到喜愛的角色。

最重要的是，模範生一定要樂於助人，特別是有需要的人。他不應該只是照顧好自己。相反地，身為模範生，他應該要盡力讓別人更好。這也就是模範生的意義：給別人一個好榜樣來學習。因此，模範生可以不僅在學業與運動上表現良好，也可以因為他的好個性而交到很多朋友。

★本文提出三個模範生應具備的特點，然後分成三段來詳細説明選擇這三點的理由，讓文章結構清楚分明，是個很好的作法。此外也提出他認為怎麼樣的人「不該是」模範生，以作為對比，更加強説服力。

2. Describing Myself

If I really must put my own image into words, I think that I would start from depicting people around me. Instead of a superficial description of my appearance, writing about my family and acquaintances can best show my personality because one can be judged by the company one keeps.

First of all, my father is a generous person. He never forces his values on me, and is always willing to understand other people's opinions. He respects my choices and offers me full support. Therefore, I learn to take responsibility for myself.

Second, my mother is the prime example of the Taiwanese spirit. She is a very active person, and easily argues with others because she enjoys meddling with others' affairs. I have her short temper, and therefore have a problem of cooperating with others. However, because of my friend, Mia, I never feel lonely.

Both of us are the only child in our families, so we keep each other company and have become bosom friends. Mia is such a diligent person, and she has excellent performance in studies because of that. She not only helps me with schoolwork problems, but inspires me that I should "study hard, and play hard." Owing to this belief, I can always derive joy from what I am doing.

With the three VIPs in my life, my picture can be easily drawn. And I hope there will be more people to color my picture in the future.

自我描述

　　如果我真的必須將自己形諸於文字，我想我會從我週遭的人開始描述。不從膚淺的外表描述下手，對於家人及朋友的描寫最能顯露出我的個性。因為觀其友可知其人。

　　首先，我父親是位大方的人，他從不強迫我接受他的價值觀，而且總是很願意瞭解其他人的意見。他尊重我的選擇並給我全然的支持，因此我學會對自己負責。

　　第二，我的母親就是台灣精神的典型代表。她很積極，也常因為多管閒事跟別人發生爭執。而我有她的急性子，所以和別人合作時常會發生些問題。不過因為我的好朋友Mia，我從未感到孤單。我們都是獨生子，所以總能互相陪伴，進而成為摯友。Mia是一個勤勉的人，所以她的課業表現相當優秀。她不只幫助我解決課業困難，也激勵了我「努力用功，努力玩」的想法。正因這個信念，我總是可以在我正從事的工作中找到樂趣。

　　有了這三位我生命中的重要人物，我的影像可以清楚的描繪出來。而我也希望未來能有更多人能夠為我的畫像著色。

★要形容自己是怎麼樣的人，總會覺得有點不好意思，不知道如何下筆。從描寫身邊的人下手，再適時從中說明這些人的性格對自己的個性有什麼影響，是個既不害羞又有創意的好方法

實戰克漏字

◆ 填充翻譯式引導作文

　　翻譯能翻得好的人，絕對也能寫出順暢的英文作文！直接開始下筆還沒有把握的話，先從把中文翻譯成英文開始做起吧！每篇文章都有中文可以參考，請照著中文填入單字片語，這樣就可以很快熟悉文章的結構、瞭解到句型如何實際運用在文章裡了。套上顏色的地方，都有套用前面的模板句型喔！

題目 ①：The Model Craze

提示：對台灣的名模風潮，請寫一文，描寫你所知道的名模及其所造成的影響。文章可不分段，或分成兩段。

　　In recent years, a supermodel trend has been sparked in the Taiwan entertainment industry. In all kinds of advertisements, we can easily see their charming figures. When it comes to 1 _____, Chiling Lin is definitely the first that 2 _____ to my mind. It is no secret that I consider her 3 _____
___

　　近幾年來，台灣的娛樂產業刮起了一陣名模風。電視和平面廣告中，隨處可見迷人的身影。而說到超級名模，林志玲絕對是第一個在我心中湧現的名字。我覺得她是全世界最美的女人，這已經不是秘密了。

　　Chiling's gentle 4 _____ beauty is known by everyone in the modeling business. Her 5 _____ skin and 6 _____ have made her a popular face. She always 7 _____ with her tall and slender body figure. Even more, she owns such a 8 _____ voice that it is capable of 9 _____
_____. She is known for having an excellent education background and high EQ, always appearing with those lovely tender eyes and a smile on

her face. Her 10 _____ personality has made her a favorite among fans. At the same time, she is the prime example of a 11 _____ Asian beauty, symbolizing that if a beauty has nothing good within, no good comes out. This is why I consider her 12 _____.

　　在模特兒業中，她以溫婉的女性美聞名。她乳白色的肌膚與美麗動人的五官也使她成為一個受歡迎的人。她總是以高挑苗條的身材吸引眾人注目。她擁有如此甜美的聲音，使男人當場融化。另外，她因為擁有良好的學歷背景與高EQ而為人稱道，臉上永遠帶著美好、溫柔的眼神與笑容。她親切的性格讓她成為粉絲的最愛。同時，**她也成為典型亞洲美女的完美範例，象徵著美女如果沒有好的內在，就不會有美麗的外表。這就是為什麼我覺得她是我的偶像。**

• 填空引導式參考解答

❶ supermodels	❺ milky white	❾ making men melt on the spot
❷ comes	❻ exquisite features	❿ amiable
❸ the most beautiful woman in the world	❼ draws everyone's attention	⓫ typical
❹ feminine	❽ sweet	⓬ my idol

題目 ②：The Most Unforgettable Person in my Lifetime

提示：請寫一文說明你最難忘的人的原因及理由。

Because of 1 _____, and because of 2 _____, Sean, a 3 _____ who came to Taiwan twenty years ago and served in a church in my neighborhood, is the most unforgettable person in my life. As a matter of fact, the reason why I came to know him in the first place was that I wished to 4 _____ my English ability. He was not a man 5 _____, but I could strongly 6 _____ his concern and encouragement for me and people around us. In addition to teaching me many English usages, he took me to the 7 _____ and 8 _____ from time to time to look after 9 _____. He often said to me, "The purpose of 10_____ knowledge is to help those 11 _____." Though I don't 12 _____ a religion, I felt deeply moved.

半因他奉獻一生幫助他人，半因他愛好和平的態度，Sean，一個來台灣二十年的傳教士，服務於我們家附近的一間教會，是我這一生最難忘的人。其實，我起先在教會認識了他是希望增強英文能力。他不是善於表達情感的人，但是我可以感受到他對我以及身邊的人的關懷及鼓勵。除了教導我許多英文用法外，他有時還會帶我去孤兒院和療養院去照顧病弱的人。他常對我說：「獲得學問的目的是要去幫助那些需要的人。」我雖然不信教，但也覺得很感動。

Last year, when he was going back to the States, I 13 _____ at the airport. He said 14 _____ that what he hoped most was that there would be less 15 _____ and more 16 _____ in Taiwan. On the bus home, I was filled with 17 _____. From Sean, I learned to 18 _____. I 19 _____ to 20 _____ for more people 21 _____ after I grow up. Personally, I think Sean is a modern day 22 _____! I pray that the day when he comes back again to Taiwan, it will not be a 23 _____ place but a 24 _____ place to live in.

　　去年，當他回美國時，我到機場給他送行，他嘆息著說他最希望台灣能少一些政治，而多一些溫暖。在我坐車回家的路上，我心中充滿了感謝。**我從**Sean**身上學到了瞭解愛和服務他人的重要性。**我下定決心長大後要為更多窮困的人奮鬥。我個人覺得，Sean根本就是個現代的聖人！我祈禱當他再度回到台灣的那天，台灣不再混亂，而是個祥和的住所。

• **填空引導式參考解答**

❶ his devotion to helping others	❾ the sick and invalid	⓱ gratitude
❷ his peace-loving attitude	❿ acquiring	⓲ understand the importance of love and serving others
❸ missionary	⓫ in need	⓳ am determined
❹ improve	⓬ practice	⓴ fight
❺ good at expressing his emotions	⓭ saw him off	㉑ in destitution
❻ feel	⓮ with a sigh	㉒ Saint
❼ orphanage	⓯ politics	㉓ chaotic
❽ sanitarium	⓰ warmth	㉔ harmonious

高階填空題

　　把文章的句型和結構都練熟了，已經有信心可以不用參考範文自己寫一篇了嗎？從這裡開始，你可以依照自己的狀況，套用模板句型練習寫作。請從以下的題目中選一個，現在就開始寫吧！

題目 ①： The Most Talented Person I've Ever Met

Because of _____, and because of _____, _____ is the person I _____. It is no secret that I consider _____.

I _____ for many reasons. First of all, _____ _____ _____.

Secondly, _____ _____. Last but not least, _____ _____ _____.

From _____ I learned to _____. This is why I find _____ my _____.

• 自由發揮的參考解答範本：

1. The Most Talented Person I've Ever Met

Because of his appreciation for multiple hobbies, and because of how good he is at everything he does, my grandfather is the person I admire most. It is no secret that I consider him the most talented person I've ever met.

I admire my grandfather's various talents for many reasons. First of all, my grandfather is a very artistic person. His oil paintings are famous in our town, and he has also held several exhibitions. Secondly, he is able to learn how to play new instruments very quickly. He randomly picked up a trumpet one day and literally mastered it the next day. Last but not least, he is also an amateur carpenter. The wooden chairs and little wagons he made for us look so good that they should be sold in stores.

From my grandfather I learned to appreciate the importance of having hobbies in life. He taught me that finding something I'm good at and enjoy doing is far more important than getting high scores on tests at school. This is why I find him my idol and inspiration.

Chapter 3
議論時事文

Part 1 | 社會議題

思路第一站

下筆前問問自己 ①：問題型時事題

問題型時事題大多和我們有切身的關係，寫作題材十分廣泛，舉凡環保問題、交通問題、社會問題、治安問題、公德心問題、青少年問題皆是。這種題目只要順著主題發揮，強調問題的嚴重性，列舉一些實際的例子，並說明問題發生的原因即可。

例如：Juvenile delinquency has had negative influence on the society. Most of these problems result from lack of care from parents.「青少年犯罪問題已經對社會造成影響。決大多數問題是因為父母疏於關懷造成。」這樣就能一句點出影響，以及問題發生的原因。

下筆前問問自己 ②：觀點型時事題

觀點型時事題顧名思義，就是要針對某一個主題發表個人的看法，可使用「第一」、「第二」、「第三」等依序列舉。若是描寫對人或物的感受，只需將感受娓娓道來即可。此類題目多半是講抽煙的害處、學校課業、廢除聯考、英文學習等，要你表達觀點。例如：First, taking the MRT is convenient. Second, it is less harmful to the environment. Third, it is very fast. 「第一，坐捷運很方便。第二，對環境沒那麼有害。第三，捷運很快。」只要依照「第一、第二、第三」的邏輯，將個人觀點一一鋪陳，就能完成文章了。

下筆前問問自己 ③：經驗型時事題

經驗型的作文題目除了描述實際的親身經歷外，大多還得再提出自己對此一經驗的看法或感受。常見的題目有逛街的經驗、打工的經驗、犯錯的經驗、學英文的經驗、比賽的經驗、學校校園生活等。

當然，若是只描寫個人經驗，和時事無法產生連結也不行。所以這種題目常會先寫出新聞，再請你舉出類似的經驗，例如由打工相關的新聞，要你延伸寫出自己打工的經驗。但無論怎麼包裝，這類型的題目還是要你寫自己的經驗，所以就算是沒聽過的新聞，也不用被它嚇到。

✏️ 下筆前問問自己 ④：喜好型時事題

喜好型時事題，是出題最頻繁的題型。由於題目為考生最熟悉的題材，因此寫作時記得選擇最簡單、最容易發揮的題材下筆就好。此類題目有：我最敬愛的老師、我最喜愛的書、我最喜歡的科目等。

此類型的題目也一樣，在講自己的喜好之外，需要與時事產生連結。例如，如果最近的新聞中提到了民眾票選的十大好書，你就可以將自己喜歡的書拿出來與這十大好書做比較討論，以與時事做連結。

✏️ 下筆前問問自己 ⑤：做法型時事題

做法型的題目，不外乎對某一特定問題提出解決方法，或如何做好一件事。在提出做法時，可以採用列舉式。常見的題目有：如何保護野生動物、如何保護樹木；另外如何改善交通、如何選擇朋友、如何用對讀書方法等亦有可能出現。

例如：In order to save wild animals, each and every one of us should try our best not to disturb them.「為了拯救野生動物，我們每個人都要努力不要打擾牠們。」

 **單字裝入袋**

時事題型多半和環境、社會議題相關，或是針對某一事件，發表自己的經驗和觀點。下列整理出在撰寫時事作文時，常用到的單字，在寫這類型作文時，可是很好用的喔！

◆ **時事題型常用動詞**

❶	估計；估量	estimate
❷	數量上超過	outnumber
❸	擁護；提倡；主張	advocate
❹	檢查；診察	examine
❺	考慮；細想	consider
❻	寧願（選擇）；更喜歡	prefer
❼	（在一定範圍內）變動；變化	range
❽	著手對付；處理	tackle
❾	是……的決定因素；形成	determine
❿	使變緊；使減少	tighten
⓫	抓住（機會）；欣然接受（提議）	embrace
⓬	（物價）下跌；（經濟）衰落	slump
⓭	大量產生；造成	spawn

◆ **時事題型常用名詞**

❶	提倡者；擁護者	advocate
❷	關係者；參與者	participant
❸	消耗量；消費量	consumption
❹	爆發	outbreak

⑤	（經濟等）突然好轉；突然轉壞	turnaround
⑥	環境保護論者；環境論者	environmentalist
⑦	規章；規則；條例	regulation
⑧	（產權）全部買下；買斷；買通	buyout
⑨	陰謀；謀叛；共謀	conspiracy
⑩	醜聞；醜事	scandal
⑪	資源；財力	resource

◆ 時事題型常用形容詞／副詞

❶	總的；全面的	overall
❷	負有法律責任的；有義務的	liable
❸	官方的；法定的；正式的	official
❹	（居住在）城市的	urban
❺	大都市的	metropolitan
❻	郊區的；近郊的	suburban
❼	明顯的；突出的	stark
❽	競爭的；競賽的	vying
❾	潛在的；可能的	potential
❿	確定地；斷然地；明確地	decidedly
⑪	漸增地；越來越多地	increasingly
⑫	戲劇性地；引人注目地	dramatically
⑬	明顯地；顯然	evidently
⑭	據說；據宣稱	allegedly

 **句型萬用包**

　　以下將時事題寫作常用到的句型列出。想知道如何寫出文章的開頭、開展、結尾，都可以在這裡找到參考用的範本。選擇幾個句型，再依不同情境調整其中的細節，就可以很快地寫出一篇文章囉。

•第一部分：文章開頭先背這些句型！

❶ 我曾經想過 _____ 。

I once thought about traveling to outer space / being an astronaut.

_____

❷ 快要_____，我幾乎
_____ 。

Nearly choking on my water / late for my first class, I hardly can say a word / have time to put on my uniform.

_____

❸ 對我來說，（名詞）大概只存在夢境中吧。

For me, romance / Mr. Right merely exists in my dreams.

_____

❹ 隨著（名詞）的蓬勃發展，_____（句子）_____ 。

With the development of the Internet / smartphones, （句子）you can know people around the world / people can go online anytime anywhere.

•第二部分：文章開展再記這些句型！

❶ 因為_____（句子）_____，所以我
_____（句子）_____ 。

Since（句子）my sister got married last year / I am already late for the meeting, I（句子）face the pressure of marriage now / will just skip it this time.

_____

❷ _____（句子）_____，因而逐漸培養出我的性格。

（句子）I have taken art lessons and piano lessons, which gradually shaped my personality.

_____

❸ 由於（名詞）進展神速，＿＿＿＿＿＿＿＿＿＿＿＿＿＿＿＿＿＿＿。

With the fast advancement of technological advances,（句子）the dream to live in outer space may not be a dream anymore.

＿＿＿＿＿＿＿＿＿＿＿＿＿＿＿＿＿＿＿＿＿＿＿＿＿＿＿＿＿＿＿＿＿＿＿＿＿

❹ 奇怪的是，＿＿＿＿＿＿（句子）＿＿＿＿＿＿＿。

Strangely enough,（句子）the stranger across the street waved at me / I think I have seen the old lady before.

＿＿＿＿＿＿＿＿＿＿＿＿＿＿＿＿＿＿＿＿＿＿＿＿＿＿＿＿＿＿＿＿＿＿＿＿＿

❺ 我常常被稱為（名詞），所以我＿＿＿＿＿＿（句子）＿＿＿＿＿＿。

Frequently referred to as a nerd / the "precious" one by my family, I（句子）don't have much confidence in myself / am totally spoiled.

＿＿＿＿＿＿＿＿＿＿＿＿＿＿＿＿＿＿＿＿＿＿＿＿＿＿＿＿＿＿＿＿＿＿＿＿＿

❻ （名詞）是我＿＿＿＿＿＿（句子）＿＿＿＿＿＿的（名詞）。

Sally / John is the girl / boy I（句子）can't get along with / like.

＿＿＿＿＿＿＿＿＿＿＿＿＿＿＿＿＿＿＿＿＿＿＿＿＿＿＿＿＿＿＿＿＿＿＿＿＿

❼ 我無法自拔地（動詞）。

I cannot help but stare at her with my tears streaming down.

＿＿＿＿＿＿＿＿＿＿＿＿＿＿＿＿＿＿＿＿＿＿＿＿＿＿＿＿＿＿＿＿＿＿＿＿＿

❽ 就我而言，我＿＿＿＿＿＿＿（句子）＿＿＿＿＿＿＿＿。

As far as I am concerned, I（句子）don't agree with what you say / can't agree with you.

＿＿＿＿＿＿＿＿＿＿＿＿＿＿＿＿＿＿＿＿＿＿＿＿＿＿＿＿＿＿＿＿＿＿＿＿＿

❾ 我（形容詞）到已經幾乎沒有辦法（動詞）。

I was so excited / angry that I could barely stand / breathe.

• 第三部分：文章收尾就用這些句型！

❶ 在現實中，我＿＿＿＿＿＿＿（句子）＿＿＿＿＿＿＿＿。

In the reality, I（句子）am just a girl who needs a lot of love from other people.

---

❷ 在另外一個層面，這樣我更能（形容詞）（動詞）。

In another aspect, it's simpler / more difficult for me to follow the rules / organize these files.

---

❸ 我認為儘管＿＿＿＿＿＿＿（句子）＿＿＿＿＿＿＿，我們還是應該＿＿＿＿（句子）＿＿＿＿＿＿。

In my opinion, although（句子）the project won't start by the end of the month, we should（句子）prepare for it early.

---

❹ 因此，我贊同（名詞）。

Therefore, I am in favor of making friends online / this plan.

---

❺（名詞）應該要歸功於＿＿＿＿＿＿（句子）＿＿＿＿＿＿。

My success / Her achievement should be attributed to（句子）my mom, who has supported me all along / her high school teacher.

---

❻ 我的人生觀在（名詞）以後有了巨大的改變。

My whole perspective changed drastically after that accident / the contest.

 模擬小示範

　　利用前面所學的「超實用單字」和「必備武器模板句型」，來練習拼出一篇完整的時事題文章吧！下面提供兩篇文章，並附上中文翻譯，現在就開始寫作套套看吧！

1. Exploration in Outer Space

I once thought about **unveiling the mysteries of outer space, contacting with extraterrestrial beings, and travelling to the planets in our solar system when I was a toddler.** Since **my father serves as an associate professor in astronomy, I have heard about myriads of stories of space-related subjects—cosmos, galaxy, meteorites, asteroids, aliens, and any other things you can think of,** which gradually shaped my personality and field of interests.

With the fast advancement of **technology**, though still far-fetched for ordinary people, **space travel has attracted the attention of some world famous magnates.** For people who earn lots of money, space travel is now considered feasible. For me, a meager salarymaker, "space travel" can be only realized in my dream—kind of pathetic but realistic. Imagine myself in the narrow cabinet of a space shuttle, sipping on a boiling hot cup of cappuccino, admiring the breathtaking spectacles of the space, taking a stroll on the rugged surface of Mars, these imaginative scenarios can "quench my thirst" for actually taking a space trip!

In the reality, I **can only sit on my rocking chair by the window in the middle of the night, light my cigar, and stare into the twinkling stars in the sky.** Strangely enough, **they seem to wink at me all at once.**

外太空探險

　　在我還是小孩時，我曾經想過**要揭開外太空的神祕面紗，與外星生物接觸，以及去外太空旅行**。因為**我爸爸是研究天文學的副教授**，所以我**聽過各式各樣有關外太空的故事**，**像是宇宙、銀河、彗星、小行星、以及外星人和各種你講得出來的事物**，因而逐漸培養出我的性格**及有關這領域的興趣**。

　　由於**科技**進步神速，雖然太空旅行對於平凡人來説仍是遙不可及，它**已吸引了許多達官顯貴們的注意**。對於擁有大把鈔票的人來説，太空旅行是相當可能的。但對我這個只有微薄薪水的人來説，這卻只是個只能在夢裡實現的夢想，有些令人同情卻是現實的。想像你自己身在太空梭的小空間內，啜飲著一杯滾燙的熱卡布奇諾，欣賞著太空中令人屏息的奇觀，漫步在火星粗糙的外表，這些想像的情節就足以像是真的去過一趟太空旅行般，止住我的渴望。

　　在現實中，我**只能在半夜，臨著窗坐在我的搖椅上，點燃我的雪茄，然後凝視著滿是閃亮星斗的天空**。奇怪的是，**這些星星好像在這一瞬間都向我眨眼睛**。

2. My Attitude toward the Opposite Sex

Nearly **crushed by heavy schoolwork,** I hardly **pay attention to my outward appearance**. Though constantly receiving insulting judgments and mocking words from my peers, I, just like other adolescents, still occasionally daydream about my princess charming—adorable face with dimples, white and tender skin, slender legs with high heels, and captivating eyes. Frequently referred to as **a "hideous monster"**, **I have very few friends of the opposite sex, let alone a girlfriend.**

For me, **romance** merely exists in my dreams. Looking into the mirror one day after school, I found myself totally unappealing: freckled face with tons of pimples and lots of ance, flabby arms, stubby legs, and lots of flab around my waist. Even so, buried under my homely appearance is a passionate heart craving for someone to explore and understand.

I am like a withering bud at the corner of the garden, waiting for some gardener to fertilize me—a pretty nice metaphor for me! One day, while I was heading to my cram school, a ravishing girl standing in front of a bubble tea shop caught my attention. **She** is the **girl** I **have had a crush on since kindergarten**. I cannot help but **stare at her with my heart beating violently**. I tried to talk to her but her abrupt reply "you should cash a reality check", though cruel yet realistic, dragged me back to reality, shattering my fantasy of having a romantic encounter. I shrugged and walked away with a broken heart.

My heart became a stagnant pool of water with no ripples at all. In another aspect, it's **easier** for me to **concentrate on my academic studies**. If we perceive things from a different angle or perspective, there is always a way out! That's life!

我對異性的態度

　　快要<u>被繁重的課業壓得喘不過氣</u>，我幾乎<u>沒有留意外表這件事</u>。雖然常常承受同儕的侮辱性批評還有嘲笑的字眼，我還是像一般青少年一樣，偶而做一下自己夢中情人的白日夢。我的夢中情人擁有有著酒窩的可人臉龐，白皙柔嫩的肌膚，穿著高跟鞋的纖細雙腿，還有迷人不償命的雙眼。我常常被稱為<u>「醜八怪」</u>，我<u>連異性友人都很少，更不用說女友了</u>。

　　對我來說，<u>浪漫愛情</u>大概只存在夢境中吧。有一天放學後我看了看鏡子中的自己，我真是醜斃了：滿佈雀斑的臉龐外加一堆粉刺跟青春痘，肥胖的雙臂，粗短的雙腿，在腰際還有一個很大的游泳圈。縱使如此，在我醜陋的外表之下還是埋藏著一顆等待某人來發掘探索的炙熱的心。我好像一個在花園角落的一顆日漸凋零的花苞，等待著某位園丁來幫我施肥。對我來說，這是一個很貼切的比喻。有一天，當我在前往補習班的路上時，一個站在泡沫紅茶店前的一個霹靂無敵大正妹，吸引了我的注意。<u>她</u>是我<u>從幼稚園開始就很喜歡的女孩</u>，我無法自拔地<u>一直死盯著她看</u>。我的心臟猛烈地跳著，我試圖跟她搭話，但她魯莽的回應：「面對現實吧。」雖殘忍但也一針見血，硬是把我拖回了現實，也把我浪漫邂逅的美夢打醒。我聳聳肩，心碎地離開了。

　　現在我的心如止水，但是在另外一個層面，這樣我<u>比較容易專注在學業上</u>。如果我們從另一個角度或觀點看事情的話，我們就不會被困在死胡同裡面。這就是人生啊！

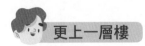
更上一層樓

　　下面再提供兩篇時事題型篇範文。請注意兩篇文章分別屬於5類中的哪一類時事題型，以及此類題型的寫作方式與技巧。參考中文翻譯下面的小分析，幫助你更熟悉此類時事題型的寫作。

1. The Advantage of Modern Technology

　　In this ever-changing modern society, the only constant factor is "change" itself. Technology advances at the crazy pace in ways not even imaginable by most people half a century ago.

　　With the invention of cell phones, people can be reached anytime and anywhere. Time devoted to work largely increases for a majority of people, which in turn creates numerous workaholics. Some people even ironically said, "TGIF should be altered to TGIM." Admittedly, communications get way more convenient than ever before with the invention of cell phone. However, we cannot deny that there are some drawbacks. First of all, many individuals are glued to the screen of the cell phone; they are therefore deprived of hobbies, sports, and time for family. People might feel more connected, but indeed their mental well-being is going to hell in a hand basket. As Martin Luther King Jr. once said, "Our scientific power has outrun our spiritual power." As urban residents, we should get used to the kaleidoscope of the high-tech and not be addicted to high-tech gadgets in our daily lives.

　　Secondly, due to the fact that personal data can be easily revealed, telephone soliciting and frauds are plaguing thousands of people nationwide. People should be wary enough and never give away any personal financial information.

　　Last, people have become generally more concerned with conspicuous consumption of material goods owing to the fact that people, especially the younger generation, want to be fancy and show off their wealth.

現代科技的優點

在這個一直不斷改變的現代社會當中，唯一一個恆久不變的因素就是「改變」本身。科技以大部分的人在五十年前都無法想像的方式發狂進步著。

隨著手機的發明，人們不論在何時何地都能被找到。對大部分的人來說，投注在工作上的時間大量的增加，而因此創造出無數的工作狂。有些人甚至諷刺地說，TGIF（Thank God It's Friday）應該要被改成TGIM（Thank God It's Monday）才對。我們必須承認，隨著手機的發明，通訊比以前都來的更方便。但是，我們也不能否認，有些缺點卻也隨之而來。首先，很多人都只專注於盯著手機螢幕，休閒活動、運動、和家人的時間都因此被剝奪了。人跟人之間或許感覺彼此的距離拉近了，但事實上他們的心靈層面卻是每況愈下。如同馬丁路德曾說：「我們科學的力量已經超越了我們精神的力量。」身為都市的居民，我們應該要習慣高科技的瞬息萬變，並且不要沉迷於生活中的高科技小玩意。

第二點，由於個人資料很容易外洩，電話推銷還有詐欺正困擾著全國數以千計的人們。大家應該要小心並且不要洩露任何個人的財務資訊。

最後，人們明顯變得越來越崇尚消費物質商品，尤其特別是年經人想要向他人炫耀財富。

★小分析：本篇在討論因科技發展，所帶來的優缺點。第一段提到科技的進步。第二段之後以手機舉例，分點列出（First of all...、Secondly,...）手機造成的問題。不過因題目只叫你寫優點，舉一堆缺點有點離題。此篇屬於問題型時事題。

2. My Thoughts on Cram Schools

Overemphasis of parents on the academic performance of their children could partly account for the cram school phenomenon. In hopes to enhance their children's class ranking and competitive edge, desperate parents commonly resort to the cram schools for fast relief. But, there is always a price to be paid. The tradeoffs are indicated as follows.

Just like any other high school student, I regularly attend cram school Monday through Friday all year round, which deprives me of extracurricular activities, sports, and hobbies. This daily routine after school renders my high school life tedious and monotonous. Admittedly, my grades did skyrocket and my folks were definitely proud of me. However, as Albert Einstein once said, "Not everything that counts can be counted, and not everything that can be counted counts," academic achievements and grades are merely "the tip of an iceberg" in our lives. Traditional teacher-centered pedagogy commonly implemented in cram schools is a salient contradiction in the definition of education. Education, in terms of etymology, means "to lead out." That is, teachers should not be the ultimate providers of knowledge but the facilitators aiding and guiding their students. If wrongly implemented, cram school "education" might strangle students' creativity and originality, further fossilizing their minds.

In the western world, highly stressing the concept of logical reasoning and critical thinking, cram schools can never exist. On account of the class size and pressure from the parents, it is next to impossible for cram schools to adjust their teaching strategies and goals. The status quo will therefore persist for some years to come. Pathetically, students become the "test-taking machines" functioning in the "examination hell." I always bear in mind that cram schools merely serve as the stepping stone toward higher education but they contradict the very nature of education itself.

我對補習班的看法

　　父母對於子女學業表現的過分強調可以部分解釋補習班現象。帶著一份能夠加強兒童在校排名和競爭力的希望，望子成龍望女成鳳的父母通常訴諸補習班得到速效。但是事情總是要付出代價的，以下將探討所付出的機會成本。

　　就像任何其他高中的學生一樣，我週一至週五全年無休地去補習，補習這件事剝奪了我的課外活動，運動和愛好。這個放學後的常態性事務使我的高中生活變得單調而乏味。我必須承認，我的成績扶搖直上，而且我的父母也為我感到驕傲。然而，正如愛因斯坦曾經說過：「並非所有重要的事情都可以被量化，也不是所有可以被量化的事情都重要。」學術成就與成績僅僅是我們生活中的「冰山一角」。在補習班當中普遍推行之傳統以教師為中心的教學法很明顯的和教育的定義有所衝突。教育以字源學的面向而論，就是引導學生走出自己的一片雲彩。也就是說，教師不應是最終的知識提供者，而是一個協助並且引導學生的促進者。補習教育如果執行方式失當的話可能會扼殺掉學生的創造力和原創性，更進一步僵化他們的思維。

　　在強調邏輯思考能力與批判推理能力的西方世界中，補習班永遠無法存在。由於班級大小與來自家長的壓力，補習班是幾乎不可能去調整教學策略和目標。這樣的狀況將因此持續再持續個好幾年的時間。可悲的是，學生成為在考試煉獄當中運作的考試機器。我會一直銘記著，補習班只是作為高等教育的墊腳石罷了，但他們違背了教育的本質。

★此篇在討論補習的觀念，屬於觀點型時事題。第二段中作者本身提出自身補習的經驗，提出他曾經經由補習成績變好，獲得了好處，但也指出補習本身會扼殺掉學生的創造力，違背教育的本質，帶出了反對的觀點。

實戰克漏字

◆ 填充翻譯式引導作文

透過前面兩篇「範文參考更上一層樓」，有沒有對時事題型更加了解了呢？現在就來試著寫寫看時事題文章吧！下面有三篇文章，請根據所提供的題目、寫作提示與中文翻譯，試著先把中文句子翻譯成英文，藉此更熟悉時事題型會用到的句型和單字，並且能順暢寫出此類文章。

題目 ①： The Internet and I

提示： 近來網路犯罪頻傳，請寫一文描寫由於網路蓬勃發展所帶來的影響及改善之道。

With the development of the Internet, 1 ＿＿＿＿＿＿ websites and 2 ＿＿＿＿＿＿ have become a 3 ＿＿＿＿＿ of 4 ＿＿＿＿＿＿, sex and scams. Some new problems, however, have 5 ＿＿＿＿＿＿ from the popularity of making friends online. 6 ＿＿＿＿＿＿ speaking, 7 ＿＿＿＿＿ is attractive but 8 ＿＿＿＿＿ as well. In the first place, some Internet friends make use of these Web sites to 9 ＿＿＿＿＿ crimes such as arranging one-night stands or 10 ＿＿＿＿＿ online. Even the gold 11 ＿＿＿＿＿ whom we used to look up to is a victim. Moreover, many crimes 12 ＿＿＿＿＿＿ exist in society have been 13 ＿＿＿＿＿ to the Internet. The commercial dispute caused by the items for 14 ＿＿＿＿＿ on online 15 ＿＿＿＿＿ websites make this convenient tool 16 ＿＿＿＿＿.

隨著網路的蓬勃發展，許多網站和聊天室開始變成賭博、色情、騙局的溫床。然而，許多問題卻源自於網路交友的普及。坦白說，網路約會有吸引力，但也有風險。首先，有些網友利用交友網站犯罪，例如安排一夜情或援助交際。甚至連我們所尊敬的奧運金牌得主都是受害者。再者，許多原本存在於社會上的犯罪轉移到網路上。拍賣網站販售物品所引起的買賣糾紛都讓這個方便的工具惡名昭彰。

Sad to say, do we have to view the use of the Internet from this 17 ＿＿＿＿＿＿? In my 18 ＿＿＿＿＿＿, although the purpose of these websites was originally well-19 _____, we should be 20 _____about our own safety. Therefore, before the 21 _____ of Internet laws, all Net users can only be as careful as possible, so they won't 22 _____ laws or get 23 _____.

　　說來可悲，我們真的只能用這種角度來看待網路的使用嗎？**我認為交友網站儘管原本立意甚佳，我們還是應該要注意自身的安全。**因此，在網路法尚未問世之前，所有網路使用者都只能盡可能的小心，以免觸犯法律或遭受傷害。

• 填空引導式參考解答

❶ numerous	❾ commit	⓱ angle
❷ chat rooms	❿ prostitution	⓲ opinion
❸ hotbed	⓫ medalist	⓳ intentioned
❹ gambling	⓬ originally	⓴ careful
❺ resulted	⓭ transferred	㉑ appearance
❻ Honestly	⓮ sale	㉒ violate
❼ Internet dating	⓯ auction	㉓ hurt
❽ risky	⓰ infamous	

提示： 第一段可以先介紹網路約會的現象。第二段可以加入自己的想法，針對網路約會進行評斷。

1 _____ ago, many 2 _____ met through a 3 _____ or through family and friends. In the modern world, however, the Internet often 4 _____ as the matchmaker, allowing 5 _____ to meet by 6 _____ of Internet dating 7 _____ or in chat rooms. Once they meet online, couples can go out 8 _____, which might be the first 9 _____ toward a happy 10 _____ relationship.

幾十年以前，很多情侶透過媒人或透過家人及朋友來認識。然而在現代社會中，網路常常扮演媒人的角色，讓陌生人藉由網路約會服務或聊天室中認識。一旦他們在線上相遇，情侶們可以出去約會，而這有可能是通往一個快樂而且長期的男女關係第一步。

As far as I am 11 _____, I am in favor of 12 _____ friends on the Internet. It is 13 _____ for us to meet everyone; nevertheless, almost everyone is 14 _____ making friends with, for each one is like a good book 15 _____ to be read 16 _____. What's more, we can meet people from every 17 _____ of the world, 18 _____ our English and 19 _____ our lives colorfully. Thus, if we can make more friends through the Internet, we may have 20 _____ to experience different 21 _____, to broaden our 22 _____, and to 23 _____ our lives. Therefore, I am in 24 _____ of making friends online.

就我而言，我同意在網路上交友。就我們來說，要認識每一個人是不可能的，然而，幾乎每個人都值得交朋友，因為每個人都像是一本值得被徹底閱讀的好書。再者，我們可以碰到全世界各個角落的人、練習我們的英文並且使我們的生活多彩多姿。因此，如果我們可以透過網路聊天交到朋友，我們有機會去體驗不同的生活型態、去拓展我們的視野並且豐富我們的生活。因此，我贊同網路交友。

• 填空引導式參考解答

❶ Decades	❾ step	⓱ corner
❷ couples	❿ long-term	⓲ practicing
❸ matchmaker	⓫ concerned	⓳ painting
❹ serves	⓬ making	⓴ opportunities
❺ strangers	⓭ impossible	㉑ lifestyles
❻ way	⓮ worth	㉒ horizons
❼ services	⓯ deserving	㉓ enrich
❽ on a date	⓰ thoroughly	㉔ favor

提示：2012年奧運結束，我國選手曾櫟騁勇奪羽量級銅牌。人生中就像是一場場的競賽，請以運動比賽做一個例子，試描述你自己或是你欣賞過的運動比賽的過程，以及你的感想。不可以純論説方式寫作，一定要提出一具體經驗作為主要內容，再延伸出經驗背後的意涵。

1 _____ all the games I have played so far, my first game in our baseball school varsity 2 _____ clear in my mind. Though considered highly 3 _____, I was an inexperienced 4 _____ in the team. In order to better prepare myself, I did 200 extra 5 _____ and sit-ups each day to 6 _____ my muscle 7 _____. Despite all the hard work I have done, I still shook like jelly before I went up. It was the 8 _____ of ninth; the 9 _____ were loaded and our team was three 10 _____ behind. I was so nervous that I could 11 _____ hold my bat.

在我打過的所有比賽中，我加入棒球隊的第一場比賽依然讓我記憶猶新。雖然被認為有天賦，但我在球隊中還是一個經驗不足的菜鳥。為了要有萬全的準備，我每天多做200個伏地挺身與仰臥起坐來增加我的肌肉強度。儘管我已經努力不少，但在上場前我還是皮皮挫。那時候九局下半，滿壘，我們三分落後，我緊張到已經幾乎沒有辦法好好握住球棒了。

The 12 _____ of the audience seemed to 13 _____ away. The air seemed to 14 _____ at that moment. I clearly heard my own 15 _____. My father's words "Don't let the fear of 16 _____ out hold you back!" started to 17 _____ in my ears. I held my breath and 18 _____ my bat with full strength. Something dramatic happened—the ball 19 _____ through the azure sky, forming a perfect 20 _____ and 21 _____ at the other side of the warning track. It was a grand slam 22 _____. The pitcher squatted by the pitcher's 23 _____ like a crestfallen rooster, furiously 24 _____ his scalp. On the other hand, I composedly ran back to the home 25 _____ and appreciated this incredible scene, ready to embrace the 26 _____ victory. I successfully 27 _____ the predicament and won that game. The audiences gave me a 28 _____ ovation right in front of the dugout. Our victory should be partly 29 _____ to my father's enlightening words, which further 30 _____ me later in my life.

觀眾的歡呼聲似乎逐漸退去。空氣似乎在當時整個凝結了。我可以清晰地聽見我的喘息聲。我父親賽前的耳提面命——「別讓害怕三振這件事

讓你放不開！」開始在我耳中迴響著。我屏息並全力揮擊，神奇的事情發生了，小白球咻地一聲劃過了蔚藍的天際，畫出了一個完美的弧線，消失在全壘打牆的另外一邊。那是一個滿貫全壘打。投手像是一隻鬥敗的公雞一樣蹲踞在投手丘旁，狂亂地抓著他的頭皮。而另外一方，我鎮靜地跑回本壘板，欣賞著這個令人無法置信的景象，並準備擁抱我們得來不易的勝利。我成功扭轉了我們的困境並且贏得了比賽。觀眾們在我們休息室前起立鼓掌歡呼。我們的勝利應該部分要歸功於我父親啟發性的文字，那些文字在之後的人生中也更進一步地激勵了我。

My whole perspective changed drastically after that game. When 31 _____ adversities or challenges, I never 32 _____ out for fear of failure. I eventually realized that a ball game can help me accumulate my life 33 _____. That sentence became my 34 _____ — I even framed it and hung it in my room as a reminder. My father, once a contortionist in our local 35 _____, passed away a year ago, but his word passed on. I will always 36 _____ with my plans and never be defeated. I clearly remember what that game taught me: Sky's the limit!

　　我的人生觀在那場比賽以後有了巨大的改變。當我面對逆境與挑戰時，我絕對不因為害怕失敗而臨陣脫逃。我最終體悟到，一場球賽也可以累積我的人生智慧，這個句子成為了我的座右銘，我甚至還把他框起來掛在我的房間裡提醒自己。我父親曾經是本地馬戲團中的軟骨功表演者，一年前去世了，但是他所說的話卻繼續延續下去。我會永遠堅持下去，決不被打敗，我清楚記得那場比賽教我的事：未來有無限可能！

• 填空引導式參考解答

❶ Among	⓭ fade	㉕ plate
❷ remained	⓮ freeze	㉖ hard-won
❸ talented	⓯ gasps	㉗ reversed
❹ rookie	⓰ striking	㉘ standing
❺ push-ups	⓱ resonate	㉙ attributed
❻ enhance	⓲ swung	㉚ inspired
❼ strength	⓳ soared	㉛ encountering
❽ bottom	⓴ curve	㉜ chickened
❾ bases	㉑ vanishing	㉝ wisdom
❿ runs	㉒ homerun	㉞ motto
⓫ barely	㉓ mound	㉟ circus
⓬ cheering	㉔ scratching	㊱ stick

 **高階填空題**

　　練習過這麼多篇時事題型作文，這裡就不再有中文翻譯可以參考，而是要你依照題目，寫出自己的狀況、經驗或觀點。下面有兩題題目，現在就來寫寫看吧！

題目 ①： The Internet and I

With the development of _____
_____
_____
_____. With the fast advancement of _____
_____
_____.

　　Frequently referred to as _____
_____, I _____
_____
_____. I was so _____ that I could barely _____. My
whole perspective changed drastically after _____
_____.

　　In my opinion, although _____
___, we should _____. Therefore, I am in favor of
_____
_____.

• 自由發揮的參考解答範本：

1. The Internet and I

With the development of new technology, it has become much easier for people to do all sorts of things on the Internet. Organize events, have video chats, play online games—you name it, the Internet offers it. However, with the fast advancement of the Internet, we also hear about all kinds of online scams. My parents often warn me not to talk to people online, because all those news articles about poor girls raped by their Internet "friends" are evidence enough that the Internet is not safe. However, I have a different opinion on this subject.

Frequently referred to as a typical nerd, I have no friends at school. The people in my class are not interested in what I am interested in, and there's no way I can carry a conversation with them without feeling awkward. On the Internet, I found people who care about the same things that I do. We can discuss things all day long, and I never feel socially inadequate when I'm talking to my online friends. On my birthday, they all sent me pictures and kind words. I was so touched I could barely speak. No one ever celebrated my birthday for me at school! My whole perspective changed drastically after my online friends came into my life.

In my opinion, although the Internet may contain hidden dangers, we should not stop using it just because of this. Therefore, I'm in favor of making friends on the Internet. If you don't talk to people just because it may be dangerous, you'll never know what you may be missing!

I once thought about _____

_____

_____. For me,

_____ merely exists in my dreams.

Strangely enough, _____

_____

___. I cannot help but _____

_____

_____.

In my opinion, although _____

___, we should _____. Therefore, I am in favor of

_____

_____.

112

2. My Thoughts on Cloning

I once thought about how having another me would be really fun when I was in kindergarten, way before I even heard about cloning technologies. I never realized that having another me would actually become possible in the near future. For me, another self had always been something that merely exists in my dreams.

Strangely enough, as if to answer my childhood prayers, the cloning technology has greatly advanced these years. Scientists have successfully cloned a sheep, and lots of other animals. They have not tried to clone a human yet (I think), but maybe, someday they will! I cannot help but tremble in excitement when I think about it.

In my opinion, although there are lots of moral problems when it comes to cloning, we should still consider developing such a technology. Just think about it we can donate organs to ourselves! Therefore, I am in favor of cloning. Someday, I hope I can get to make friends with another me!

思路第一站

✏️下筆前問問自己 ① ：作文所要探討的時事議題為何？

What? Who? When? Where? Why? How?下筆前先想想這個時事議題的內容，還蓋哪些人事時地物，並寫出自己的看法。寫作時可以不用對時事議題有非常深入、專業的評析，但至少要展現出自己對此議題的基本認知及看法。讓我們以題目The most impressive campaign for environmental protection.（最令人印象深刻的環保運動）為例：

• What? 什麼事？

可以先用一句話概述這個新聞議題的內容。在這裡就可以說 The most impressive campaign for environmental protection is the strike initiated by a Swedish girl. （我最難忘的一項環保運動就是一位瑞典少女發起的罷課活動。）

• Who? 誰？

例如 Greta Thunberg refused to attend school lessons until Sweden's general election drew attention to the climate crisis. （格雷塔·童貝里拒絕去學校上課，直到氣候危機成為瑞典大選重視的議題。）

• When& Where 時間&地點

例如 She initiate the campaign in Sweden in 2018. （她於2018年在瑞典發起了這個運動。）

• Why? 為什麼？

例如I admire the initiator of the campaign because she is determined and inspiring. （我尊敬這個運動的發起人，因為她很有決心而且具啟發性。）

• How? 如何做？

例如I will make efforts to protect the environment, too. （我也會努力保護環境。）

撰寫與時事議題相關的作文時，可以在第一段先簡述自己對這個新聞議題的了解，描述這個時事議題的相關人、事、物，或者事件發生的原因、影響。

✒ 下筆前問問自己②：這個事件或時事議題對自己的重要性為何。

寫作文的時候，不用像新聞報導，把細節交代得很清楚，只要平常有在關注新聞，對於這個時事議題會如何影響自己的生活有些基本的了解和想法就可以了。

例如，你可以説：Starting in August 2018, she skipped school and spent her days on propaganda of global climate strike in front of the Swedish Parliament. In 2019, she inspired 4 million people to join the global climate strike.（2018年八月，她開始罷課並且在瑞典國會前面宣傳全球為氣候罷工罷課的運動。2019年，她發動了4百萬人加入全球氣候罷課運動。）

以這邊的主題為例，可以強調這個新聞議題會引起你注意的重點。例如，你可以説：This environmental protection campaign gets my attention because it is initiated by a common girl who just sticks to her faith and took actions.（我會注意到這個環保運動是因為它是由一位平凡但能堅實信念並採取行動的女孩所發起的。）

這麼一來，時事議題對於讀者來説就更有相關性了。

✒ 下筆前問問自己③：簡述本身會如何因應相關的改變。

不管是政治、金融、環保相關的新聞，都是互相關聯、都會影響民生。可以簡述這則時事議題會對讀者的生活產生如何的影響，並且提出自己的反思，簡述本身會如何因應相關的趨勢。

例如，你可以説：Greta Thunberg's proposal makes me realize that it is necessary to have governments put emphasis on environmental issues, for implementing policies to limit pollution is vital.（格雷塔·童貝里的提議使我了解必須要使政府重視環境議題，因為實行政策來限制污染是必要的。）

I will show more concerns about climate change and do my part to mitigate the human impact on the environment.（我會更加注意氣候變遷的情況並且盡一己之力去減輕人類對環境的影響。）

時事議題大多顯得嚴肅，為了不要使自己的寫作顯得脱離現實，可以盡量將所論述的時事議題和生活做連結，例如政治會引響經濟民生物價等面向，環境污染會直接影響人體的健康等等。

 **單字裝入袋**

　　看國際新聞的時候可以多注意有哪些較常報導的議題，例如環保議題、人權運動、金融貿易等等，記下相關的單字。寫作時常需要表達自己的看法，相關的單字也可應用在這類的作文中。

◆ 環保議題相關單字

❶	污染	pollution = contamination
❷	對生態無害的	eco-friendly
❸	環境保護	environmental protection
❹	全球暖化	global warming
❺	溫室效應	greenhouse effect
❻	溫室氣體	greenhouse gas
❼	氣候變遷	climate change
❽	二氧化碳	carbon dioxide
❾	甲烷	methane
❿	臭氧層	ozone
⓫	生物多樣性	biodiversity
⓬	林木減少	deforestation
⓭	復育森林	reforestation
⓮	棲息地破壞	habitat destruction
⓯	臭氧層破壞	ozone depletion
⓰	二氧化碳排放量	carbon dioxide emission
⓱	煙；氣（有害的）	fume
⓲	PM2.5懸浮微粒	particulate matter 2.5
⓳	酸雨	acid rain
⓴	化石燃料	fossil fuel
㉑	替代能源／永續能源	alternative/ sustainable energy

◆ 人權運動新聞相關單字

❶	基本人權	fundamental human rights
❷	性別平等	gender equality
❸	同性婚姻	same-sex marriage
❹	合法化	legalize
❺	勞工權益	labor right
❻	基本工資	minimum wage
❼	工作場所衛生	workplace hygiene and sanitation
❽	員工福利	employee benefits
❾	難民	refugee
❿	收容所	refugee shelter
⓫	人道救援	humanitarian aid
⓬	特赦	amnesty
⓭	政治庇護	political asylum
⓮	遣返	repatriation
⓯	引渡	extradition

◆ 金融貿易新聞相關單字

❶	貿易戰	trade war
❷	關稅	tariff
❸	貿易協定	trade agreement
❹	自由經濟貿易區	Free Economic Pilot Zone
❺	區域貿易協定	Regional Trading Agreement
❻	嚴重的	serious / severe / fully-fledged
❼	加密貨幣	cryptocurrency
❽	虛擬貨幣	virtual currency

⑨	物聯網	the Internet of things
⑩	跨國公司	multinational corporation
⑪	財團	consortium
⑫	紓困	bailout
⑬	網路商店	cyber shop
⑭	實體商店	brick-and-mortar shops

◆ 表達意見的單字

❶	同意	agree
❷	不同意	disagree
❸	意見	opinion
❹	疑慮	concern
❺	建議	suggestion
❻	假設	assumption
❼	說明	illustration
❽	解釋	explain
❾	贊成	support
❿	不贊成	disapproval

句型萬用包

　　開始下筆寫作前，總要想好一篇作文要如何開頭、承接、結尾。快來把以下的句型套色的部份當作模板，然後在黑色畫底線的部份依照自己的狀況放入適合的單字（想不出填什麼的話，也可以可參考前面「實用單字」的部份找尋靈感）。這樣就能輕鬆完成考場必備的超實用金句、一口氣加好幾分！

• **第一部分：文章開頭先背這些句型！**

❶（名詞）是當前人們最需要重視的議題之一；它對人們的生活有（形容詞）的影響。Climate change / Trade war / Human right is one of the most important issues that people should show concern about; it has significant / devastating / inevitable influence on people's life.

❷ 無可否認的，注意（國際議題／時事議題）是很重要的。（政治／經濟／環保／人權）議題，雖然不太是人們日常生活討論話題，卻是和我們的生活息息相關。
Undeniably, it is significant to catch up with the issues of international affairs / current events. Though people don't often talk about the matters about political / economic / environmental protection / human right issues in their daily conversation, these issues are actually closely related to our daily life.

❸ 當我讀到／看到這則新聞時，我覺得很（形容詞）。（名詞）的議題比我想的更加（形容詞）。
When I read about / watched the news, I felt shocked/ astonished/ astounded/ stunned/ thunderstruck/ petrified. The issue of environmental protection / human right / political ideology / trade war is much severer / more complicated / devastating / daunting than I had thought.

❹ 我了解到解決這個議題需要（名詞）。
I realized that to resolve this issue, more emphasis on related topics / greater cooperation among governments / more devotion from non-government organizations is required.

• 第二部分：文章開展再記這些句型！

❶ （動詞）了一場（名詞），影響多人的生活。

A demonstration / strike / environmental protection campaign / trade war happened/ occurred/ took place/ arose, which brought changes to many people's life.

---

❷ （名詞）所說的話令我印象深刻，使我了解對個議題過於無知不太適當。

The words of the campaign initiator/ organizational representative / political leader were imprinted in my mind, which made me realize that it is inappropriate to stay ignorant about this issue.

---

❸ 如果人們對於這個議題保持過於（形容詞）的態度，事態會變得更加嚴重。

If people remain a(n) indifferent/ unconcerned/ detached/ unsympathetic/ apathetic/ impervious/ careless/ heedless/ inattentive attitude toward this issue, the situation would get worse.

• 第三部分：文章收尾就用這些句型！

❶ 每個人都應該對這個議題（動詞）。

Everyone should pay more attention on this issue / do their part to improve the situation.

---

❷ 這個（名詞）改變了我對這個議題的（名詞）。

The news report / editorial / video clip in the Internet changed my idea/ thought/ view/ opinion/ interpretation/ hypothesis/ notion about this issue.

---

❸ 我開始思考如何（動詞），以改善情況或者防止情況（動詞）。

I began to think about how to make efforts/ devotion/ contribution/ efforts to improve the situation or keep the condition from deteriorating/ worsening/ exacerbating.

❹ 我（動詞）只要 _____（句子）_____，狀況就會逐漸改善。

I am sure/ certain/ convinced that as long as the（句子）government implements relevant projects / people begin to change their behaviors, things would be different.

❺ 就目前的情況看來，（名詞）對於改善這個議題扮演相當重要的角色。

Based on the current situation, international institutions/ regional associations/ international enterprises/ non-government organizations play an important role in resolving this issue.

❻ 人們常常會（動詞）（名詞）。

People tend to underestimate/ underrate/ miscalculate/ misjudge the impact of this issue/ the damage caused by this problem.

❼ 對許多人來說，這次的（名詞）是一個（名詞）。

To many people, this incident /disaster /riot /fluctuation is a wake-up call/ an alarm/ warning sign.

 **模擬小示範**

連接超實用的單字和好用的必備模板句型，就能拼出一篇完整的文章囉！

1. Global Warming

Global warming is one of the greatest challenges that human beings are facing. Though many people don't feel a lot of changes in their daily life, the impact of the global warming has actually brought about many changes in the environment.

One of the most obvious effects of global warming is extreme weather. As the weather patterns are rapidly changing in all parts of the world, many aspects of our life would be influenced. For example, with drastic increase of rainfall in certain areas, some animals have to leave their natural habitat. With higher frequency of heavy precipitation, more floods occur, leading to animal migration and deaths of plants. On the other hand, the extreme heat and droughts in various regions around the world has cause threat to the local residents. Changes in weather also lead to potential risks for human health for the seasonal temperature variation could become less predictable.

As a citizen of the global village, I realized that it's time to show more concern to the global warming issue. To do my part in mitigating the damage that human has caused to the earth, I shall reduce my carbon footprint by taking public transportation more often. I would also support environmental protection campaigns to urge authorities to take measures to resolve this issue.

全球暖化

全球暖化人類所正面臨到的最大考驗之一。雖然許多人不會覺得日常生活中有很多改變，全球暖化的衝擊其實已經對環境造成很多影響。

全球暖化其中一個最明顯的影響是極端氣候。當全球各地的天氣型態快速轉變，我們生活有許多面向都會受到影響。例如，某些地區的雨量暴增，造成一些動物必須要離開他們的自然棲息地。因為較常出現大量降水，有更多洪水發生，造成動物遷徙和植物死亡。另一方面，全球各地許多地區的極端高溫和乾旱對當地的居民造成威脅。天氣改變可能對人類的健康帶來潛在的風險，因為季節的溫度變化變得比較難預測。

作為一個地球村的公民，我了解到該是時候對全球暖化議題表示關心。為了盡一己之力來減緩人類對地球造成的損害，我應該要更常搭乘大眾交通工具，以減少碳足跡。我也會支持環保運動，呼籲當局要採取措施來解決這個問題。

2. Non-Government Organizations

Non-government organizations are the institutions devoted to philanthropic causes. These institutions are not funded by a single country, and they are not operating for making profit. Some well-known NGOs include Red Cross, World Wildlife Fund (WWF), and UNICEF. Over the past two decades, NGOs have become larger, more sophisticated, and more professionalized. More volunteers have joined such organizations. They want to contribute their expertise, such as accounting, medical practice, or legal profession for making positive changes in the community.

Working or volunteering in a non-government organization could be an unforgettable and inspiring experience. Since the volunteers may need to travel to different regions around the world for charity work, it is a good chance to improve the language proficiency and sharpen the interpersonal skills. To a student like me, it could be very helpful for my personal growth. If I could have a chance to work for a non-government organization, I would join UNICEF (United Nations International Children's Emergency Fund). I've been concerning about the welfare of disadvantaged children in my community. I would offer them help by donating money or volunteering to offer tutor lesson for kids in the remote village where educational resources have been scarce. With the experience, I aspire to expand my horizon and offer help underprivileged children in other areas, too. Hopefully, someday I could realize this goal and make contribution for the world.

非政府組織

　　非政府組織是投入慈善工作的機構。這些機構不是由單一國家所資助，而它們營運也不是為了獲利。有些知名的非政府組織，包括紅十字會、世界野生動物基金、聯合國兒童基金會等。過去二十年來，非政府組織變得規模更大、組織更縝密、更加專業化。更多志工加入這樣的團體。他們希望貢獻自己的專業能力，像是會計、醫療、或法律專業，為社群帶來正向的改變。

　　在非政府組織工作或者擔任志工會是一個難忘且深具啟發性的經驗。因為志工可能必須要在世界各地不同的區域之間旅行，這會是一個增進語言能力和提升人際溝通能力的好機會。對於像我這樣的學生來說，這對我的個人成長會很有幫助。如果我有機會為一個非政府組織工作，我想加入聯合國兒童基金會(UNICEF)。我一直在關注我周遭弱勢兒童的福祉。我會透過捐錢、或者自願到教育資源缺乏的偏遠地區去給小朋友上課。有了這些經驗，我立志要拓展視野，並且幫助其他地區的弱勢兒童。希望有一天我能實現這個目標，並且對世界做出貢獻。

更上一層樓

　　學會使用模板句型寫出一篇漂亮的文章後，還可以怎麼在一些小地方讓文章錦上添花呢？

1. Is Referendum a Good Idea?

　　In the modern world, democracy has become a mainstream value that is highly regarded by many people. In a democratic country, citizens can participate in major decision-making process, such as choosing the legislative representatives or voting for important issues that may have impact on everyone's life. In many countries, referendum has become a common practice, which can be considered a display of the core value of democracy: the citizens can express their ideas with their votes. In such decision-making procedure, people follow the 'majority rule.' That is, the idea that is supported by over half of the population would be put into practice.

　　In my point of view, the referendum is not always the best method to bring about the best solution. Although referendum is considered a good idea by many people for the citizens have their say in significant matters for the nation, it may sometimes cause problems. Take the 2016 United Kingdom European Union membership referendum for example. Although the referendum result was that Britain would leave European Union, the 'smooth and orderly' EU exit seems to be a very difficult task, and situation in the country have been in a turbulent state. Based on my personalobservation, referendum may not be a good idea. Voters may make inappropriate choice because of misleading propaganda. Also, if the proportion of the 'majority' is not significantly larger than the 'minority,' the referendum result may not have been strongly supported by public opinion. Therefore, I think the referendum procedure and relevant regulations should amended to make the system more sophisticated.

在現代世界，民主已經成為一個許多人高度重視的價值。在民主國家中，公民可以參加重大的決策過程，像是選舉立法代表或者投票決定可能會影響所有人生活的重要議題。在許多國家，公投成為一個普遍的措施，它可以被視為是民主核心價值的展現：公民可以透過投票表達他們的意見。在這樣的決策過程中，人們遵從「多數決定」。也就是說，有超過半數人口支持的想法會被付諸實行。

就我的意見來說，公投不一定是找出最佳解決方式的最好方法。雖然許多人認為公投是個好主意，因為公民可以在國家重大事務上有發聲的機會，它有時候也會造成問題。以2016年英國脫歐公投為例。雖然公投結果是英國要離開歐盟，似乎很難達成「順利且合宜的」脫歐，而該國處於不安定的狀況。根據我的觀察，公投可能不是一個好主意。選民可能會因為誤導的宣傳而做出不適合的決定。此外，如果「多數」的比例沒有明顯大於「少數」的比例，公投結果可能並沒有受到民意的強烈支持。因此，我認為公投程序和相關的規定應該要修正來使這個系統更佳精密。

★ 這篇文章不但有條理地提出自己對公投這件事情的認知，也舉出了實際例子，來說明自己對公投的看法，顯示出好的作文架構。

2. Is developing Crypto Currency necessary?

Over the past few years, cryptocurrency has become a significant trend in the global economy. Nowadays, 'Bitcoin,' one of the crypto currencies, become the new buzzword. Many people consider this cryptocurrency as a tool that made smart investors make millions in just one or two years. When Bitcoin first came to existence in 2009, it was traded at a low value. In the following years, it experienced exponential growth and brought investors tremendous profit.

Many people know Bitcoin as an investment tool, but it is actually a currency system established on block chain technology. Cryptocurrency has received mixed opinions. People support the development of cryptocurrency focus on its advantages. For example, it allows instant fund transfer. Also, the decentralized application frees the currency from influence of political conditions. Advocates think cryptocurrency and blockchain technology can bring revolutionary changes in the economy on a global scale. However, some people are against crypto currency for its lack of regulations and the shady origins. The complexity and variety of crypto coins may also cause higher risks of scams.

Considering the above-mentioned factors, I wouldn't take developing crypto currency to be the best choice. Despite the great convenience, it may expose users in risks in many aspects. The fluctuation in the currency system is one of my concerns. Also, the block chain technology is not accessible and comprehensible to everyone. Personally, I still prefer to make purchase in the traditional currency for its legitimacy of record keeping appears more trustworthy to me.

發展加密貨幣是必要的嗎？

在過去幾年中，加密貨幣成為全球經濟中一個重要的趨勢。現在，其中一種加密貨幣「比特幣」成為新的熱門話題。許多人認為這種加密貨幣是幫助聰明投資者可以在一、兩年之內賺進百萬的投資工具。比特幣在2009年一開始出現的時候，是以低價在交易。在接下來的幾年之中，它呈現指數型的成長，為投資人帶來大量的收益。

許多人認為比特幣是一種投資的工具，但它其實是一種建立在區塊鏈科技之上的貨幣系統。加密貨幣一直是毀譽參半。支持發展加密貨幣的人著重在它的好處上。例如，它允許立即的資金轉移。此外，去中心化的操作方式，使加密貨幣不受政治情況的影響。擁護者認為加密貨幣和區塊鏈科技可以為全球經濟帶來革命性的改變。然而，有些人反對因為加密貨幣缺乏管制、來源可疑而反對它。加密貨幣的複雜性和多樣性可能也會造成較高的詐騙風險。

考慮到上述的因素，我不會將發展加密貨幣當成是最好的選擇。儘管相當便利，它還是會讓使用者在許多方面承受風險。加密貨幣系統的波動幅度是使我擔心的原因之一。此外，區塊鏈科技不是每個人都能夠取得並理解的。就個人來說，我比較傾向用傳統貨幣買東西，因為我覺得它的合法性和紀錄準確性比較值得信任。

實戰克漏字

◆ **填充翻譯式引導作文**

翻譯能翻得好的人，絕對也能寫出順暢的英文作文！直接開始下筆還沒有把握的話，先從把中文翻譯成英文開始做起吧！每篇文章都有中文可以參考，請照著中文填入單字片語，這樣就可以很快熟悉文章的結構、瞭解到句型如何實際運用在文章裡了。套上顏色的地方，都有套用前面的模板句型喔！

題目 ①： AI 科技的應用

提示：第一段寫出AI科技的應用及影響。
第二段寫出你對AI科技應用的看法。

Artificial intelligence (AI) is an1 _____trending in the modern world. It is widely 2 _____in our daily life. Simply put, AI is a system that can be 'trained' to 3_____ the effectiveness and efficiency of the 4_____ and machines.

人工智慧AI是現代社會中最重要的趨勢之一。它廣泛應用於我們的日常生活中。簡單來說，AI是一個系統，可以「被訓練」來優化工具和機器的效能及效率。

AI is most 5_____ used in the IoT system. The gadgets are connected to the Internet, and the information is stored and 6 _____ to increase the performance of the machine.

AI 常用在物聯網的系統中。這些工具連上網路，資訊被貯存並且分析，以增加機器的效能。

For 7 _____, AI-based information system is 8 _____ to sedans to assist driver in navigating the 9 _____. The system can receive information from Internet about traffic flow on the 10_____ This can help driver avoid being 11 _____ in the traffic jam. Also, the AI system can help the driver 12 _____ to 13 _____conditions to avoid accident, or 14 _____ the harm of a car crash.

舉例來說，AI為基礎的資訊系統被應用在轎車上已協助駕駛操作車輛。這個系統可以由網路上接收有關沿路交通流量的資料。這可以幫助駕駛避免遇到塞車。此外，AI系統可以幫助駕駛對預期之外的情況作出回應以避免發生意外，或者減少車禍帶來的損害。

15 _____ AI has made our life much more convenient than before, people have diverse views on this topic. Some people think that AI could be 16_____ by come malicious units, which may threat the security of common civilians. For example, 17_____an autocratic government intends to monitor the citizens, they can have 18_____ to the personal information of the citizens. Under the 19 _____, people may not have the freedom to express their true thoughts.

雖然AI使我們的生活比以前便利許多，人們對於AI還是有不同的看法。有些人覺得AI可能會被惡意的組織濫用，對一般人民的安全造成威脅。舉例來說，當一個獨裁政府企圖監控人民的時候，他們可以取得人民的個人資訊。在這個情況下，人們可能就沒有表達真正感受的自由了。

Others think that overreliance on AI may have 20_____ effect on the originality and uniqueness of individuals. 21 _____ the advancement of AI, it can not only take over the mechanic and repetitive work in the manufacturing industry,but it could 22_____do tasks that involve lots of planning and calculation, like playing chess.

其他人認為過度依賴AI可能會對每個人的原創性和獨特性有負面的影響。隨著AI的進步，它不僅可以接替製造業當中機械化和重複性質的工作，也可以完成像下棋這種需要大量計畫與計算的工作。

In my point of 23_____, AI has great influence on our life, but it may not have control over our life. As long as we keep enhancing our competence, we could utilize the technology 24_____ than worry about that AI technology would conquer and ruin the human world.

在我看來，AI對我們的生活有很大的影響，但它可能不會控制我們的生活。只要我們持續增進自己的能力，我們就可以利用這項科技，而不是擔心AI會征服且毀滅人類世界。

• 填空引導式參考解答

❶	important	❾	vehicle	⑰	when
❷	applied	❿	route	⑱	access
❸	optimize	⑪	trapped	⑲	circumstances
❹	gadgets	⑫	react	⑳	negative
❺	commonly	⑬	unexpected	㉑	With
❻	analyzed	⑭	reduce	㉒	also
❼	example	⑮	Though	㉓	view
❽	applied	⑯	abused	㉔	rather

•填空引導式參考解答

　　With the rapid 1_____ in traffic system, it is much easier for people to travel around the world. 2_____trips would be a routine for some merchant, political leaders, or people who often go on recreational travels. 3 _____the distance between countries could be shortened with the 4 _____ air traffic service, it is much easier for a 5 _____ disease to spread from country to country.

　　隨著交通系統的進步，人們要在世界各地旅行變得更加容易。橫跨大洲的旅行對商人、政治領袖、或者常常為娛樂目的而旅行的人們來說，像是家常便飯。雖然發展成熟的航空服務使國與國之間的距離縮短了，傳染疾病也更容易從一個國家傳到另一個國家。

　　In the old days, an epidemic outbreak may not be able to 6_____ its influence to other regions, and it is easier for the local government to curb the epidemic from breaking. 7 _____, as people travel between different regions more often, the 8 _____ for the virus to be brought to different place increases, 9_____ may lead to pandemic of the disease.

　　早先，傳染病的爆發不太可能影響到其他的區域，而當地政府也比較能夠控制疫情。但是，隨著人們越來越常往來不同的區域之間，病毒被帶往不同地區的可能性增加，可能造成疾病的大流行。

　　10 _____ the circumstance, international 11 _____ in the is necessary to prevent a disease from 12_____ across countries. When an epidemic is detected in a place, the local government should reveal the 13_____ to the international society so that other countries could take 14_____. The governments could enforce quarantine inspection at custom, and inform travelers about the risks of 15 _____the disease.

在這個情況下，要防止疾病在國際間擴散，國際的合作就相當重要。當傳染病在一個地區被發現，當地政府就應該要將訊息對國際社會公開，其他國家才能採取防護措施。各國政府應該要加強海關檢疫作業，並且告知旅客感染疾病的風險。

Then, international travelers should follow the 16_____ of the ground staff at the airport to complete the 17_____ procedures. Also, the airline passengers should be aware of the initial 18_____ of the disease and report to the authorities 19_____ when they feel unwell after the trip to the epidemic-stricken area. When a 20_____ system among countries is built, it should be easier to battle the diseases like SARS, Avian flu, and African Swine fever.

然後，國際旅客應該要聽從機場地勤人員的指示完成檢疫的流程。此外，航空公司的乘客應該要了解這種疾病的初期症狀，如果到疫區旅行回來之後有不舒服，要向有關當局匯報。如果可以建立國際之間合作的系統，要對抗SARS、禽流感、非洲豬瘟這類的疾病應該會比較容易。

• 填空引導式參考解答

❶ improvement	❽ likelihood	⓯ contacting
❷ Cross-continental	❾ which	⓰ instruction
❸ Though	❿ Under	⓱ quarantine
❹ sophisticated	⓫ cooperation	⓲ symptoms
❺ contagious	⓬ spreading	⓳ concerned
❻ extend	⓭ condition	⓴ collaborative
❼ However	⓮ precautions	

 **高階填空題**

把文章的句型和結構都練熟了，已經有信心可以不用參考範文自己寫一篇了嗎？從這裡開始，你可以依照自己的狀況，套用模板句型練習寫作。請從以下的題目中選一個，現在就開始寫吧！

題目 ①： Climate Refugees

When it comes to _____, we often think of _____
_____. However, _____
_____.

Climate refugees are _____
_____. _____
_____ because of _____ _____
_____. Take _____ for example. Citizens of the
country _____
__. Many _____ suffered from _____
_____
_____
_____. Another example is _____, _____
_____
____. People in the country are expecting _____
_____
___.

Though it seems too late and too difficult to _____
_____, I believe _____
_____
____. On the one hand, we could _____
_____. On the other hand, _____
_____
_____ By doing so, everyone can resolve the
problem together.

• 自由發揮的參考解答範本：

1. Climate Refugee

When it comes to refugees, we often think of people who are forced to leave their home country because of the civil war or persecution. However, a new kind of refugee have been gaining attention in recent years—the climate refugees.

Climate refugees are the people who have to head for a foreign country to seek shelter. Their homeland is no longer habitable because of natural disasters caused by extreme weather and drastic climate change. Take Syrian for example. Citizens of the country was struck by a severe drought for three consecutive years. Many farmers suffered from crop failure and livestock deaths, and they had to move away from their own land and seek jobs at big cities. Another example is Kiribati, a Pacific island nation located midway between Australia and Hawaii. People in the country are expecting a large-scale migration for the country may be entirely under water in 30 to 50 years.

Though it seems too late and too difficult to do anything for mitigating the climate change, I believe there are something we could do to assist the climate refugees. On the one hand, we could introduce legislation so that more countries could accommodate the climate refugees. On the other hand, it is still necessary for every to do their part in reducing greenhouse gas emission and help alleviate the global warming effect. By doing so, everyone can resolve the problem together.

_____ is one of the most commonly-discussed topics in recent years. People have always _____ _____ and several large corporations have _____

_____

_____

As far as I know, _____

_____ for the purposes of _____

_____

_____. The U.S. and Russia, the Cold War rivals, _____

_____. On the other hand, _____

_____. Soon after _____

_____, _____

_____.

Despite the fact that _____

_____ _____

_____, I _____

_____. For one thing, _____ _____

_____. For another, _____

_____. In my point of view,

_____ _____.

2. Space competition

Space competition is one of the most commonly-discussed topics in recent years. People have always been curious about the universe, and some countries and several large corporations have devoted to developing technology which makes it possible for people to have commercial space trips and exploration into deeper space.

As far as I know, several major countries have been advancing their space technology for the purposes of improving human beings' knowledge about outer space but also display their political power in the international society. The U.S. and Russia, the Cold War rivals, have both been displaying their ability to develop space technology. On the other hand, two renowned enterprises have been trying to make commercial spaceflight possible. Soon after the space trip project are announced, some billionaires expressed their interest in participating such pioneering projects.

Despite the fact that advanced space technology indicates huge progress in human's techniques and knowledge, I wouldn't take space race as the most important goal. For one thing, looking for a colony in space doesn't seem practical. For another, there are many other issues that require immediate attention and solution on earth, such as environmental protection. In my point of view, the governments and enterprises should devote more efforts to deal with these problems.

Part 3 學術研究

 思路第一站

在學習過程中，很多人會遇到要撰寫一篇小論文的情形，而考試的時候，偶爾有會遇到要撰寫一篇陳述自己對某個議題看法的文章。寫學術文章的時候，通常需具備以下的架構：

✎ 下筆前問問自己 ①：引言（Introduction）—如何引導讀者進入主題

• 主旨

可以在Topic sentence 就指出這篇文章所要傳達的中心主旨為何，開門見山，一目瞭然。例如：Subsidizing pre-schools is essential in improving the society.（提供幼兒園補助對於社會進步來說相當重要。）

• 動機及重要性

引言的段落也需要說明做這個學術研究的動機、或者對這個議題抱持某項立場的原因。同時說明，研究這個議題的重要性為何、或者採取這個立場，可以帶來什麼好處。例如：Education is important for the development of an individual, and early-year schooling can be very helpful for building positive character traits.（教育對個人發展很重要，而幼兒教育對於建立正向人格很有幫助。）

• 簡述架構

這個段落的結尾，可以簡述之後的文章內容或架構。例如：In the following sections, I will illustrate the idea with actual examples and statistical proof for the significance of the idea.（在接下來的段落中，將會以實際例子以及數據資料佐證來說明這個概念的重要性。）

這樣一來，讀者可以在閱讀引言之後就清楚掌握作者所想要傳達的中心主旨，準備好接受後面文章將會提到的資訊。

🖊 下筆前問問自己 ②：支持論點（supporting sentences）

• 說明理由

在Supporting sentence 的段落，需向讀者具體説明為何支持Topic sentence 提出的立場。例如：Subsidizing pre-schools is a welfare for children of underprivileged families. It also helps to relieve the burden of their parents.（補助幼兒園是對弱勢家庭孩童的福利。它也會幫助減輕這些父母的負擔。）

• 引用研究或名言

在撰寫學術論文或作文的時候，可以引述前人的研究或者名言佳句來支持自己的論點。例如：Franklin said that "an investment in knowledge pays the best interest." Thus, subsidies for educational institutions is essential.（富蘭克林曾説「對知識的投資會有最好的利益」所以，對教育的補助金是很重要的。）

• 提供數據資料

一般的作文可能會舉例、或者陳述理由。例如：The research conducted by a U.S. socialist indicated that over 90 percent of people who have attended pre-school achieve higher social status when they grow up.（一位美國社會學家的研究指出，唸過幼兒園的人當中有百分之90長大後可以達到較高的社會地位。）

🖊 下筆前問問自己③：結論（conclusion）

• 總結論點

作文的結尾，可以總結先前的論點。例如：With the above-mentioned reasons, subsidies for pre-schools plays a significant role in the development of children, families, and the society.（基於上述的理由，對幼兒元的補助金對於兒童、家庭、及社會的發展都很重要。）

• 提供建議

除了摘要、重申前述的論點之外，也應提出建議。例如：The government should allot proper amount of money from the annual budget to subsidize pre-schools.（政府應該由年度預算中分配適當的金額來補助幼兒園。）

單字裝入袋

　　有些概念可以用到不同的單字來表達，寫文章時可以多使用一些學術常用的詞彙，例如方法可以說"way"，在學術的文章中則可以用 "method"、"approach"。以下列出一些常用在學術文章中的單字。

❶	分析	analysis
❷	方法	approach / method
❸	領域	area / field
❹	評估	assessment / evaluation
❺	假設	assume
❻	當局	authority
❼	可取得的	available
❽	獲益	benefit
❾	概念	concept
❿	一致	consistent
⓫	重要的	constitutional / significant / essential
⓬	情境	context / situation / circumstance
⓭	合約	contract
⓮	造成	create / cause
⓯	資料	data / statistics
⓰	定義	definition
⓱	衍生	derived
⓲	分佈	distribution
⓳	成立	established
⓴	估計	estimate /
㉑	證據	evidence
㉒	因素	factor
㉓	功能	function
㉔	辨別	identified

㉕	指出	indicate
㉖	牽涉到	involve
㉗	議題	issue
㉘	主要的	major
㉙	原則	principle
㉚	流程	procedure / process
㉛	研究	research
㉜	特定的	specific
㉝	理論	theory
㉞	變數	variable

◆ 引言部分常用單字／片語

❶	由……組成	constitutes
❷	理論的發展	theoretical development
❸	目標	aims & objectives
❹	研究動機	study motivation
❺	研究重要性	research niche / significance of the work
❻	文獻缺漏	gap in the literature
❼	概念架構	conceptual framework
❽	普遍採用的	widely adapted

◆ 支持主旨段落常用的單字

❶	研究發現	research findings
❷	研究結果	research results
❸	趨勢	trends
❹	主張	argue (v) / argument (n)
❺	指出	indicate / reveal / demonstrate / illustrate
❻	調查	investigate / look into

❼	啟發	inspire (v) / inspiration (n)
❽	比較	comparison
❾	差異	differences / discrepancies
❿	證實	confirm / verify
⓫	與⋯⋯一致	correspond to
⓬	明顯的	obvious / clear / apparent
⓭	與⋯⋯有關	associated with / related to
⓮	解釋	illustrate / explain
⓯	觀點	viewpoint / standpoint
⓰	影響	impact / influence

◆ 結論段落常用單字

❶	結論	conclude (v) conclusion (n)
❷	摘要	in summary
❸	結果	result / outcome
❹	一般來說	generally speaking / Overall
❺	調查	investigation / survey
❻	潛在的	potential
❼	推薦	recommendation
❽	保證	warranted
❾	適用於	applied to...
❿	處理	be addressed to
⓫	探索	explore
⓬	情境	context / situation / circumstance

句型萬用包

　　開始下筆寫作前，總要想好一篇作文要如何開頭、承接、結尾。快來把以下的句型套色的部份當作模板，然後在黑色畫底線的部份依照自己的狀況放入適合的單字（想不出填什麼的話，也可以可參考前面「實用單字」的部份找尋靈感）。這樣就能輕鬆完成考場必備的超實用金句、一口氣加好幾分！

・第一部分：文章開頭先背這些句型！

❶ 過去幾十年以來，（主題）在（事件）中一直扮演重要的角色。

In the past few decades, the revised versions of curriculum guidelines have played an important role in the innovation of educational system.

❷ 在（事件）的過程中，（主題）對（相關的事物）有很大的影響力。

In the process of innovating the mandatory events, the revised curriculum guidelines have great impact on how the teachers implement the courses.

❸ 在（領域）當中，最重要的研究議題是（主題）。

One of the major topics to be investigated in the field of educational renovation is the washback effect of the change on the major exams.

❹ 一個（主題）常見的問題就是（對於問題的描述）。

A well-known problem with the revision of curriculum guideline is that teachers may be bewildered about how to implement the new principles without a clear understanding about possible changes in the college entrance exam.

❺ 為了要解決（相關議題）的問題，我們應該要研究（主題）。

To rectify the problem of insufficient preparation of teachers for implementing the new curriculum guidelines, we should investigate on teachers' perception of the new principles, which can inspire authorities concerned to arrange on-the-job training courses.

• 第二部分：文章開展再記這些句型！

❶ （相關）研究顯示（某件與主題相關事的重要性）。

Studies/ Relevant researches have shown that teachers' perception about the revised curriculum guidelines is closely related to the efficiency of implementing innovative ideas in education system.

---

❷ 已經有些相關的措施來處理（與主題相關的議題）。

The authorities concerned have made several attempts to solve the issue that teachers need more support in implementing the innovated curriculum.

---

❸ 主要的目標是要發展一個成熟的方法（來解決與主題相關的問題）。

The aim is to develop more sophisticated method to enhance/ raise/ strengthen the teachers' understanding on the revised curriculum guidelines and help them have better competence to put the course principles into practice.

• 第三部分：文章收尾就用這些句型！

❶ 為了（達成與主題有關的目標），（相關單位）將會（採取相應的措施）。

To promote the new curriculum, the local Ministry of Education office would organize seminars to introduce the innovate ideas.

---

❷ 因為有（名詞）的（名詞），（與主題相關的現象）將會獲得改善。

With the detailed explanation and practical examples offered on the seminar, the problem that teachers have insufficient understanding about the pedagogical innovation would be resolved.

---

❸ 這個（形容詞）的措施也會對（與主題相關議題）有正面的幫助。

The new/ enforced/ direct/ key measure would also have positive effect on the efficiency of education.

---

❹ 總之，（與主題相關的措施）是一個（形容詞）的（措施）。

In sum, organizing the seminars to enhance teachers' comprehension and motivation to implement the new curriculum is an essential/ pivotal/ necessary measure.

連接超實用的單字和好用的必備模板句型，就能拼出一篇完整的文章囉！

1. Bilingual Education

Over the past few years, **the promotion of bilingual education** has been a controversial issue; **people have different views on whether the innovative practices in educational system.** Some people say that it is essential to integrate English into different subjects in the curriculum, while others think immersion in English is not the best choice.

For those who support bilingual education, high English proficiency is the key to success. It is assumed that if students can learn English while learning the subject content, students can use English better both in their academic work and in daily conversation. This can make students gain some advantages in the competitive society.

On the other hand, people who are against bilingual education think that overemphasizing English throughout the curriculum may hinder the learning of students' first language. Also, students may not be able to comprehend the course content well if the lessons are not delivered in their mother tongue. This may have negative impact in learning of academic subjects and the leaning of second language (English).

Some experts have made suggestions **regarding this issue.** In order to avoid the "bipolar distribution of English proficiency" which be worsened by implementation of bilingual education, the government should consider 'equity' rather than 'equality.' That is, they should consider students' need while incorporating English exposure throughout the curriculum rather than providing the language input in all classes that may seem overwhelming to some students.

雙語教育

在過去幾年，**推廣雙語教育**一直是個具爭議的議題；**人們對於這種教育體系中的創新有不同的看法**。有些人認為有必要將英語融合至課程當中不同的科目，而有些人認為沈浸式英語融入課程中並不是最好的選擇。

支持雙語教育的人認為，好的英語能力是成功的關鍵。他們認為如果學生可以一面學習學科內容、一面學習英文，就可以在學業上和日常生活對話中將英文使用地更好。這可以讓學生在競爭的社會中更有優勢。

另一方面，反對雙語教育的人們認為過度在課程各個面向中強調英文可能會阻礙學生第一語言的學習。此外，如果課程內容不是用他們的母語呈現，學生可能無法理解。這會對於他們的學科學習以及第二語言（英文）學習有負面的影響。

有些專家已經**對此議題**提出相關建議。「英語能力的雙峰現象」可能會因為實行雙語教育而更加惡化，為了避免這個現象，政府應該先考慮「公平」而非「平等」的概念。也就是說，他們在整個課程中納入更多接觸英語機會的時候，應該考慮到學生的需求，而不是提供過多、會讓一些學生無法承受的語言輸入機會。

2. The Length of a School Day

One of the major topics to be investigated in the field of **education renovation** is **the length of a school day.** Some people think that students can benefit more from the extended school days, while others think the shorter school days are better for students' development and maturity.

The supporters of extending school days consider longer learning time at school may help underprivileged children and their families. They think that more hours in academic training would never do harm students' development. Also, the additional courses and comprehensive activities after the formal lessons at schools is a way to keep students from poor families from being affected by gangsters in the community.

Skeptics of longer school days point out that high achieving countries like Finland and Singapore have opted to maximize the learning and collaboration time within an appropriate length of schedule. To them, shorter school days allow students more freedom for arrange their after-school time, which helps them explore the possibilities such as gaining work experience or devoting to community service.

To **maximize the effectiveness of school days and help students reach a school-life balance**, experts have **offered some suggestions**. For one thing, the school-life balance, experts have offered some suggestions. For one thing, the education system can offer remedial lessons and club activities for students who need them. Also, the schools would coordinate educational resources in the community as well as offering guidance for students in terms of part-time work. Schools can offer students assistance in arranging after-school time rather than lengthening the school day.

學校一天的上課長度

__教育變革__的其中一個主要應調查的議題是__學校一天的長度__。有些人認為延長學校一天的常度對學生是有益的，而有些人認為上學時間短一點對於學生的發展和成熟比較好。

支持延長上學時間的人認為，學生在學校待比較久，可以幫助弱勢的孩童和家庭。他們認為學術訓練的時數延長，對學生的發展不會有害處。此外，額外的課程以及正式課程之後各式各樣的學校活動，是可以讓貧窮家庭學生免於受到社區幫派份子影響的方法。

不支持延長上學時間的人指出，芬蘭和新加坡等高度發展的國家，都選擇在適當長度的上學時間當中，盡量達到最大的學習和合作效果。對他們來說，上學時間短一點可以讓學生有更多自由安排課後時間，幫助學生探索不同的可能性，像是獲得工作經驗或者投入社區服務等等。

為了__要讓上學時間效率最大化，並且幫助學生達成課業與生活之間的平衡__，專家__提出一些建議__。一方面，教育系統可以提供補救教學課程和社團活動給需要的學生就好。此外，學校可以整合社區當中的教育資源並且提供學生打工的輔導。學校可以提供學生規劃課後時間的協助而不是延長上學的時間。

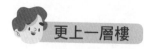

學會使用模板句型寫出一篇漂亮的文章後，還可以怎麼在一些小地方讓文章錦上添花呢？

1. Regulations on Social Media

With the prevalence of Internet and the convenience it brings in spreading information, a commonly-discussed issue is how to implement proper regulations on social media.

The popularity of social media like Facebook and Twitter has made information about politics, economy, and environmental issues assessible for more people. However, a well-known problem behind the trend is that fake news and irrational remarks may mislead people and cause panic or argument among people. The impact of such phenomenon may be more serious than many people have though. While anyone can initiate a campaign to for justice like MeToo, the impact of fake news spread through social media on the US presidential election should not be ignored.

To rectify the problem of **twisted information that may lead people to make inappropriate political or financial decisions as well as eliminate the disputes caused by biased comments**, proper regulations on social media should be implemented. Authorities concerned should establish proper laws and remain the neutrality of audit committee. Hopefully, the new system could maintain the speech independence and credibility of online posts at the same time.

對於社群媒體的管控

隨著網路的普及,以及它使傳播資訊更加便利,如何針對社群媒體執行適當規範也成為一個常被討論的議題。

Facebook和Twitter等網站受歡迎的程度,使有關政治、經濟、以及環境議題相關的資訊更容易被人們所取得。但是,這個趨勢背後有個明顯的問題,就是假新聞可能誤導民眾並且造成恐慌或引起紛爭。這種現象造成的衝擊可能比許多人所想得更為嚴重。雖然每個人都可以發起像MeToo這樣尋求正義的運動,透過社群媒體傳的假新聞對美國總統大選的影響也不容忽視。

為了解決**錯誤訊息可能導致人們做出不適當的政治或財務決定的問題、並且減少偏激言論帶來的紛爭**,應該要對社群媒體採取適當的規範。有關當局應該制定適當的法律並且維持審查委員會的中立。希望新的系統可以同時維持言論獨立性以及線上發文的可信度。

★這篇文章不僅列出社群媒體應受到規範的原因,也舉出實例、並提出了具體的建議,不僅依循學術文章應有的架構,更可以啟發讀者對這個議題有更深的思考。

2. The Effect of Smartphone on Learning

The prevalence of smartphone has significant impact on the students' learning efficiency. Some people consider smartphone a gadget that can facilitate learning, while others think of using smartphone an addictive activity that can impede learning outcome.

Some studies have shown that the presence of the smartphone can distract learners' attention, hindering learning effect. A study published in the journal Computers and Human Behavior indicated that cell phones tend to reduce concentration and memory. The researchers found that some students even suffer from nomophobia—the fear of being without access to the cell phone. The addiction of technology also has negative effect on students' performance on quizzes.

On the other hand, some pedagogical workers claimed that smartphones can facilitate students' learning. Some experiments conducted on secondary school pupils have proved application of smartphones can increase students' motivation in learning. Access of online learning resources can also contribute to upgrading the curriculum.

Experts have been trying to minimize the negative effects of smartphones on learning; they intend to incorporate this technology in the educational procedure. In a word, **discipline and proper guidance for students would be essential for making smartphones a helpful tool rather than a hindrance in students learning.**

智慧型手機對學習的影響

　　手機的普及對於學生學習效果有很大的影響。有些人認為智慧型手機是一個可以增進學習的工具，而有些人認為使用智慧型手機是讓人上癮的活動，會妨礙學習成果。

　　有些研究指出，智慧型手機的出現會使學習者分心，降低學習的效果。有一個在《電腦與人類行為》期刊中發表的研究指出，手機常會降低專注力和記憶力。研究者發現，有些學生會患有「無手機恐懼症」——害怕手機不在身邊。對這種科技上癮也對學生在小考的表現有負面的影響。

　　另一方面，有些教育工作者宣稱智慧型手機可以促進學生學習。有些在中等學校進行的實驗證明智慧型手機可以增加學生的學習動機。使用線上學習資源也可以使課程升級。

　　專家一直在嘗試減少智慧型手機對學習的負面影響；他們試圖要將這個科技應用在教育的過程中。簡而言之，**如果要讓手機在學習過程中成為有用的工具，而不是對學生學習的阻礙，給予學生紀律和適當引導是很重要的。**

★實際提出研究的結果，呈現正面和反面的觀點，並且在結尾的時候做出綜合的評論。

◆ 填充翻譯式引導作文

　　翻譯能翻得好的人，絕對也能寫出順暢的英文作文！直接開始下筆還沒有把握的話，先從把中文翻譯成英文開始做起吧！每篇文章都有中文可以參考，請照著中文填入單字片語，這樣就可以很快熟悉文章的結構、瞭解到句型如何實際運用在文章裡了。套上顏色的地方，都有套用前面的模板句型喔！

題目 ①： Developing Tourism in Taiwan

提示： 第一段描述發展觀光業的好處與壞處。
第二段如何發展台灣的觀光業較為適宜。

　　The development of tourism in Taiwan is one of the 1 _____ issues when it comes to 2 _____ the local economy. People have 3 _____ views about promoting tourist industry in Taiwan. 4 _____ tourism industry thrives, local people can have more job 5 _____, and the local custom and cultural 6 _____ can be better preserved. Since more tourists come to Taiwan, there will be 7_____ demand for accommodation and 8 _____ service, which could bring about more work opportunities. On the other hand, for the purpose of 9 _____ local culture to tourists from other countries, people may be willing to 10 _____ more efforts in 11 _____ lost traditions. The authorities concerned have been making efforts in offering 12 _____ and guidance to tourist agencies in recent years.

　　發展台灣觀光業是談到促進本地經濟時一個重要的議題。人們對於促進台灣的觀光業有不同的看法。隨著觀光產業興盛，本地人可以有更多的工作機會，而且本地的習俗和文化的特色可以被保存地比較好。因為有更多觀光客來台灣，對於住宿和餐飲服務的需求也會更多，就會帶來更多的工作機會。另一方面，為了介紹本地的文化給其他國家的觀光客，人們會願意投入努力來復興已經失傳的傳統。有關當局近年來一直在努力提供旅行社諮詢服務以及指導。

　　To develop a more 13 _____ method to enhance tourism, several aspects have to be taken into 14 _____. First of all, it is necessary to take proper 15 _____ in registering and managing foreign tourist to avoid the 16 _____ of illegal immigrants. A well-organized 17 _____ should be built to eliminate human-trafficking 18 _____ of tour group. On the other hand, it is also important to remain the 19 _____ between environmental protection and 20 _____ the scenic spot. With 21 _____ gaining popularity, there are more itineraries for tours that would cause less 22 _____ while making people aware of the need to protect the environment. In sum, while boosting 23 _____ by promoting tourism in Taiwan, local security and environmental 24 _____ should not be ignored.

為了發展出一個更精密的方法來促進觀光產業，有一些面向應該要考慮到。首先，有必要採取適當措施來登記與管理外國旅客，以防止非法移民的問題。應該要見建立一個縝密的系統來防止偽裝成旅行團的人口走私。另一方面，在環境保護以及宣傳景點之間取得平衡也是重要的。隨著生態旅遊業越來越受歡迎，有更多的旅遊行程是為了減少損害並且提升人們的環保意識。總而言之，利用發展台灣觀光業來促進經濟的同時，本地的安全和環境永續也不該被忽略。

• 填空引導式參考解答

❶ essential	❾ introducing	⑰ system
❷ boosting	❿ devote	⑱ disguised
❸ diverse	⑪ reviving	⑲ balance
❹ As	⑫ consultation	⑳ promoting
❺ opportunities	⑬ sophisticated	㉑ ecotourism
❻ features	⑭ consideration	㉒ damage
❼ greater	⑮ measures	㉓ economy
❽ catering	⑯ problem	㉔ sustainability

提示：有些人認為設置動物園是限制動物的活動範圍，而且為了商業利益犧牲動物的自由；有些人認為設置動物園可以保育動物、並且有教育意義，對於動物和人類來說都是有益處的。請提出你的觀點，說明設置動物園是否合理、有正面或負面的影響。

Zoos are great places to see. Visitors can see the 1 _____ animals from all over the world, which can 2 _____ their horizons. However, there are different 3 _____ about the establishment of the zoo. Some people consider zoos a good facility, 4 _____ others think zoos could do more harm than good.

動物園是很適合參觀的地方。參觀者可以看到來自世界各地的迷人動物，幫助他們拓展視野。然而，對於建立動物園，人們有些不同的看法。有些人認為動物園是一個好的設施，而有些人認為動物園弊多於利。

Supporters of building zoos think that 5 _____ the zoos is helpful in conserving animals, and the 6 _____ facilities in the zoos can raise 7 _____ of animal conservation. Visitors of the zoo can have better 8 _____ about the features of different species, and they could become more 9 _____ about maintaining habitats for these animals. Another 10 _____ of constructing zoos is that endangered animals can be 11 _____ and protected in the zoos. This is helpful for the survival of the 12 _____ animals.

支持建立動物園的人認為建立動物園有助於保育動物，而動物園當中的教育設施可以提昇人們對動物保育的意識。拜訪動物園的人可以對不同物種有更多的了解，他們會更關心要保護那些動物的棲息地。另一個建立動物園的好處是瀕危的動物可以在動物園中被復育和保護。這可以幫助受到威脅的動物生存。

13 _____ to the idea of building zoos, on the other hand, think that people are just using animals to 14 _____ themselves, and this is not fair for the precious creatures 15 _____ in the zoo. To them, zoos are mostly built for 16 _____ purposes rather than for education or animal 17 _____. Also, without proper 18 _____, the

zoo animals would have their immunity weakened over the years of being 19 _____ to the zoo.

　　另一方面，反對建立動物園的人認為人們只是利用動物娛樂自己，而這對這些被困在動物園裡的珍貴動物並不公平。對他們來說，動物園建立，大多是為了商業的目的、而不是為了教育或者保育動物。此外，沒有適當管理，動物園裡的動物，受限於動物園當中多年之後，免疫能力會變弱。

Based on the 20 _____ mentioned above, zoos can be of benefit, but they need to be under 21 _____ supervision to prevent some negative 22 _____. The zoo staff should be well-trained, and the 23 _____ should have the management plans 24 _____ by the authorities concerned.

　　基於以上提到的因素，動物園可以是有好處的，但是他們受到適當監督來預防一些負面的效果。動物園工作人員應該要受到適當訓練，而有關當局也應該要審核動物園的管理計畫。

•填空引導式參考解答

❶ fascinating	❾ concerned	⑰ conservation
❷ broaden	❿ benefit	⑱ management
❸ perspectives	⓫ nurtured	⑲ limited
❹ while	⓬ threatened	⑳ factors
❺ building	⓭ Opponents	㉑ proper
❻ educational	⓮ entertain	㉒ effect
❼ awareness	⓯ confined	㉓ administrator
❽ understanding	⓰ commercial	㉔ scrutinized

 高階填空題

把文章的句型和結構都練熟了，已經有信心可以不用參考範文自己寫一篇了嗎？從這裡開始，你可以依照自己的狀況，套用模板句型練習寫作。請從以下的題目中選一個，現在就開始寫吧！

題目 ① : Rail transit in Taiwan

When it comes to traffic infrastructure in Taiwan, many people think of the _____
_____.

The construction of the system has brought great convenience to residents in the metropolitan areas. However, _____
_____. _____.
Some people consider _____ _____
_____, while others _____ _____
_____.

To some people, _____
_____. According to the experts, a train is much more efficient than the car or a bus in terms of _____.
A train of the metro system is much faster than the car. Besides, _____
_____ _____
_____. This illustrates that railway transit system could make the road less crowded.

In contrast, _____
_____. _____.
They think that _____ _____
_____. Also, _____ _____
_____.

With the above-mentioned factors taken into consideration, _____
_____. However, _____
_____
_____.

1. Rail transit in Taiwan

When it comes to traffic infrastructure in Taiwan, many people think of the well-developed High-Speed Rail system, Taipei Metro system, and the Kaohsiung Rapid Transit System.

The construction of the system has brought great convenience to residents in the metropolitan areas. However, people have diverse views about extending the railway system. Some people consider the railway system the best solution for public transportation, while others think that the cost and harm of constructing railway systems outweigh its benefit.

To some people, the rail transit such as the metro system is the best way to alleviate the heavy traffic in the urban area. According to the experts, a train is much more efficient than the car or a bus in terms of transporting passengers during rush hours. A train of the metro system is much faster than the car. Besides, as more people are taking the metro system or light rail train, the traffic on the road would be eased. This illustrates that railway transit system could make the road less crowded.

In contrast, some people are opposed to extending rail transit system to different areas. They think that during the construction work of the rail transit system, the road would be even more crowded. Also, if the rapid transit system extending into the suburban areas are not frequently used, it would be operated in deficit.

With the above-mentioned factors taken into consideration, the government could take rail transit a good option for enhancing the efficiency of public transportation system. However, a thorough plan for enhancing usage rate and proper allocation of budget will be the prioritized issues to consider.

題目 ② : Medical Practice Claim

Nowadays, people are more aware of _____
_____. Under the circumstance, _____
_____. When the patients or their fam
ilies_____, they would
claim that _____. This
often does harm to both the medical personnel and the patients. The former
may feel distressed for being accused of _____
_____. The latter, on the other hand, may feel agonized
for suffering not only for the illness or injury but also for the treatment in the
hospital.

To solve the problem, _____
_____. First of all, _____
_____
_____
_____. The doctors and
nurses should_____.
Secondly, _____
__. When the patients can_____
_____, they _____,
which could _____.

In sum, medical malpractice is something that everyone wants to avoid.
To minimize the harm such cases may cause, _____
_____ _____.

2. Medical Practice Claim

Nowadays, people are more aware of protecting their rights. Under the circumstance, more disputes have occurred in the medical care cases. When the patients or their families have doubts about the outcome of medical practice, they would claim that they have suffered from malpractice of the medical practitioners. This often does harm to both the medical personnel and the patients. The former may feel distressed for being accused of a conduct which was done to help the patient but end up to bring about an undesired outcome. The latter, on the other hand, may feel agonized for suffering not only for the illness or injury but also for the treatment in the hospital.

To solve the problem, some experts have proposed several possible solutions. First of all, authorities concerned should provide professional training to help medical practitioners avoid such blunder. The doctors and nurses should also get mental health support so that they would remain calm and make proper decisions under the intense situations. Secondly, a care system for victims of medical malpractice should be established. When the patients can get appeased and offered compensation about the matter, they might feel less frustrated, which could make the medical practice claims less complicated and time-consuming.

In sum, medical malpractice is something that everyone wants to avoid. To minimize the harm such cases may cause, the medical professionals, the patients, and the government should work together.

Chapter 4
看圖寫作文

Part 1 ▶ 圖表分析
Part 2 ▶ 連環圖片
Part 3 ▶ 描寫照片

Part 1 圖表分析

思路第一站

✏️下筆前問問自己 ①：先說明是哪一種圖表！

常見的圖表包括柱狀圖（bar graph）、線型圖（line graph）、圓餅圖（pie chart）或表格（table）等。除了點明是哪一種圖表以外，更重要的是要說明這個圖表的主題是什麼？是用來傳達怎樣的訊息？例如，如果這張圖表的主題是一百名高中生最想要的寵物種類，就可以這麼說：A hundred high school students were interviewed on what kind of pet they want the most. The results are shown in this bar graph.「一百名高中生被訪問他們最想要哪種寵物。結果如這張柱狀圖所示。」

你也可以直接破題，並點出數據。例如：As we can see from the pie chart, 30% of high school students favor huskies, and 26% favor sheepdogs.「正如圓餅圖所示，三成的高中生偏好哈士奇，而二成六喜愛牧羊犬。」

✏️下筆前問問自己 ②：再描述整體趨勢、特別的現象！

圖表中總會有幾項特別突出，如在圓餅圖中比例特別大一塊、或是在柱狀圖中就只有某一根特別短之類的。這種時候，一定要把這種特別的狀況提出來描述。例如如果你發現在一百名高中生中，高達七十名想要養狗，遠遠勝過其他種類的動物，就非得提一下這個狀況不可：Seventy out of one hundred students said they wanted dogs as a pet.「一百名中有七十個學生說他們想要狗當寵物。」

若是線型圖，多半是用來表達「演變」的狀況。像是如果要表示從2000年到2012年中，班上有手機的學生數量，就不會用圓餅圖。如果從線型圖中發現有手機的人數一直在增加，就可以把這個趨勢點出來，甚至預

測未來可能的狀況：It's obvious in this line graph that every year more and more students have cell phones. In 2016, perhaps, it will be mandatory for all students to have cell phones!「從這線型圖可以明顯看出每年都有越來越多學生有手機。也許到了2016年，學生們都會被規定一定要有手機才行！」

🖊 下筆前問問自己 ③：也可以討論自己的狀況！

要是每個人都只分析圖表中的數字而已，文章會千篇一律，閱卷老師也會看到睡著。要讓自己的文章與眾不同、吸引注意，就可以加入自己的親身體驗。例如當你發現一百名學生中有七十名都想養狗，而覺得很驚訝：難道他們不會想養其他的動物嗎？這種時候就可以寫：I'm surprised that so many students want dogs. What about birds and cats? Aren't fish good pets too?「我很驚訝這麼多學生想要狗。鳥和貓呢？魚難道不是好的寵物嗎？」

除了討論自己的狀況外，針對圖表提供意見也很重要，而且可以為全文作畫龍點睛之效。例如: According to the picture, we can assume that 2% of customers of Apple switched to Sony Ericsson, and that it is about time for Apple to think of a new marketing strategy.「依據圖表我們可以推測2% Apple 的顧客轉移至Sony Ericsson；因此，Apple 應該擬定一個新的銷售策略。」如此一來，除了分析圖表，我們還能很有邏輯的提出建議。

不過，要注意的是撰寫圖表首重分析，分析要盡量客觀，且應該避免口語跟情緒化字眼。所以就算你很討厭狗，也不要說出什麼「這些受訪的學生真沒品味」之類的話。而若題目中只要你描述圖表的狀況，沒有提到任何分析方面的事情，那就最好不要加入自己的感想，且盡量使用精簡的文字，以免被視為離題。

 單字裝入袋

　　要學會寫一篇作文前，最重要的是要先有足夠的字彙，以下提供描述經驗相關的作文絕對好用的單字！

◆ 描述數據變化的單字

　　圖表中若涉及了兩個以上的時間，就一定要寫數據的變化。變化的種類一般有增加、減少、波動、不變，通常用動詞＋副詞，或者形容詞＋名詞來表示。

　　常用的單字如下：

表示增加的動詞			
增加 increase	上升 rise	竄升 jump	飆升 shoot up
上升 go up	成長 grow	湧升 surge	爬升 climb

表示減少的動詞		
減少 decrease	掉落 fall	下沉 sink
下降 go down	被減少 is reduced	墜落 dip
衰退 decline	掉落 drop	墜落 plunge

形容詞	
慢慢的 slow	適當的 moderate
漸漸的 gradual	顯著的 significant
穩定的 steady	大幅的 sharp
快速的 rapid	戲劇性的 dramatic
些微的 slight	顯著的 drastic

表示增加的名詞		
增加 increase	竄升 jump	成長 growth
上升 rise	湧升 surge	

表示減少的名詞		
減少 decrease	縮減 reduction	下降 fall
衰退 decline	掉落 drop	

表示維持不變的單字片語	
維持不變 remain the same	維持平穩 remain stable
達到穩定 reach a plateau	維持穩定 remain constant
穩定 stabilize	

◆ 說明數據意義常用動詞

❶	指出	indicate
❷	揭露	reveal
❸	假設	assume
❹	闡明	illustrate
❺	指出	point out
❻	預料	predict
❼	提出	present
❽	顯示	show
❾	猜想	suppose

◆ 描述比例的單字

❶	百分之七十五（四分之三）	75 percent = three quarters
❷	百分之六十六（三分之二）	66 percent = two-thirds
❸	百分之五十（一半）	50 percent = half
❹	百分之三十三（三分之一）	33 percent = a third
❺	百分之二十五（四分之一）	25 percent = a quarter
❻	百分之二十（五分之一）	20 percent = one-fifth

 **句型萬用包**

　　開始下筆寫作前，總要想好一篇作文要如何開頭、承接、結尾。快來把以下的句型套色的部份當作模板，然後在黑色畫底線的部份依照自己的狀況放入適合的單字（想不出填什麼的話，也可以可參考前面「實用單字」的部份找尋靈感）。這樣就能輕鬆完成考場必備的超實用金句、一口氣加好幾分！

•第一部分：文章開頭先背這些句型！

❶ 這張（名詞）顯示（名詞子句）的概況。

The pie chart / line graph / table shows the general picture of the ways students use their computers / people's preferences in movies / the way people think about music.

---

❷ 這張（名詞）顯示在（數字）年中，（名詞子句）有哪些改變。

This pie chart / line graph / bar graph shows the change of people's preferences in books / opinions on new technology / feelings about idols over a four / ten / sixteen-year period.

---

❸ 這張（名詞）顯示在（時間）與（時間）的時間之間，（名詞子句）的數量。

The graph / table / chart shows the number of students who have iPhones / girls who have boyfriends / people who have pets between 2011 and 2012 / October and December / the 20th and the 30th .

---

❹ 這張（名詞）顯示（名詞）與（名詞）這些人對（名詞）的選擇有什麼差別。

The bar graph / table / pie chart illustrates the difference between male students and female students / girls and boys / adults and teenagers in choices of snacks / fruit / transportation .

---

❺ 在這張（名詞）裡，（動詞）了人們如何（動詞）。

It is shown / exhibited / demonstrated in this graph / chart / table how people spend their vacations / sleep / go to work.

❻ 這是一張（名詞），顯示一次有關於（名詞子句）的（名詞）的結果。

This is a bar graph / chart / table that shows the results of a survey / questionnaire / interview on people's opinions on their salary / the ways students spend their allowance / the way students think about their parents.

• **第二部分：文章開展再記這些句型！**

❶ 整體來說，他們花（比例）的（名詞）來做（動詞+ing子句）這樣的事。

Overall, they spend two-thirds / twenty percent / one-fourths of their weekends / time / money surfing the Internet / making pancakes / buying clothes.

❷ 整體來說，（名詞）的數量從（時間）到（時間）這個時間，呈現（名詞）的狀態。

Overall, the number of students / rich people / cars shows an increase / decrease / rise from 2011 / January / 10 o'clock to summer / Monday / March.

❸ （名詞）這個東西（形容詞）地領先（名詞）這個東西百分之（數字）。

Motorcycles / Cats / Strawberries takes a huge / little / surprising lead of 15 / 25 / 50 percent over bicycles / mice / bananas.

❹ （名詞）只有（數字）%，明顯地不受歡迎。

Swimming / Snakes / Pineapples, which has a meager proportion of 5 / 3 / 10 percent, apparently is under disfavor.

❺ 相對地，（名詞）這個東西佔了（名詞）的（比例）比例。

In contrast, dancing / Mexican food / water takes up one-third / two-thirds / 30 percent of people's weekends / the timetable / my afternoons.

❻ 我們可以從這張（名詞）看出（名詞）這些人都喜歡（名詞）多過（名詞）。

We can see from this **chart / graph / table** that **students / women / people** prefer bananas / vegetables / telephones over apples / meat / cell phones.

•第三部分：文章收尾就用這些句型！

❶ 整體來說，從（時間）到（時間）這段時間，在（名詞）這方面有（形容詞）的改變。

Overall, from **2010 / February / Monday** to **winter / June / 9 o'clock**, there was **no / little / a huge** change in average income / people's preferences in clothing / people's love for pizzas.

---

❷ 結論是，大部分來說，（名詞）對（名詞）這些人來說是用來（動詞），而（名詞）選擇（名詞）則是為了（動詞）。

In conclusion, mostly, **food / juice / books** for **men / students / elderly people** are to **entertain / earn money / stay** slim whereas **women / adults / babies** opt for **drinks / milk / television** to enjoy themselves / satisfy their needs / have fun.

---

❸ 這張（名詞）明確地顯示，（名詞）把（名詞）看作是生活中不可或缺的一部分。

This **chart / graph / table** clearly illustrates that **children / women / fathers** view cell phones / cosmetics / music as an indispensable part of their lives.

---

❹ 根據這張（名詞），我們可以預期在未來會有更多（名詞）能夠（動詞）。

According to this **bar graph / line graph / table**, we can expect that, in the future, more and more **families / girls / students** will have televisions in their homes / enjoy books / like rock music.

---

❺ 結論是，（**n.+所有格**）這些人對（**名詞**）這些東西的喜好隨著時間（**動詞**）。

To conclude, people's / students' / boys' preferences for book genres / ice cream flavors / girlfriend types fluctuate / remain stable / remain the same with time.

---

❻ 我很（**形容詞**）看到我是多數／少數。

I'm very surprised / glad / sad to see that I'm in the majority / minority.

　　連接超實用的單字和好用的必備模板句型，就能拼出一篇完整的文章囉！這裡就有兩篇例子，並附上翻譯。就照著這個方法來套套看吧！

1. Time Arrangement on Weekends

　　下方的圓餅圖是有關NBA高中的學生在週末時對各項活動時間分配平均的調查。寫一篇短文分析說明此數據，並與你自己的時間表作比較。

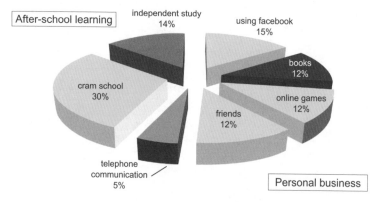

Time Arrangement on Weekends

　　The **pie chart** shows the general picture of **the way students in NBA high school allocate their time on weekends.** Overall, they spend **two-thirds** of **their schedule dealing with personal business, using facebook, reading books, playing online games, hanging out with friends and talking on the phone respectively.** Among them, **using facebook** takes a little lead of **15** percent over **books, games and friends**, all of which have equal shares of 12 percent. **Telephone communication**, which has a meager proportion of **5** percent, apparently is under disfavor now that contacting friends has been a lot easier, more convenient, and cheaper via the Internet. In contrast, **after-school learning** takes up **one-third** of the **timetable**, with an amazing division of 30 percent on the cram school, twice more than that on independent study.

Compared with the above schedule, my weekends are outlined likewise as study for 60 percent and leisure, 40 percent. Yet the arrangement differs. Mostly, I study and discuss schoolwork with classmates in school. In addition, there are a number of differences in leisure activities. Firstly, while using facebook and online games account for half of the leisure time in NBA High School, the two of them take the least proportion in my schedule. What parallels with the pie chart is the telephone hours, which I don't take much interest in either, since my friends and I stick together for most of the daytime.

In conclusion, while there are different choices between how NBA students and I arrange the weekends, as high school students, the contour of the timetable is similar.

週末的時間分配

　　這張**圓餅圖**顯示**NBA高中的學生在週末使用時間方式**的概況。整體來說，他們花**三分之二**的**時間來處理個人的事務，各為使用臉書、看書、玩網路遊戲、和朋友一起玩、講電話**。在這之中，**使用臉書**有**15%，稍稍領先書、遊戲和朋友**，這三項都同樣有12%。而**電話聯絡**只有小小的**5**%，明顯地不受歡迎，因為現在使用網路聯絡朋友更簡單、更方便、更便宜。相對的，**課後學習**佔了**時間表**的**三分之一**，而且驚人地有30%的部份都在補習班，比獨立讀書多了兩倍。

　　與以上的時間表相比，我的週末大致也一樣，讀書佔60%，休閒佔40%，但分配稍有不同。大部分的時候我都在學校讀書並和同學討論課業。另外，在休閒活動方面也有一些不同。首先，對NBA高中的學生來說使用臉書和網路遊戲佔了一半的休閒時間，但它們兩個在我的時間表佔了最少的部分。和圓餅圖狀況相同的是電話時間，我也對那個沒什麼興趣，因為我和我的朋友白天大部分的時間都在一起。

　　結論是，雖然NBA的學生跟我分配週末時間的選擇方式有很多不同，身為高中生，時間表大致上還是相似的。

2. Average Household Income

以下是二〇〇九年到二〇一二年間台灣某城市的平均家庭年收入圖，請寫一段敘述來說明四年間平均家庭年收入的變化，並説明自己的感覺。

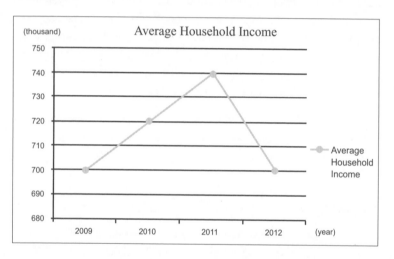

The above **chart** shows the change in **average yearly income** over a **four-year** period. From 2009 through 2011, average income rose steadily at a rate of $20,000 per year. However, from 2011 to 2012, incomes dropped $40,000 and returned to the average yearly income of 2009.

Overall, from **2009** to **2012**, there was **no** change in **average household income**. However, this doesn't mean that no changes occurred between 2009 and 2012—the average household income did rise, it's just that it dropped again in 2012.

To me, it is a bit sad to see that the average household income went down this year. We can actually feel it happening in our everyday lives—my parents spend money much more carefully these days. They don't like taking us to eat out anymore, and we even keep a box of coupons so we can save as much money on our purchases as possible. I hope that the average household income will be on the rise again soon, so that my parents will take us out to have steak again!

平均家庭收入

以上的**表格**顯示**四年內平均年收入**的改變。從2009到2011，平均收入穩定地以一年20000元的速率上升。但是從2011到2012，收入跌落了40000元，到2009年的平均年收入。

整體來說，從**2009**到**2012**年，**平均家庭收入沒有**改變。但是，這並不表示從2009到2012沒有發生任何改變：平均的家庭收入是有上升，只是在2012下降罷了。

對我來說，看到今年的家庭平均收入降低是有點難過的事。我們事實上可以感覺到這在我們每天的生活中發生。我的父母這一陣子花錢都小心多了。他們不再喜歡帶我們出去吃飯，而我們甚至有一盒折價券，讓我們可以在買東西時盡可能地省錢。我希望家庭平均收入能趕快再升高，我父母才願意再帶我們出去吃牛排！

 **更上一層樓**

　　學會使用模板句型寫出一篇漂亮的文章後，還可以怎麼在一些小地方讓文章錦上添花呢？看看其他同學的作品，注意他們有哪些地方值得學習，加入這些特色，讓文章更有變化、更加分！

1. Number of Students Enrolled at U-Fun English Language School

　　以下這個圖表顯示來自彰化、嘉義、台南、高雄、屏東宇凡英文的學生，在2011年和2012年這兩年間的入學人數狀況。請寫一段敘述來說明有哪些變化。

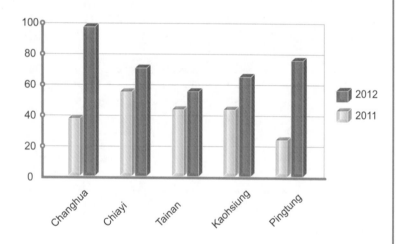

　　The graph shows the number of students enrolled at U-Fun English Language School between 2011 and 2012. We can see, for example, that the number of students in Pingtung rose from thirty students in 2011 to eighty students in 2012. Moreover, in 2011, Chiayi students outnumbered those from any other city. Overall, there are many students in Changhua.

1. 宇凡英語教室的學生人數

這張表顯示2011和2012之間，在宇凡英語教室登記入學的學生人數。舉例來說，我們可以看到屏東的學生從2011的30名成長到2012的80名。還有，在2011，嘉義的學生比任何其他城市都多。整體來說，彰化有很多學生。

★本文提出幾點從圖表中看出的狀況，包含學生人數的增加、和學生人數的多寡。但實在太短了，且雜亂、沒有組織，而以「整體來說，彰化有很多學生」來結尾也不太好，應將其他縣市的學生狀況也一起放入結論中。

2. Preferences of Ice Cream Flavors

以下這張圖表是訪問了20名男學生與20名女學生喜歡的冰淇淋口味的結果，每個人都可以選一種以上。請寫一篇文章來描述這張圖表，並加入自己的感想。

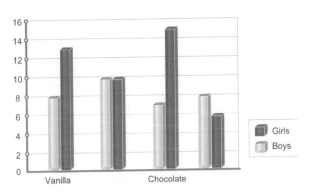

Twenty male students and twenty female students were interviewed on their favorite ice cream flavors. They can choose more than one flavor if they want to. This bar graph illustrates the results of this survey. We can see from this chart that an overwhelming number of 15 out of 20 girls chose chocolate flavored ice cream, while only seven boys picked chocolate. We can also see that more boys seem to prefer mango flavored ice cream than girls, and that the same number of boys and girls enjoy mint chocolate chip ice cream.

This bar graph surprised me somewhat because I am a girl and yet I can't imagine how so many girls love chocolate ice cream. Chocolate ice cream tastes terrible! I love chocolate, but I still can't stand chocolate ice cream. On the other hand, I'm glad that many share my love for vanilla ice cream. Overall, this chart shows that my preference is a bit different, but not too different from other girls'.

喜歡的冰淇淋口味

　　20名男學生與20名女學生被訪問他們最喜歡的冰淇淋口味。他們如果想要，可以選超過一種口味。這張柱狀圖顯示這個問卷的結果。我們可以從這張圖表看到20名女生中有15名之多的人選了巧克力口味的冰淇淋，而只有7名男生選了巧克力。我們也可以看到似乎有更多男生比女生更喜歡芒果口味的冰淇淋，而有一樣數量的男生與女生喜歡薄荷巧克力口味的冰淇淋。

　　這張柱狀圖讓我有點驚訝，因為我是女生，而我實在無法想像怎麼會有這麼多女生喜歡巧克力冰淇淋。巧克力冰淇淋實在不好吃！我喜歡巧克力，但我還是沒辦法忍受巧克力冰淇淋。另一方面，我很高興有這麼多人跟我一樣喜歡香草冰淇淋。整體來説，這張圖顯示我的喜好和其他女生有一點點不一樣，但也不是太不一樣。

★當題目提到要你説出自己的想法時，可別一直講自己的想法而忘了與圖表做連結。本文最後將自己的狀況與圖表中的其他女生做比較，就是不錯的作法。另外，本文中的數字有時用英文寫出，有時用阿拉伯數字，應該要統一選用其中一種就好。

3. Students' Preferences on Pets

　　以下這個圖表是訪問了20名男學生與20名女學生「想要的寵物」的結果。請寫一篇文章來描述這個圖表，並與自己的狀況比較。

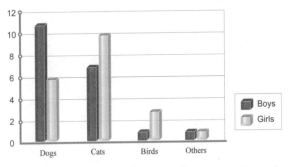

This chart shows us what kind of pets the twenty girls and twenty boys that are interviewed want. We can tell from the chart that among these twenty girls, more of them want cats than dogs. Boys, on the other hand, prefer dogs over cats. Birds are not too popular, but at least they have more votes than other animals—only one boy and one girl voted for "others", which is kind of sad considering how many animals there are besides dogs, cats and birds.

I am a girl, but unlike the girls that were interviewed, I'm more of a dog person than a cat person. I feel like cats are always judging you with their condescending eyes. Dogs are much friendlier! However, the one pet I really want is a hippo. Porcupines come in a close second. Also wombats, rabbits, and a baby leopard! I don't understand how so few students chose "others". Are they too stupid to understand that there are amazing animals that are not cats or dogs?

學生想要的寵物

　　這張圖表顯示受訪的20名女生和20名男生想要的寵物種類。我們可以從這張圖表看出在20名女生中，想要貓的人比想要狗的人多。另一方面，男生想要狗的比想要貓的人多。鳥不太受歡迎，但牠們至少比其他動物有更多票。只有一個男生和一個女生投給「其他」，這有點悲哀，因為在狗、貓和鳥以外還有這麼多種動物。

　　我是個女生，但和那些受訪的女生不同，我比較喜歡狗而較不喜歡貓。我覺得貓總是用高高在上的眼神批判地看著你。狗就友善多了！不過，我真正想要的寵物是河馬，豪豬則是第二名。我還想要袋熊、兔子和花豹寶寶！我不懂怎麼會有這麼少學生選了「其他」。他們是笨到不懂貓和狗以外還有很多很棒的動物嗎？

★不但比較了自己與其他學生的選擇有哪些差別，也具體地提出了喜歡狗而不喜歡貓的理由，相當有說服力。不過最後面沒有必要人身攻擊說受訪的學生太笨了，可能會被扣分，最好要避免。

實戰克漏字

◆ 填充翻譯式引導作文

翻譯能翻得好的人，絕對也能寫出順暢的英文作文！直接開始下筆還沒有把握的話，先從把中文翻譯成英文開始做起吧！每篇文章都有中文可以參考，請照著中文填入單字片語，這樣就可以很快熟悉文章的結構、瞭解到句型如何實際運用在文章裡了。

> **題目 ①：** Students' Preferences in Snacks

下方的圖表列出男、女學生喜歡的點心選項。寫一篇至少兩段的文章，分析解說圖表，並與你個人喜歡的喜好做比較。

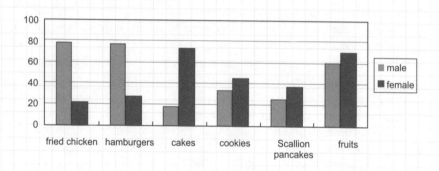

The 1 _____ illustrates the difference between male and female students in 2 _____ of 3 _____. Apparently, boys prefer 4 _____ and 5 _____ food whereas girls favor sweets. For boys, fried chicken and hamburgers win the most 6 _____, both accounting for over 75 percent. Bread and Scallion pancakes come next, with a 7 _____ difference from the top two by 8 _____ 10 to 15 percent. Cakes, which have a 9 _____ proportion of less than 20 percent, apparently are under 10 _____. On the other hand, girls' likes and dislikes go 11 _____ opposite to those of boys. Well-loved 12 _____ for boys are least popular with girls, while cakes and cookies, which barely 13 _____ boys, hit girls' top choice.

　　這張柱狀圖描述男女學生對點心選擇的差別。明顯地，男生喜歡油炸和鹹的食物，而女生喜歡吃甜的。對男生來說，炸雞和漢堡得到最多票，都有超過75%。接下來是麵包和蔥油餅，離前兩名降了大概10到15%。蛋糕只有小小的20%以下，明顯地不受歡迎。另一方面，女生喜歡和討厭的東西和男生的喜好完全相反。受到男生喜愛的點心最不受女生歡迎，而蛋糕和餅乾都幾乎不吸引男生，卻是女生的最佳選擇。

　　Interestingly, among the 14 _____, boy and girl students do share one thing in common—their love for fruits. 60 percent of boys and 70 percent of girls have fruits for snacks according to the figure. As a girl, my choices are similar with most female students, only that fruits come first and then cakes and cookies. In conclusion, mostly, snacks for boys are to 15 _____ hunger whereas girls opt for sweets to acquire a sense of 16 _____. Yet without doubt, boys and girls at this stage are health-conscious to a certain degree, for over half of them would take fruits during meals.

　　有趣的是，在眾多不同之中，男女學生有一件事相同：他們對水果的喜好。根據數據，60%的男生和70%的女生都吃水果當點心。身為女生，我的選擇和大部分的女學生類似，只是水果是第一名，再來才是蛋糕和餅乾。結論是，大致上點心對男生來說是滿足食慾，而女生選擇甜點來得到安慰舒適的感覺。但毋庸置疑，這個階段的男女生都到某種程度地注重健康，因為他們超過一半的人都會在吃飯時吃水果。

● 填空引導式參考解答

❶ bar graph	❼ slight	⓭ attract
❷ choices	❽ roughly	⓮ diversities
❸ snacks	❾ meager	⓯ satiate
❹ fried	❿ disfavor	⓰ comfort
❺ salty	⓫ drastically	
❻ votes	⓬ refreshments	

高階填空題

　　把文章的句型和結構都練熟了，已經有信心可以不用參考範文自己寫一篇了嗎？從這裡開始，你可以依照自己的狀況，套用模板句型練習寫作。請從以下的題目中選一個，現在就開始寫吧！

題目 ①： Preferences for Fruit

　　100名高中女生受訪詢問她們最喜歡的水果是哪一種。以下的圓餅圖為訪問結果，請寫一篇短文描述這張圖的內容。

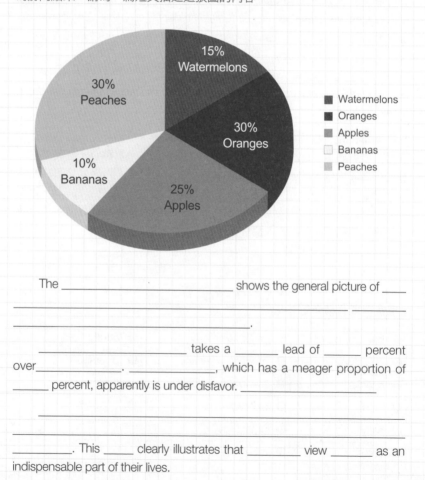

The _____ shows the general picture of _____

_____ _____

_____.

_____ takes a _____ lead of _____ percent

over_____. _____, which has a meager proportion of

_____ percent, apparently is under disfavor. _____

_____

_____

_____. This _____ clearly illustrates that _____ view _____ as an

indispensable part of their lives.

• 自由發揮的參考解答範本：

1. Preferences for Fruit

The pie chart shows the general picture of high school girls' preferences for fruit. Peaches take a slight lead of 30 percent over the other kinds of fruit. Bananas, which have a meager proportion of 10 percent, apparently are under disfavor. However, the differences are not really huge—oranges, apples and watermelons, though having different numbers of votes, are not really so different in terms of popularity.

One thing is certain, though—none of the 100 girls interviewed answered that they did not like any fruit. This chart clearly illustrates that high school girls view fruit, no matter what kind, as an indispensable part of their lives.

思路第一站

下筆前問問自己 ①：抓出圖片重點

進行連環圖片的寫作時，使用「定體→審圖→立意→聯想」的四步驟，能幫助你全盤掌握圖片重點。首先讓我們找出圖片中的主角是誰吧：

• 定體：主體是誰？

看圖作文中，畫面的主體往往是人物。要從畫面中人物的形體、相貌、服飾等，弄清人物的性別、年齡、身分；從人物的表情、動作，推測人物在想什麼。確認主角的個人檔案（定體）之後，接下來便是要觀察跟主角互動的事件、地點和時間。

• 審圖：觀察圖片中的周圍環境

一張只有主角的圖片，是無法開展成一篇故事的。因此需要觀察圖片中的周圍環境，弄清事件發生的時間、地點以及和事件有關的物品，此步驟也就是「審圖」。

下筆前問問自己 ②：安排故事架構並完成作文

• 立意：訂出寫作題旨

根據圖片的事件、時間與地點，你可以從中發展出不同的寫作路線；集合上述所有的條件，把事情的來龍去脈交代清楚，建構出一篇完整的作文。這個步驟的寫作，也就是「立意」。

• 聯想：佈局作文內容，加上聯想畫龍點睛

雖然有人物，有景物，但沒有聲音，也不會動。而看圖作文，則要借助於圖片提供的形象進行合理想像，把圖上的人物寫活。經過前面的「定體→審圖→立意」三步驟，此時寫作要注意，按照從整體到部分，由遠到近等順序，言之有序；要抓住重點，突出中心。利用已掌握的事件、地點

和時間等寫作素材，將作文寫得「有色有聲」，既有事物的靜態，還有事物的動態；將靜止的畫面「活動化」，平面的事物「立體化」，就是一篇生動又充滿感情的連環作文了。

✏️ 下筆前問問自己 ③：看圖作文還需要注意什麼？

• 選擇陳述觀點

撰寫故事時，可以從很多種觀點切入：你可以是故事中的某個角色（會用I / We第一人稱），或是講故事的旁觀者（會用He / She / They第三人稱）。在寫作時，你可以幫主角取好名字，這樣可以避免一直出現 our English teacher 或是 the classmate sitting next to me 這樣重複的單字。要注意的是，全文只能選定一個觀點，且主詞、時態及相關描述都必須配合這個觀點。

• 使用正確時態

注意「時態」的掌握：一般看圖寫作都是描述文或記敘文，寫的都是過去已發生的事，主要都要用「過去式」。若遇到中間有一些說明是「習慣」或是「不變的真理」，則可用現在式。

• 聯想相關詞彙

為了避免內文多次重複出現相同的字，有時候要尋找相關的替代詞彙。例如：

中文說法	英文寫法	其他替換寫法
「寫」東西	to write	to scribble、to jot down
「信件」	note	letter、message
「生氣」	angry	furious、irritated

以下將提供四篇連環圖片的作文作為示範，並為該幅連環圖片整理出適合的好用單字與模板句型（因為每一篇連環圖片寫作會因為圖片情境的不同，架構出不同的故事內容，所以單字與模板句型也不會是固定的）。快來看看不同的看圖寫作方式吧！

Chapter 4 看圖寫作文

181

連環圖片作文你可以這樣寫！①

　　看圖寫作有趣的地方在於，同樣的圖片讓不同的人來寫，會發展出完全不一樣的有趣情節。在看完圖片後，必須先思考整篇文章的架構，試著將文章分段描述，通常會分成三段，第一段是故事的開頭，首先要點出故事的主旨，接下來便是故事開展，最後一段是故事結尾。常見的結尾方式是藉由這篇故事，主角得到了什麼啟示、教訓，或是結尾出現意外發展，讓大家都大吃一驚。快看看以下四篇連環圖片的寫作實例是如何開頭、發展故事，結尾又是如何撰寫的吧！

> **題目：** The Most Unforgettable Birthday Present
>
> **提示：** 請仔細觀察以下三幅連環圖片的內容，寫出一個涵蓋連環圖片內容並有完整結局的故事。

The Most Unforgettable Birthday Present
最難忘懷的生日禮物

　　Last Friday was **my girlfriend Jane**'s **birthday**, and we planned to spend a whole joyful evening. Contrary to my expectation, though, I **got a pile of papers to do in the office and had to work overtime.** As a consequence, it was not until **eight o'clock in the evening** that **I finally got all my work over with**. After leaving the office, I rushed into a jewelry shop and chose a beautiful pearl necklace as Jane's birthday present. As soon as **I walked out of the shop**, **I violently collided with a passerby**, which immediately caused a swelling on my forehead, and dropped the present on the pavement.

<u>上週五</u>是我女朋友Jane的生日，我們原先計劃要開心地度過一整晚。然而事與願違的是，我要在公司處理一堆報告還得加班。結果，一直到八點鐘，我才終於將所有的工作完成。在離開公司後，我趕緊到一家珠寶店並選了一條美麗的珍珠項鍊當作Jane的生日禮物。就當我一走出商店，我狠狠地撞上一位行人，額頭上立刻腫了個包，而禮物也掉落在人行道上。

　　In the midst of chaos, despite the bruise and dizziness, I picked up the present and hurried on my way to meet Jane. Running toward the destination, I apologized for <u>my lateness</u> and handed over the present to <u>Jane</u>. When Jane tore the gift box open and took the stuff out, she looked really confused. Much to <u>my astonishment</u>, <u>the gift inside was not the beautiful pearl necklace at all but a necktie instead</u>! I mistakenly took the present when accidentally bumping against that passerby!

　　在混亂中，我顧不得瘀青與暈眩，拾起了禮物並繼續趕去和Jane碰面。我三步併作兩步地到達了目的地，為遲到一事向Jane道歉並且將禮物遞給她。當Jane拆開了禮物包裝盒並拿出裡頭的東西時，她看起來一臉困惑。讓<u>我十分驚訝</u>的是，<u>裡頭的禮物不是那條美麗的珍珠項鍊，而是一條領帶</u>！原來我在意外撞上那位行人時，拿錯了禮物。

　　I got dumbstruck on the spot and felt extremely embarrassed for my carelessness. Jane, being a sweet and considerate girl, smiled gently at me and said that she would always treasure the necktie because it was the most unforgettable <u>birthday present she</u> had ever received.

　　我當場呆若木雞，也對我的粗心感到十分不好意思。不過溫柔又體貼的Jane，溫和地對我微笑，還說她會永遠珍藏這條領帶，因為這是<u>她</u>收過最難忘的<u>生日禮物</u>了。

★注意描述已發生的故事需要用過去式。此篇文章的起承轉合，其「起」、「承」是第一、二段；第二段最後面主角拿錯禮物是「轉」。接著第三段是「合」，以女友出人意表地接受了錯拿的禮物來作結。

 單字裝入袋

❶	喜悅地；令人高興地	joyfully
❷	與……相反	contrary to
❸	（一）堆	pile
❹	結果	consequence
❺	珠寶店	jewelry shop
❻	項鍊	necklace
❼	與……相撞	collide (with + sb.)
❽	行人	passerby
❾	腫脹；隆起物	swelling
❿	掉下；落下	drop
⓫	混亂	chaos
⓬	向……道歉	apologize (to + sb.)
⓭	禮物盒	gift box
⓮	驚訝	astonishment
⓯	領帶	necktie
⓰	錯誤地	mistakenly
⓱	震驚到說不出話	dumbstruck
⓲	不謹慎	carelessness
⓳	體貼的	considerate
⓴	難以忘記的	unforgettable

句型萬用包

❶ _____ 是 _____ 的 _____ 。

Last Friday was my girlfriend Jane's birthday.

_____

❷ 事與願違的是，我 _____ 。

Contrary to my expectation, I got a pile of papers to do in the office and had to work overtime.

_____

❸ 一直到 _____ ，才 _____ 。

It was not until eight o'clock in the evening that I finally got all my work over with.

_____

❹ 就當 _____ ，_____ 。

As soon as I walked out of the shop, I violently collided with a passerby.

_____

❺ 我三步併作兩步地到達了目的地，為 _____ 向 _____ 道歉。

Running toward the destination, I apologized for my lateness to Jane.

_____

❻ 讓 _____ 的是，_____ ！

Much to my astonishment, the gift inside was not the beautiful pearl necklace at all but a necktie instead!

_____

❼ 這是 _____ 收過最難忘的 _____ 了。

It was the most unforgettable birthday present she had ever received.

題目： Determination against the Fate

提示： 請仔細觀察以下三幅連環圖片的內容，寫出一個涵蓋連環圖片內容並有完整結局的故事。

Determination Against the Fate
面對命運所展現的堅定

Well goes an old saying, "**One thorn of experience is worth a whole wilderness of warning**." For me, there's a memory that has always remained vivid in my mind. **Chi-Ming, my best buddy in the period of my junior high school days**, was the most unforgettable person in my life. He was born in a rich family, but everything changed after **his father departed his life in a car accident when he entered senior high school**.

俗話說的好：「**一次深刻的經歷，抵得過上千百次的告誡**」。對我來說，有段記憶一直在我心裡不曾淡去。**志明是我國中時期的最佳拍檔**，也是我生命中最難以忘懷的人。他出生於一個富裕的家庭，但**當他進入高中就讀時，他的父親在一場車禍中辭世**，而他生命的一切也變得不同。

What's worse, drowned in the sorrowful atmosphere, his mom did nothing but hang around, which led to financial difficulty in his family. Fortunately, Chi-Ming transformed himself into an independent youth. He became diligent and positive instead of discouraged. Soon after the event, he worked part-time, including serving as a fruit harvester and a courier delivering gas tanks. In that way, he not only supported his family but also paid his way through senior high school as well as college.

更糟的是，在沉浸於哀傷中的氣氛下，他的媽媽成天無所事事，而此舉也讓他的家庭陷入了財務困難。幸運的是，志明轉變成為一位獨立的年輕人。他變得勤勞積極，而不是意志消沉。不久之後，他兼差打工，包含當採果員以及瓦斯外送員。在那樣的情況下，他不只撐起了他的家庭，也讓自己可以完成高中及大學學業。

Note-worthily, it was his revival and aggressive attitude that won him praise and admiration. I will remember **his inspiration** to me permanently because **I have learned his determination against the fate**.

值得注意的是，是他的振作以及進取的態度為他贏得了讚揚與欽佩。我將會永遠記得<u>他</u>給我的<u>鼓舞</u>，因為<u>**我學到了他在面對命運時展現的堅定決心**</u>。

★此篇文章的起承轉合，其「起」、「承」是第一、二段；第二段中間描述志明在困境下，依舊支撐家庭並完成學業是「轉」。第三段主角表示自己會以志明當榜樣，在面對命運時會展現堅定是「合」，為文章畫下完美的句點。

 單字裝入袋

❶	刺；荊棘	thorn
❷	回憶	memory
❸	鮮明的	vivid
❹	好朋友；夥伴〔口語用法〕	buddy
❺	離開	depart
❻	車禍	car accident
❼	沉溺在……	drown in
❽	閒晃	hang around
❾	經濟上有困難	financial difficulty
❿	轉變為	transform into
⓫	勤奮的	diligent
⓬	沮喪；洩氣	discouraged
⓭	兼職；打工	part-time job
⓮	任職	serve
⓯	外送員；信差	courier
⓰	賺錢以供費用	pay one's way through
⓱	值得注意地	note-worthily
⓲	重新振作	revival
⓳	讚揚；稱讚	praise
⓴	鼓舞	inspiration
㉑	決心	determination

 句型萬用包

❶ 俗話說的好：「_____」。

Well goes an old saying, "One thorn of experience is worth a whole wilderness of warning."

❷ 對我來說，這段記憶一直在我心裡不曾淡去。

For me, the memory has always remained vivid in my mind.

❸ （人名，補充說明）是我生命中最難以忘懷的人。

Chi-Ming, the best buddy in the period of my junior high school days, was the most unforgettable person in my life.

❹ 但_____之後，一切都改變了。

But everything changed after his father departed his life in a car accident when he entered senior high school.

❺ 更糟的是，_____（句子）_____。

What's worse, his mom did nothing but hang around.

❻ 幸運的是，_____（句子）_____。

Fortunately, Chi-Ming transformed himself into an independent youth.

❼ 我將會永遠記得（名詞）給我的（名詞），因為_____（句子）_____。

I will remember his inspiration to me permanently because I have learned his determination against the fate.

題目： A Terrifying but Unforgettable Weekend

提示： 請仔細觀察以下四幅連環圖片的內容，寫出一個涵蓋連環圖片內容並有完整結局的故事。

A Terrifying but Unforgettable Weekend
一個驚駭卻難忘的週末

  Judy, who worked from Monday through Friday, went to **the department store** for **shopping as her pastime on the weekend**. The department store was having an anniversary sale; as a result, it was crowded there. Filled with happiness, **Judy decided to purchase a lot of things which she liked as a reward for her hard work**. All of a sudden, a teenager moved close to her, stole her purse, and escaped right away.

Never did **Judy** think such **a misery** would happen! She was stricken with astonishment and did not know what to do next. All **she** could do was **scream**, hoping **someone would help her**.

　　Judy，平日週一至週五要工作，**在週末時**去**百貨公司購物當作消遣**。這家百貨公司正在舉辦週年慶特賣，因此相當擁擠。**Judy**滿是喜悅，**她決定要採買很多她喜歡的東西來當作她辛勤工作的犒賞**。突然之間，一位少年接近她，偷了她的皮包，並且立刻逃跑。**Judy**從來沒想過這樣的**慘劇**會發生。她飽受驚嚇，不知道接下來該如何是好。**她**唯一能做的就是**尖叫**，並希望**有人能夠幫忙她**。

　　Seeing the teenager running far away from her, Judy fell into despair. Then on the way the teenager fled, she saw an old man wearing sunglasses sitting on a bench under the tree with a cane on his left hand. Regarding him as a blind man, she just wanted to leave in disappointment. Out of the blue, the old man stood up and rushed to capture the teen thief! It turned out that **the old man was a police officer in disguise**. Since many robberies happened in the department store on weekends, the authorities decided to take action. Thanks to **the police officer**'s help, **Judy had a terrifying but unforgettable weekend**.

　　眼見那位少年跑得離她越來越遠，Judy陷入了絕望。然後在少年逃跑的路上，她看到一位老人戴著太陽眼鏡，坐在樹下的板凳上，左手還拿著一根拐杖。她認為那位老人是個盲人，想說只好帶著失望離開。出乎意料地，那位老人站了起來並衝過去抓住了那位年輕小偷。原來**那位老人是由一位警官所假扮的**。因為有許多搶案都發生在週末的百貨公司裡，當局決定要採取行動。感謝有那位**警官**的協助，**Judy度過了一個驚駭卻難忘的週末**。

> ★本題的主軸很明確，就是關於偷竊搶劫的事件，但別忘記須用過去式。第一段，先陳述故事發生的背景，並在最後帶入第二張圖片遇到小偷的情況。進入第三張圖片，一樣使用普通敘述文替後續發展鋪陳。最後一張圖片雖然是自己想像，不妨用意外的結局收尾，文章更有驚喜。

 **單字裝入袋**

❶	消遣；休閒	pastime
❷	週年慶	anniversary sale
❸	擁擠的	crowded
❹	購買	purchase
❺	獎勵	reward
❻	年輕人；青少年	teenager
❼	偷竊	steal
❽	逃跑	escape
❾	慘劇；悲傷的事	misery
❿	受打擊的	stricken
⓫	尖叫	scream
⓬	絕望	despair
⓭	逃走	flee（過去式為fled）
⓮	太陽眼鏡	sunglasses
⓯	拐杖	cane
⓰	盲眼的；失明的	blind
⓱	意外地	out of the blue
⓲	逮住	capture
⓳	假裝；喬裝	in disguise
⓴	搶劫案	robbery
㉑	官方；當局	authority
㉒	採取行動	take action
㉓	恐怖的	terrifying

句型萬用包

❶（人名）去（名詞），為了_____。

Judy went to the department store for shopping as her pastime on the weekend.

_____

❷ _____ 滿是喜悅，_____。

Filled with happiness, Judy decided to purchase a lot of things which she liked as a reward for her hard work.

_____

❸（人名）從來沒想過這樣的（名詞）會發生。

Never did Judy think such a misery would happen!

_____

❹ _____唯一能做的就是_____，並希望_____。

All she could do was scream, hoping someone would help her.

_____

❺ 原來_____（句子）_____。

It turned out that the old man was disguised by a police officer.

_____

❻ 感謝有（名詞）的協助，_____（句子）_____。

Thanks to the police officer's help, Judy had a terrifying but unforgettable weekend.

 模擬小示範

◆ **填充翻譯式引導作文**

　　看完前面四篇連環圖片的範例後，現在動手來試寫看圖作文的句子吧！以下提供三題連環圖片題目，每一題由四張圖片組成。請先仔細看每一題的題目與提示，再參考中文翻譯來作答。你需要試寫的句子是關鍵句的部分（即套色處）。只要能寫出關鍵句，完成一篇看圖作文就不再是難事了！現在就來實際練習看看吧！

> **題目 ①**：Being Careful Is Always Better

> **提示**：第一段開門見山描述你做了一個噩夢，並且敘述在遊樂園發生的事情。第二段針對這個噩夢，描述你從中學到的教訓。

　　Last night, I dreamed 1 _____ that I went to 2 _____ with 3 _____. We were both extremely excited when we stepped into the amusement park with a balloon and a lollipop held in our hands. Sue grabbed my arm and happily told me that she wanted to try the roller coaster first. Though I was always afraid of thrilling things like roller coasters, I agreed to do so. After waiting in line for 4 _____, we couldn't wait to 5 _____, excitedly 6 _____ in ecstasy. In about a minute, the roller coaster started to move slowly, and then dived at an amazing speed. I turned to my left to see whether Sue enjoyed the thrill as well. To my horror, 7 _____!

昨天晚上，我夢見一場嚇人的夢，是關於我和我的好友Sue一起去遊樂園。我們兩個人踏進遊樂園時，手上拿著氣球和棒棒糖，覺得非常興奮。Sue抓著我的手，高興地告訴我她想要先去搭雲霄飛車。雖然我對於像雲霄飛車這類刺激的事情很害怕，我還是答應她了。排隊排了快一個鐘頭後，我們等不及要搭上雲霄飛車的第一節車廂，瘋狂地大叫和揮舞我們的雙手。大約一分鐘後，雲霄飛車慢慢啟動，隨即快速俯衝。我轉向左側，想要看看Sue是否一樣玩得盡興。讓我驚嚇的是，我旁邊的座位竟然沒有人！

I became dumbstruck, only wanting to get out of the cart and find out what's going on. After leaving the roller coaster, I walked alone for about ten minutes, pondering over any possibilities of Sue's disappearance. All of a sudden, I heard somebody crying and raised my head toward the source of it. Shocked, I couldn't say a word with my jaw falling to the ground. Sue 8 _____ with her shirt hooked on the rail of the roller coaster! She struggled to free herself, but it only made the condition worse. It was at the moment she fell from the place she was hooked on that I woke up, my forehead covered with cold sweat.

我當場呆若木雞，一心想要離開車廂查看事情的原委。從雲霄飛車下來之後，我獨自走了約10分鐘，猜想Sue消失的各種可能原因。突然之間，我聽見有人哭喊，抬起頭往叫聲看去。我嚇到了，說不出話下巴幾乎掉到地上。Sue的衣服勾住了雲霄飛車的鐵軌，她整個人吊在半空中。她掙扎著想脫困，但卻讓情況變得更危急。就當衣服勾住處鬆掉，她掉下來的同時，我醒了過來，額頭上冒出了一堆冷汗。

After the horrible nightmare, I can only say that whether in reality or not, to be more careful is always much better.

這場駭人的噩夢過後，我只能說無論是夢或現實，小心一點總是上策。

• 填空引導式參考解答

❶	a thrilling dream	❺	sit in the first cart of the roller coaster
❷	the amusement park	❻	yelling and waving our arms
❸	my friend, Sue	❼	there was nobody sitting next to me
❹	almost an hour	❽	was hanging in the air

題目 ②： Be Content with What You Have

提示： 以故事開頭的作文，往往結尾會以一個道理作結。此篇第一段描述兩隻金魚異想天開的計劃。第二段以教訓結尾，提供簡單卻富涵哲理的寓意。

Two goldfish 1 _____ day in, day out. On one side of it was a tiny door. One of the goldfish said to the other, "I bet that door leads to a land 2 _____ and 3 _____. If we could only open it, we'd be rich. Why don't we 4 _____?" The other goldfish agreed eagerly. Together, they set about trying out different combinations on the combination lock that secured the door.

　　兩隻金魚日復一日被關在水族箱裡面。水族箱的一側有一扇小門。其中一隻金魚跟另一隻金魚說：「我跟你打賭，那扇門會通往一處滿是黃金和寶藏，以及有取之不盡食物的土地。只要我們能打開那扇門，我們就發財了。我們何不試試看呢？」另一隻金魚完全贊成。兩隻金魚嘗試了各種密碼組合，想要打開門上的密碼鎖。

It seemed to be a near-impossible task, but one day, miraculously, their plan succeeded. The goldfish gave the lock a twirl 5 _____, and it 6 _____. Trembling with anticipation, they 7 _____—only to see 8 _____, and the water 9 _____ in their tank rushing out 10 _____ in a torrent.

這似乎是一項不可能的任務，不過就在某天，奇蹟似地，兩隻金魚的計劃成功了。一隻金魚用魚鰭轉開了鎖，門就應聲打開了。兩隻金魚興奮期待著，推開了小門，卻只看到門的另一側空無一物，而且水族箱裡讓牠們賴以維生的水，順著開口一傾而出。

This story warns of the consequences of greed, and proves that the grass is not always greener in somebody else's pasture. It's important to be contented with what you have, rather than always striving for something beyond reach.

這個故事警告我們，貪婪會招致的結果。而且並不是別人牧場裡的草才更綠（別人的東西不一定好）。重要的是，要對現況感到滿足，而不是總想要取得你伸手不可觸及之物。

• 填空引導式參考解答

❶ were trapped in a tank	❻ clicked open
❷ full of gold and treasure	❼ pushed open the door
❸ an endless supply of food	❽ nothing on the other side
❹ give it a shot	❾ that kept them alive
❺ with their fins	❿ from the opening

試寫完連環圖片作文的句型後，現在開始我們把中文翻譯拿掉，請你根據所提供的連環圖型，試著自由發揮寫出一篇最符合圖片的作文。作答保留部分句子，方便讓你串聯文章。空白處請發揮你的創意，填入任何適合的句子或短句，長短不限。以下有兩個題目，都練習寫看看吧！寫完作文後，還可以參考後面自由發揮的範本，了解一下雖然是同樣的連環圖型，但也會有不同的寫法喔！

題目 ①：The Old Man's Intimate Partner

_____. Bruce, who was in his elderly age of 75, had a sympathetic heart. _____

_____. _____

_____. _____

_____, what he did most every day was make a cup of tea, and sit on the sofa, dozing off from time to time.

One morning, he was woken up from his sleep by a shrill bark. _____

_____. When coming

outside, he saw a horrible sight—a young man was maltreating a stray dog.
_____ _____
_____. _____ _____
_____. On seeing this, _____ _____
_____. After the guy finally ran away, he slowly walked near
the poor dog, _____ _____. _____
_____. Fearing that it might be bullied again, Bruce took the dog
back home. _____ _____
____.
    _____
    _____.

• 自由發揮的參考解答範本：

1. The Old Man's Intimate Partner

In a brick house on the outskirts lived a poor, old man. Bruce, who was in his elderly age of 75, had a sympathetic heart. Years ago, his wife and two children lost their lives in a car accident, leaving him alone. Even so, he still plucked up courage to live by himself, but he had to walk on crutches. Because he had broken his leg while repairing his leaking roof, what he did most every day was make a cup of tea, and sit on the sofa, dozing off from time to time.

One morning, he was woken up from his sleep by a shrill bark. To figure out what was going on, he took his cane and stepped out of the house. When coming outside, he saw a horrible sight—a young man was maltreating a stray dog. he was trampling on it with his foot. To the elderly man's anger, he even threw a ball at the dog. On seeing this, Bruce yelled at him, and threatened to call the police. After the guy finally ran away, he slowly walked near the poor dog, trying to see if it was okay. Luckily, it wasn't badly hurt. Fearing that it might be bullied again, Bruce took it back home. From then on, he fed milk and other nutrients to the dog in spite of his poverty. He named the dog "Paul" in memory of his late son. Gradually, they became intimate partners.

題目 ②：Honesty Is the Best Policy

_____, May got up from the bed in great astonishment, _____ _____ _____. What's worse, _____ _____ _____. It was apparent to her that she would definitely be late for the class, _____. "_____ _____," May told herself.

_____, with a pale countenance May told her mother that she might have caught a fever. Of course she was merely pretending, but May's mother regarded her daughter's trick as the fatigue caused by excessive study. Accordingly the deeply worried mother in no time drove her daughter to see the doctor for further diagnosis.

_____ _____

_____ _____

_____ _____
_____ _____
_____ _____
_____ .

• 自由發揮的參考解答範本：

2. Honesty Is the Best Policy

Last Monday, May got up from the bed in great astonishment, as she noticed that it was almost two minutes left to eight in the morning. What's worse, she suddenly recalled that she forgot to finish the assignment for the English class started from 8:10. It was apparent to her that she would definitely be late for the class, and be scolded by the teacher for not submitting her homework. "I must find an excuse to avoid all the trouble," May told herself.

Dressed in the uniform and carrying her schoolbag, with a pale countenance May told her mother that she might have caught a fever. Of course she was merely pretending, but May's mother regarded her daughter's trick as the fatigue caused by excessive study. Accordingly the deeply worried mother in no time drove her daughter to see the doctor for further diagnosis. That was a cold morning, and a large number of the patients crowded the little clinic. Due to the limited time, although after the fast but hasty checkup, May was not caught lying about the sickness, she still had to take certain pills every several hours. She was even grounded in her room, which made the young girl bored to tears. If she had the chance to turn back the time, May would have been honest and accepted the punishment she deserved for not fulfilling her duty as a student.

Part 3 | 描寫照片

思路第一站

🖊 下筆前問問自己 ①：文章開頭：設定照片主題

　　照片題型寫作多以寫人、記事、寫景物為主，所以同樣可以運用 What? Who? When? Where? Why? How? 這5W1H的寫作技巧。首先先找出圖中的主角是誰？是男生或女生？是人物或事物？場景是在都市或鄉村？利用「5W1H」，幫助釐清可以用來寫作的線索，然後抓住這條線索，寫出文章的開頭。

　　例如：The woman standing in the water is picking shells and behind her are several yachts.「那個站在水中的女人正在撿貝殼，而她後面有許多小艇。」即可點出who、where、以及what。然後，再依照圖片細微處繼續補充描述。

🖊 下筆前問問自己 ②：文章開展：運用想像力

　　單幅的照片圖型因為只有一張圖，所以只能展示一件事的部分內容，因此利用「5W1H」觀察後，得到的寫作素材可能不完整。所以在面對照片圖型時，我們要學會如何從一張照片呈現的畫面，想像出故事的過去以及未來；也就是運用想像力，幫故事杜撰以前曾經發生的事情，並且賦予故事未來的變化與結果，以此便能順利開展文章，加深照片本身的故事性，並且利用杜撰出的故事未來發展，鋪陳準備文章作結。

　　例如：From her facial expression, I can tell that she is absorbed in what she's doing.「從她的表情，我可以猜到她一定很陶醉在撿貝殼。」運用想像力，為圖片多做補充。內容就會看起來更豐富，與其他人的不同。

✏️ 下筆前問問自己 ③：文章結尾：一定要有個完整的收尾

千萬不要只是把照片裡看到的情境寫完就沒了！好的文章結尾，可以讓整篇文章頓時變得生動有趣，或是引人入勝。常見的照片題型結尾，會根據文章開展時所鋪陳的劇情，延伸出本篇的高潮劇情，或是藉此機會提出寓意，讓人有所頓悟，或是見好就收，讓故事留下想像空間。只要確認結尾有涵蓋前面的開頭與開展，就是一個完整的收尾。

「照片題型篇」因為每張照片的情境皆不同，發展出不同的故事內容，因此會運用到的單字與句型，也不是固定而能套用在每張照片的。以下「照片題型你可以這樣寫」將提供四篇照片題型當作寫作示範，會針對當張照片整理出適合此照片情境的單字與模板句型，同學們可以藉此學到不同情境下的實用單字與句型。

連環圖片作文你可以這樣寫！①

　　照片題型是相當有趣的作文考試題型。它除了考驗同學在「經驗敘述」、「人物描述」、「地方敘述」三大題型所學到的描述技巧與功力，最重要的是，照片題型可以讓同學發揮天馬行空的想像力，根據照片的圖像，架構出一篇充滿趣味的作文。以下提供四篇照片題型的寫作實例，每一篇皆提供寫作提示。同學可以仔細看看，每篇故事如何開頭、開展和結尾。也可以參考每篇的「模板必備武器一單字」和「模板必備武器一句型」，練習寫出一篇精采又生動的文章！

題目①：Planking

提示：第一段敘述你對此現象的了解。第二段敘述你所知道關於這個現象的優缺點，並提出個人看法。

Planking 仆街

Of all kinds of **Internet trends**, **planking might not be the most famous one yet**, but no one can deny its rapid and wide spread over the social networks, such as Facebook. One doesn't have to be **a stunt performer** to **perform planking**—as a matter of a fact, it involves lying down flat on the ground or the surface of an object. From its appearance, **this simple movement is meaningless, and a little silly**. However, youngsters don't think so. They plank on every possible place, posting the photos of their poses on the Internet, and win the praise and appreciation from friends or other Internet users. From where I stand, **if they continue to compete with each other on planking, it might incur some unimaginable accidents**.

在所有的**網路流行事物中**，**仆街或許還不是最知名的**，但沒有人會否認這個活動在像 facebook 等社群網站上是越傳越廣且越傳越快速。並非是**特技演員**才能**表演這個動作**一說穿了，仆街就只是將臉部朝下並直挺挺地趴在地面或任何物體的表面上。乍看之下，**這個簡單的動作不僅沒有任何意義，甚至還有點蠢**。然而年輕人們可不這麼認為。他們不僅在各種地方仆街，還把拍下的照片上傳到網路上供朋友與其他網友們觀看分享，藉此爭取他人的讚美與認同。就我看來，**如果他們持續要以仆街來分出高下，可能會招致難以想像的不幸事故。**

In Australia, a young adult lost his life for planking on a balcony railing on the seventh floor, because he failed to keep his balance. Ironically, even though there is news about casualties in planking one after another, it still catches on. **Planking** can be great fun, but **people should not do it unscrupulously when this kind of activity jeopardizes the importance of their health and safety.** Ultimately, it is not worth **being in a wheelchair for your whole life to take a funny photo to impress somebody you don't know on the Internet.**

在澳洲，有一位年輕男子因為在七層樓高的陽台欄杆上仆街時失去平衡而喪生。諷刺的是，即使有傷亡消息接二連三傳出，仆街依舊持續風行。**仆街**是可以很有趣的，但**在其超過健康與安全的重要程度時，人們就不應該恣意妄為**。總的說來，**要是為了讓網路上某個陌生人對你逗趣的仆街照片有印象，卻換來一輩子得在輪椅上度過**，絕對不值得。

單字裝入袋

❶	潮流	trend
❷	仆街	planking
❸	否認	deny
❹	快速的	rapid
❺	散播、散布	spread
❻	社群網路	social network
❼	特技、危險的動作	stunt
❽	平坦地	flat
❾	外表、表象	appearance
❿	無意義的	meaningless
⓫	傻的、愚蠢的	silly
⓬	年輕人	youngster
⓭	張貼照片到網路上	post
⓮	讚賞	praise
⓯	與……競賽	compete
⓰	招致（危險）	incur
⓱	無法想像的	unimaginable
⓲	欄杆	railing
⓳	平衡	balance
⓴	諷刺地	ironically
㉑	傷亡人數	casualty
㉒	肆無忌憚地	unscrupulously
㉓	危害	jeopardize
㉔	安全	safety
㉕	一生、終身	lifetime
㉖	輪椅	wheelchair
㉗	使……印象深刻	impress

句型萬用包

❶ 在所有的＿＿＿＿＿＿＿＿ 中，＿＿＿＿＿＿＿＿＿＿＿＿＿＿＿＿＿ 。
Of all kinds of Internet trends, planking might not be the most famous one yet.

＿＿＿＿＿＿＿＿＿＿＿＿＿＿＿＿＿＿＿＿＿＿＿＿＿＿＿＿＿＿＿＿

❷ 並非是 ＿＿＿＿＿＿＿＿＿ 才能 ＿＿＿＿＿＿＿＿＿ 。
One doesn't have to be a stunt man to perform planking.

＿＿＿＿＿＿＿＿＿＿＿＿＿＿＿＿＿＿＿＿＿＿＿＿＿＿＿＿＿＿＿＿

❸ 乍看之下，＿＿＿＿＿＿＿＿＿＿＿＿＿＿＿＿＿＿＿＿＿＿＿＿＿＿ 。
From its appearance, this simple movement is meaningless, and a little silly.

＿＿＿＿＿＿＿＿＿＿＿＿＿＿＿＿＿＿＿＿＿＿＿＿＿＿＿＿＿＿＿＿

❹ 就我看來，＿＿＿＿＿＿＿＿＿＿＿＿＿＿＿＿＿＿＿＿＿＿＿＿＿ 。
From where I stand, if they continue to compete with each other on planking, it might incur some unimaginable accidents.

＿＿＿＿＿＿＿＿＿＿＿＿＿＿＿＿＿＿＿＿＿＿＿＿＿＿＿＿＿＿＿＿

❺ ＿＿＿＿ 是可以很有趣的，但 ＿＿＿＿＿＿＿＿＿＿＿＿＿＿＿＿＿＿＿ 。
Planking can be great fun, but people should not do it unscrupulously when this kind of activity jeopardizes the importance of their health and safety.

＿＿＿＿＿＿＿＿＿＿＿＿＿＿＿＿＿＿＿＿＿＿＿＿＿＿＿＿＿＿＿＿

❻ ＿＿＿＿＿＿＿＿＿＿＿＿＿＿＿＿＿＿＿＿＿＿＿＿＿＿，絕對不值得。
It is not worth being in a wheelchair for your whole life to take a funny photo to impress somebody you don't know on the Internet.

連環圖片作文你可以這樣寫！②

題目 ②： Drug Abuse

提示： 第一段敘述你對毒品問題的了解。第二段敘述在你認識的人之中是否有人吸毒，若有，敘述你的感想。若無，請提出解決毒品問題的對策。

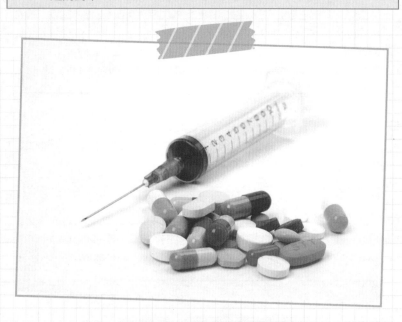

Drug Abuse 毒品成癮

Among **youngsters** nowadays, **drug abuse** has become a more and more **serious problem and caused widespread concerns.** At the beginning, because of **having curiosity** and because of **wanting to show their courage in front of their peers**, they start taking drugs. Others take drugs because they are hopeless, depressed and frustrated. Once they start taking it, they will come to be addicted and after a while, they can't live without drugs. **Taking drugs will** not only **destroy one's health and future** but also **cause critical problems for society**.

　　近來在**青少年**中，**吸毒**已經成為一個愈來愈**嚴重的問題並引起廣泛的關切**。一開始，一半因為**好奇**，一半因為**想在同儕之前展現勇氣**，他們開始吸毒。其他人吸毒是因為他們感到無望、憂鬱，以及挫折。一旦他們開始吸食，他們就會上癮，但過了一陣子，他們就不能沒有毒品。**吸食毒品不僅會毀滅一個人的健康及前程**，也會給**社會造成棘手的問題**。

Of all the people I know, there **is one guy who takes drugs**. Unfortunately, he was my beloved and respected father. Before being addicted, my father, who was good-tempered and easygoing, always helped my mom with housework. **The happy hours when he took me out to play basketball or swim** are the memories that I would never forget. Later, perhaps because of the influence of bad friends or the discouragement of unemployment, he started to take drugs. Every time he came to **crave drugs**, he **changed into someone I didn't know**. Now, my father has left us for a long time. Nobody knows where he is now. The fact is that everytime I think of him, I **can't help but cry my eyes out**. Therefore, being someone who witnessed how drugs can break his family, I completely understand its dangerous qualities. No matter what makes people take drugs, we can say for sure that drugs will definitely harm their bodies and mind.

　　在我認識的人之中，有**一個人吸毒**。不幸的是，他曾是我摯愛及尊敬的父親。在上癮之前，好脾氣而且好相處的父親總是幫忙媽媽做家事。**他帶我去打籃球或游泳的快樂時光**是我難以忘懷的記憶。後來或許受到壞朋友的影響或失業的挫折，他開始吸毒。每次他**發作**，他就會**變成一個我完全不認識的人**。現在父親已經離開我們很久了，沒有人知道他現在身在何處。事實是，每當我想起他時，我總是**忍不住潸然淚下**。因此，做為一個目擊毒品如何毀滅他的家庭的人，我徹底了解吸毒的壞處。但不論何種原因使人吸毒，我們可以確信的是毒品必定對人們的身心造成傷害。

單字裝入袋

❶	年輕人	youngster
❷	藥物濫用	drug abuse
❸	造成	cause
❹	關切	concern
❺	好奇、好奇心	curiosity
❻	表現	show
❼	同儕	peer
❽	服用藥物	take drugs
❾	沒救的	hopeless
❿	憂鬱的	depressed
⓫	（對藥物、酒精）上癮的	addicted
⓬	破壞、摧毀	destroy
⓭	棘手的、危急的	critical
⓮	敬重的	respected
⓯	脾氣好的	good-tempered
⓰	好相處的	easygoing
⓱	家事	housework
⓲	影響	influence
⓳	失業	unemployment
⓴	潸然淚下	cry one's eyes out
㉑	目睹	witness
㉒	特質	quality
㉓	傷害	harm

句型萬用包

❶ 近來在 _____ 中，_____ 已經成為一個愈來愈 _____ 。

Among youngsters nowadays, drug abuse has become a more and more serious problem and caused widespread concerns.

---

❷ 一開始，一半因為 _____，一半因為 _____ 。

At the beginning, because of having curiosity and because of wanting to show their courage in front of their peers.

---

❸ _____ 不僅會 _____ ，也會 _____ 。

Taking drugs will not only destroy one's health and future but also cause critical problems for society.

---

❹ 在我認識的人之中，有 _____ 。

Of all the people I know, there is one guy who takes drugs.

---

❺ _____ 是我難以忘懷的記憶。

The happy hours when he took me out to play basketball or swim are the memories that I would never forget.

---

❻ 每次他 _____ ，他就會 _____ 。

Every time he came to crave drugs, he changed into someone I didn't know.

---

❼ 事實是，每當我想起他時，我總是 _____ 。

The fact is that everytime I think of him, I can't help but cry my eyes out.

模擬小示範

◆ 填充翻譯式引導作文

　　看完前面四篇照片題型的範例後，現在動手來試寫照片題型的句子吧！以下提供三題照片題型題目，請先仔細看每一題的題目與提示，再參考中文翻譯在套色的關鍵句中填入答案，完成一篇照片題型作文就不再是難事了！現在就來實際練習看看吧！

題目 ①：Making the Earth a Better Place

提示：請根據圖片的場景，描述這種現象可能發生的原因，並合理說明將來可能會發生的情況和目前人類能做的事。第一段描述此種現象帶來的問題，第二段則敘述為了改善此現象人類所做的努力並作結。

According to the 1 _____, Global warming, resulting from excessive carbon dioxide and other gasses, has 2 _____ the rise of average temperature in recent decades. At the same time, global climate has shown obvious changes all around the world, such as icebergs melting as well as continuous typhoons and droughts. 3 _____ in this picture, the climate change significantly 4 _____ both the Arctic and the Antarctic circles. With the fast rate of ice melting at the North Pole, Polar bears died from hunger because they cannot catch seals for food. On the other hand, penguin chicks are frozen to death because of the continuous rainstorms at the South Pole. 5 _____ the extreme climate transformation, it is 6 _____ that polar bears and king penguins would go 7 _____ very soon.

　　根據科學家的觀察，由於過度的二氧化碳和其他氣體所引起的全球暖化，在近幾十年來已經造成了平均溫度的升高。同時，全球的氣候在世界

各地已經表現出明顯的變化，比方說冰山的融解以及持續不斷的颱風和旱災。一如在圖片中所見，氣候變化很明顯地衝擊了北極圈和南極圈。隨著在北極冰山的快速融解速度，北極熊因為抓不到海豹為食，而死於飢餓。另一方面，小企鵝們也在南極持續斷的暴風雨中凍死了。由於這個極大的氣候轉變，北極熊和國王企鵝預估在短期內將會絕種。

To 8 _____ the aggravation of global climate change, 9 _____ 140 countries signed the Kyoto protocol in 1997, and in 2009, an important conference in Copenhagen, Denmark, 10 _____ at 11 _____ global warming. To our disappointment, although the objective of the treaty is to stabilize greenhouse gas concentrations in the atmosphere at a level that would prevent dangerous interference with the climate system, the treaty itself actually sets no mandatory limits on greenhouse gas emissions for individual countries and contains no enforcement mechanisms. 12 _____ is that with the circulation of air and the ocean tides, the 13 _____ of unusual climate is no longer regionalized. Any damage to the environment would affect other parts of the globe. Therefore, as members of the 14 _____, each of us has a 15 _____ to play in protecting the environment and 16 _____ the Earth 17 _____ to live in.

為了避免全球氣候轉變惡化下去，超過了140個國家在1997年簽訂了京都議定書，而在2009丹麥的哥本哈根會議重點是在對抗全球暖化。讓我們失望的是，雖然協議簽署的目的，就是穩定溫室氣體在大氣層中的濃度，以避免對大氣系統造成干擾。但協約本身其實並無對個別國家的溫室氣體排放強制設限，也沒有包含任何的強制機制。真相是，由於大氣和海洋潮汐的循環，不尋常的氣候影響不再只是區域化而已。任何對於環境的傷害都會影響到全球的其他部分。因此，作為地球村的成員，我們每一個人都要扮演一種角色，以保護環境並且使地球成為更好的居住地方。

• 填空引導式參考解答

❶ observation of scientists	❼ extinct	⑬ influence
❷ contributed to	❽ prevent	⑭ global village
❸ As you can see	❾ more than	⑮ role
❹ affects	❿ aiming	⑯ making
❺ Due to	⑪ fighting against	⑰ a better place
❻ estimated	⑫ The truth	

提示：請根據圖片中的場景，描述他們正在從事的活動，並合理說明近
年來該項活動快速流行的原因及其優點。全文共三段，第一段敘
述點出此項活動為何，第二段敘述此活動的優點，並且帶出最後
一段的作結。

In the past few years, 1 _____ of Taiwanese have suddenly
2 _____ the bicycle as if it were a startling new invention. A
3 _____ bike enthusiasm 4 _____ the land and bicycle
production 5 _____ to 6 _____ the demand around the island.

　　在過去幾年間，數十萬台灣人似乎視自行車為驚奇新發明，突然樂意
接受自行車風潮。自行車熱潮席捲這塊土地，台灣的自行車生產量暴增以
供給這項需求。

　　Originally, bicycles are popular only with children and only a few
adults. Now, national preoccupation with high petrol price, air pollution and
physical fitness has brought the bike back to the forefront—particularly with
adults. 7 _____ costing lots of bucks and 8 _____ to the

pollution problems, biking is a completely 9 _____ and clean form of transportation that doesn't 10 _____ carbon dioxide emissions. The only fuel it burns is our own calories! Biking is also quiet, a huge plus for all of us suffering from the ill effects of noise pollution. Moreover, leisurely 11 _____ will 12 _____ levels of euphoria-producing hormones 13 _____ endorphins, which means we can 14 _____ away our blues.

原本自行車只受到孩童和少數大人的喜愛,但現在,國家所關注汽油價格高漲、空氣汙染,與身體健康等議題,都讓自行車重回主流一尤其是成人之間。並非花大錢然後增加汙染問題,自行車是一種完全節約且乾淨的交通運輸模式,不會製造二氧化碳排放量。它唯一會燃燒的燃料,就是我們的卡路里!騎乘自行車也相當安靜,對於受到噪音汙染負面影響的我們是一大益處。除此之外,優閒的自行車行有助於增加腦內啡,一種會引發愉悅感受的荷爾蒙,因此我們能「騎」走憂鬱。

All in all biking is a totally environment-friendly exercise not only for the outer 15 _____ we live in but the inner part of our human bodies.

騎乘自行車是一項全然環保的運動,不只對我們居住的四周環境,更是人體內部的環保。

• 填空引導式參考解答

❶ hundreds of thousands	❻ meet	⑪ bike rides
❷ embraced	❼ Rather than	⑫ boost
❸ wave of	❽ adding	⑬ called
❹ swept	❾ economical	⑭ bike
❺ soared	❿ produce	⑮ surroundings

高階填空題

　　練習寫完前面三篇照片題型的句子，現在開始我們把中文翻譯拿掉，請你根據所提供的照片，試著自由發揮寫出一篇最符合照片的英文作文。作答保留提供部分句子，方便讓你串聯文章。空白處請發揮你的創意，填入任何適合的句子或短句，長短不限。以下有兩個題目，都練習著寫看看吧！寫完作文後，還可以參考自由發揮的解答範本，了解一下雖然是同樣的照片題型，但也會有不同的寫法喔！

題目 ①： Traffic Problems

　　Traffic is undoubtedly a serious problem facing residents of Taiwan. The island's drivers are _____. Cars, trucks and motorcycles _____ _____

_____ _____

_____ _____

_____ _____. To

solve these problems, _____ _____
___.

    Firstly, _____
__. Secondly, _____
_____ _____
_____. Most important of all, _____
_____ _____
_____ _____
_____ _____. Perhaps one day we can really enjoy
more orderly traffic.

• 自由發揮的參考解答範本：

---

1. Traffic Problems

    Traffic is undoubtedly a serious problem facing residents of Taiwan. The island's drivers are notorious for their disregard to traffic rules. Cars, trucks and motorcycles weave in and out through the traffic at dangerously high speeds. Illegal passings, drunk driving and running through red lights are not unusual. What's worse, exasperating traffic jams can be seen everywhere as the number of motor vehicles grows rapidly. To solve these problems, I think the following measures must be taken immediately.

    Firstly, road regulations should be strictly enacted to deter violations. Secondly, the authorities concerned ought to improve public transportation systems to reduce people's need of private cars. Most important of all, drivers must be educated and even reeducated on road safety. Only through the cooperation between the government and the citizens can we have a better traffic condition. Perhaps one day we can really enjoy more orderly traffic.

Chapter 5
書信聲明文

Part 1 正式信函

思路第一站

在工作上、學業上、或者生活中，常會有需要寫信的情況，書信有各式各樣的功能，正式的信函包含求職信、推薦信、提案信、邀請信、催繳信、訂單處理信等等，通常會依照固定的架構來撰寫。寫正式信函的時候，通常需具備以下的架構：

✏️ 書信架構 ①：引言（introduction）

• 問候

如果想要緩和語氣，在信件一開始會有一、兩個問候的句子，表達對對方的關心，例如：I hope this letter reaches you in good spirits.（希望收到這封信時您一切安好。）

• 提及雙方之間的關係

引言的段落也需要提及前次雙方接觸、碰面或聯絡時所提到的事項，喚起對方的記憶，以便進行後續的溝通。例如：We appreciate you for giving an impressive presentation at our study club last week, and many of our club members found your talk rather inspiring.（我們很感謝您上週在我們的讀書會上發表一個令人印象深刻的演說，需多成員都覺得深受啟發。）

• 簡述信件目的

進入主題之前，可以先說明這個信件主要的目的。例如：We are very honored to invite you to be a keynote speaker at the Spring Conference.（我們很榮幸邀請您來擔任春季研討會的主題演講者。）這樣一來，讀者可以在閱讀引言之後就清楚掌握作者所想要傳達的中心主旨，準備好接受後面信件所要聯絡的事項。

✏️ 信件架構 ②：主要聯絡事項（main body）

在main body的部分，可以說明信件主要的目的，例如邀請、詢問、道歉、慰問等等。

- 邀請

可以說明邀請的目的與場合。例如：Please join us for a farewell party in honor of Amy Frank, who is leaving Oracle to pursue other business interests.（敬邀參與Amy Frank的歡送會，她將要離開甲骨文公司另覓其他事業。）

- 接受

說明接受對方提出的求職、邀請、或提案等。常見的例子包括接受邀請，例如：We accept your kind invitation with great pleasure.（我們欣然接受您的盛情邀約。）或者接受對方的報價，例如：Your bid of $8,000 for the interior refurbishment of our reception room has been accepted.（您提案以8000元美金為我們的接待室做內部裝修已獲接受。）

- 婉拒

說明婉拒對方提出的求職、邀請、或提案等。常見的例子包括婉拒求職信函，例如：At this time there does not appear to be a position with us that is suited to your admittedly fine qualifications.（目前我們沒有職缺符合您的優秀資歷。）或者婉拒信用卡申請，例如：We have reviewed your credit application and regret to inform you that we are unable to offer you a bank card at this time.（我們已經查過您的信用申請，很遺憾通知您，我們此次無法將銀行卡提供給您。）

下筆前問問自己 ③：回覆事項（reply）

- 回覆事項

信件結尾可以說明對請對方確認或回應的事項。例如：Please refer to the enclosed catalogue and contract and call us should you have any questions.（請參閱附檔的型錄以及合約，有任何問題歡迎打電話詢問。）

- 期限與其他細節

信件結尾可以向對方確認細節。例如：I am happy discuss new patient education strategies at the conference, but would you let me know how much time you have allotted me?（我很樂意在研討會上面討論新的衛教策略，但是可以請您告知您安排多長時間給我做這場演講嗎？）

- 期待雙方的合作

結尾時可以加上對雙方聯繫的正向回應，例如：We look forward to working with you.（我們期待與您共事。）或者 We offer this contract extension with our compliments.（我們以此合約展延信件向您致意。）

 **單字裝入袋**

書寫信件的時候，可以依照溝通事項的不同，選用下列的單字：

◆感謝信函常用單字

❶	欣賞	appreciate
❷	親切的	gracious
❸	有品味的	tasteful
❹	慷慨的	bountiful
❺	感激的	grateful
❻	好客的	hospitable
❼	珍惜的	cherished
❽	感激的	indebted
❾	心胸寬大的	largehearted
❿	難忘的	memorable
⓫	受寵若驚的	flattered
⓬	喜出望外的	overjoyed
⓭	獨一無二的	one-of-a-kind
⓮	慷慨	generosity

◆致歉信函常用單字

❶	健忘地	absentmindedly
❷	意外的	accidental
❸	承認（錯誤）	admit/ acknowledged

❹	笨拙的	awkward
❺	犯錯	blunder/ fault
❻	粗心的	inadvertent
❼	疏忽	negligence
❽	欠缺考慮的	thoughtless
❾	不充分的	insufficient/ in adequate
❿	錯誤的	erroneous
⓫	改正	rectify
⓬	彌補	compensate
⓭	退還款項	reimburse
⓮	修理	repair

◆ 邀請函常用單字

❶	出席	attend
❷	場合	occasion
❸	致敬	salute
❹	取消	cancel
❺	喜慶日	fete
❻	愉悅	pleasure
❼	隆重慶祝	solemnize
❽	慶祝	celebration

⑨	榮幸	honor
⑩	延後	postpone
⑪	歡迎	welcome
⑫	紀念	commemorate
⑬	就任	installation
⑭	深感欣喜	rejoice

◆ 求職信函常用單字

❶	申請	apply
❷	合資格的	qualified
❸	回應	response
❹	附上	enclose
❺	招募	recruitment
❻	簡章	prospectus
❼	提案	proposal
❽	文件	document
❾	條款	provision / terms
❿	政策	policy
⑪	附加的	attached
⑫	闡述	illustrate
⑬	總結	summarize

⑭	雇用	employ
⑮	證書	credential
⑯	專業的	professional
⑰	背景	background
⑱	機會	opportunity

◆ 抱怨/客訴信件常用單字

❶	故障	breakdown/ malfunction
❷	遺漏	omission
❸	品質較差的	inferior
❹	有瑕疵的	flawed
❺	受損的	damaged
❻	收費過高的	overcharged
❼	不專業的	unprofessional
❽	沒有事實根據的	unjustifiable
❾	不一致的	inconsistent
❿	扭曲事實的	mispresented

句型萬用包

　　開始下筆寫作前，總要想好一篇作文要如何開頭、承接、結尾。快來把以下的句型套色的部份當作模板，然後在黑色畫底線的部份依照自己的狀況放入適合的單字（想不出填什麼的話，也可以可參考前面「實用單字」的部份找尋靈感）。這樣就能輕鬆完成考場必備的超實用金句、一口氣加好幾分！

• 第一部分：文章開頭先背這些句型！

❶ 問候對方（收信愉快的慣用語）。

I hope this email finds you well.
/ I hope this email reaches you in good spirits.
/ I hope you are having a wonderful day.

---

❷ 感謝您主動聯絡我們（與此封信件相關的事項）。

Thank you for reaching out to us regarding the matter about the construction work in collaboration with Harvey Crane Construction.

---

❸ 回應您（前封信件的），（相對應的作為）

In response to your letter asking for support for the Wildlife Conservation Foundation, I am enclosing a check for $500.

---

❹ 我要回覆您（某項計畫／議題）並進行後續聯絡。

I am getting back to you for the follow-up of the Berkeley Online Learning System Project.

---

❺ 如同之前 承諾/提及，（與信件主旨相關的事項）。

As promised / As mentioned previously, All-City Science fare would be postponed until this September.

•第二部分：文章開展再記這些句型！

❶ 我們感到（表示高興、遺憾、榮幸）要在此通知您（信件主旨相關的事項）。

例：We are pleased to inform you that your application for admission to Summerhill School has been accepted.

例：It is with reluctance that we have to inform you that your application was not accepted.

---

❷ 請參閱附檔（以查看相關的資訊）。

Please find the enclosed / attached file for the meeting date, the list of guest speakers, and the topics of the talks for the conference.

---

❸ 希望可以獲得（信件相關主題）更進一步的資訊。

I am interested in receiving information / learning more about the job duties and responsibilities of the position you are recruiting.

•第三部分：文章收尾就用這些句型！

❶ 希望可以盡快得到回覆。

Please reply at your earliest convenience. / Looking forward to hearing from you soon.

---

❷ 希望可以得到正面的回覆。

Hoping for a favorable reply, I am.

---

❸ 希望可以有其他的安排。

I hope you are able to make other arrangement.

---

❹ 謝謝您考慮我的提案/申請。

Thank you for considering my application. / Thank you for taking time reviewing my proposal.

 模擬小示範

連接超實用的單字和好用的必備模板句型，就能拼出一篇完整的文章囉！

● ● ●

1. 求職信

Dear Ms. Gibson,

I hope this email reaches you in good spirits.

I am wiring this letter in response to your recruitment ad in Saturday's paper seeking someone experienced with computer simulation for adaptive antenna system. I'm really interested in applying for the position. Firstly, there aren't that many openings in this field. Secondly, my experience and background match almost precisely what you appear to need.

I was intrigued when I contacted with the human resource personnel through the phone number given in the ad and discovered that this is your company. I have never forgot reading several of your research papers when I was writing my master's thesis. Your studies were the most inspiring researches for my academic work.

Please find the enclosed file **for my resume.** After reviewing my educational background and experience, I hope you will agree that an interview might be interesting for both of us.

Best regards,
Emily Watson

求職信

親愛的吉勃遜小姐，

展信愉快。

這封信是為了回應上星期六報紙上的適應性天線陣列電腦模擬人員職缺的徵才廣告而寫的。我很希望能申請這個職缺。首先，在這個領域的職缺沒有那麼多。再者，我的經驗和背景能符合貴公司的需要。

透過廣告上的聯絡電話接觸貴公司人力資源部門人員時，我很高興地發現到這是您所經營的公司。我從未忘記在撰寫我碩士論文的時候讀過幾篇您的論文。您的文章是對我學術工作最有啟發的研究之一。

我的履歷如附檔，敬請參閱。在您審核過我的教育背景以及經驗之後，希望您會同意與我的面談對雙方都是有益的。

敬祝 愉快

艾蜜莉‧華森

2. 提案信

Dear Mr. Morris,

I hope you are having a wonderful day.

Thank you for reaching us regarding **the itinerary for the package tour of Green Island.** As mentioned in the previous letters, **we need to make an itinerary for promotion of tours in the peak season of summer.** Would you be interested in a 1,200-word piece analyzing the benefits of staying with a host family with the advantages of staying in a hotel. Some people seek an in-depth tour when they visit this island, hoping to experience more local customs. In contrast, some people just look for the relaxation in the island; they hope to away from the hustle and bustles in urban life with the concierge taking care of every trivial thing for them. Please find the enclosed file for the article **when you make arrangement of the itinerary.** This way, we can design tours that catering to tourists and travelers with different expectations.

Please reply at your earliest convenience **about your ideas regarding this issue so that we could complete this project in time.**

Best regards,
Ariana Grande

提案信

莫里斯先生您好,

展信愉快。

謝謝您來信聯絡**綠島套裝行程規劃的事宜**。如同前幾封信件所提到的,**我們需要計畫一個於夏季旅遊旺季推廣的旅遊行程。**可否請您看一下這篇1200字的文章,當中分析住宿在當地招待家庭的家中以及住宿在飯店兩者各自的好處。有些人來到島上是希望進行深度旅遊,體驗更多當地的風俗。而有些人來到這個島上是為了放鬆,想要遠離都市生活,由飯店禮賓人員幫他們處理瑣事。**當您在安排旅遊行程時,**請參閱附檔中的文章。這樣的話,我們可以設計出符合遊客和旅行者各自不同的需求。

請盡快回覆**您對這個議題的想法,這樣我們才能夠即時完成這個計畫。**

敬祝 愉快

亞利安那 · 格蘭德

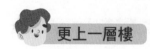
更上一層樓

學會使用模板句型寫出一篇漂亮的文章後，還可以怎麼在一些小地方讓文章錦上添花呢？

1. Response Letter

Dear Mr. Palmer,

I hope this email finds you well.

Thank you for reaching out to us regarding **the infestation in our Fortune cereal.** We feel sorry that you had this experience, and we'd like to show you that we share your concern.

We take consumer satisfaction as our top priority when managing any affair in the company, and we sincerely regret your recent experience with our product. Our company has a well-established product inspection procedure, and we carefully examine each lot of the raw materials on its arrival. We have sanitarians check on out manufacturing plant continually. Also, we visit our suppliers' facilities regularly to ensure nothing is contaminated in the process of production. Besides, food samples are collected all through the manufacturing process and are analyzed in our laboratories. This has been our standard operating procedure to ensure the production of high-quality, insect-free products.

We have been investigating in the case that you reported to us about the flawed product. It has been brought to the attention of the concerned company officials.

Thank you for taking time communicating with us.

Best regards,

Richard Wang

Customer service representative

Fortune Food Co., Ltd.

回覆抱怨信

帕默先生，您好

展信愉快。

謝謝您來信告知我們**幸運玉米片裡發現蟲子的案件。**我們很抱歉讓您有這樣的遭遇，並希望讓您知道我們跟您一樣關切此事。

在處理公司事務的時候，我們將顧客滿意度視為最重要的目標，而我們對於您最近使用我們產品有不好的遭遇感到遺憾。我們公司有完善的產品檢查制度，而我們會小心地檢查每一批送抵的原料。公共衛生官員會持續監督我們的製造工廠。此外，我們會定期拜訪我們供應商的設施來確定製造過程是沒有污染的。另外，我們會在生產過程中採取食物樣本並且送到我們的實驗室分析。這一直是我們為了確保高品質、無蟲害產品所採用的標準作業流程。

我們已經在調查您回報給我們關於瑕疵產品的案例。已交由公司相關高層處理。

謝謝您花時間與我們溝通。

幸運食品客戶服務代表

李察‧王 敬上

★這篇文章具備了信件的基礎架構，並且有條理地將主旨與內文呈現出來，信件標明公司的立場與作為，並且對於顧客反映事項表示尊重與感謝。

2. Response Letter

Dear Ms. Simpson,

I am getting back to you regarding **the problem with your Neatly Electronic Digital Computerized Hairdryer.**

We understand that your appliance is still under warranty, but we are unable to repair it for you free of charge. As specified in the terms of the warranty, any irreversible damage caused by customers' inappropriate use of the hair dryers would render the warranty null and void. The machine was plugged into a European 220-volt outlet when it was intended for use only with 110-volt outlets or for 220-volt outlets with a converter. We actually have a small tag affixed near the plug warning to use only 110-volt current. Please find the attached file for the electronic version of the user's manual, which you have received a printed copy inside the pack of the product.

If you wish to repair the machine at the cost of 100 dollars, please reply to us at your earliest convenience. Otherwise, we have to return it to you.

We are regretful to inform you that we could not make an exception for you because the warrant terms have specified the conditions of complimentary repair. We'd really appreciate your understanding.

Best regards,

Diana Lesley

Customer Service Representative, Neatly Co., Ltd.

回覆抱怨信

辛普森小姐，您好，

這封信是回應**您對於尼特莉電子數位吹風機的問題。**

我們理解您的吹風機仍在保固期間，但是我們無法免費為您修理吹風機。如同保證書條文所明訂的內容，任何因為顧客不當操作吹風機而造成的不可逆損害，會使保固無效。這個吹風機被接到歐洲220伏特的插座，但它僅能使用於110伏特的插座，或者需透過變壓器才能插入220伏特的插座。我們其實有在插頭旁邊貼上小標籤提醒只能使用110伏特的電流。請參閱附檔中的電子檔使用手冊，而您的產品包裝當中已經附有一份紙本的使用手冊了。

如果您希望支付100元來修理這台機器，請盡快回覆我們。否則，我們會將機器退還給您。

我們很遺憾要通知您無法為了破例，因為保固條款中已經說明免費維修的狀況了。我們會很感謝您的諒解。

尼特莉有限公司 客服代表

黛安娜‧萊斯禮 敬上

★應用基本的信件架構、使用常用的句型，並且有條理地說明無法提供商品保固免費維修服務的原因。

實戰克漏字

◆ 填充翻譯式引導作文

翻譯能翻得好的人，絕對也能寫出順暢的英文作文！直接開始下筆還沒有把握的話，先從把中文翻譯成英文開始做起吧！每篇文章都有中文可以參考，請照著中文填入單字片語，這樣就可以很快熟悉文章的結構、瞭解到句型如何實際運用在文章裡了。套上顏色的地方，都有套用前面的模板句型喔！

題目 ①： Invitation

提示： 第一段簡介組織的宗旨和活動。
　　　第二段說明邀請對方加入的原因及回覆的方式。

Dear Eddie Redmayne,

I am 1 _____ to inform you that the 2 _____ of Glory Community Anti-Crack Coalition extend a cordial 3 _____ to you to join our fellowship and help us to maintain the quality of life we enjoy. The 4 _____ was formed eight months ago to oppose the activity and effects of 5 _____ drug use and stop trafficking in Golden City and especially in the Glory neighborhood. We are a dedicated group of 6 _____ who feel that an involved citizenry is our best 7 _____ to the social problems that challenge our community. We feel that your 8 _____ with neighborhood healthcare and your 9 _____ to help the local youngsters would make you a valuable 10 _____ of our coalition.

艾迪‧瑞德曼先生您好

我很榮幸通知您，光榮社區反禁藥聯盟的成員誠摯邀請您參加我們的組織並協助維持現有的生活水準。這個聯盟是在八個月之前成立，目的在反對禁藥使用的活動以及影響，並且遏止黃金市、尤其是光榮社區當中禁藥偷渡的情況。我們是一群志工，我們相信影響著社區的社會問題需要透過公民的參與才能解決。我們覺得，由於您在社區健康照護上的經驗，以及您對於幫助本地年輕人的熱情，您會是我們聯盟寶貴的一位成員。

The Glory Community Anti-Crack Coalition would hold events to 11 _____ local people's knowledge about 12 _____ drugs to eliminate the negative 13 _____ they have on our next generation. We also make 14 _____ propaganda on anti-drug programs. Also, we hold bi-weekly meetings to 15 _____ current projects and plan future 16_____. The Golden City council already has two delegates to the coalition, but your name has been 17 _____ several times as a 18 _____ social worker; we feel that you would be of great 19 _____ to our association.

Please reply about the possibility of your participation at your earliest 20_____. Thank you!

Sincerely,
Lily Lucas
Chairperson of Glory Community Anti-Crack Coalition

　　光榮社區反禁藥聯盟會舉辦活動來加強本地人對於非法禁藥的知識，以便遏止亦禁藥對我們下一代的負面影響。我們也會持續宣傳反禁藥的活動。此外，我們每兩週有一次聚會來更新目前專案以及規劃未來的活動。黃金市議會已經有兩位代表參加本聯盟，但作為一位認真投入的社會工作者，你的名字已經被提到過好幾次，我們覺得您會是我們協會很強的助力。

　　請盡快回覆您參加本協會的可能性。謝謝您！
光明社區反禁藥聯盟理事長
莉莉・盧卡斯 敬上

• 填空引導式參考解答

❶ honored	❽ experience	⓯ update
❷ members	❾ enthusiasm	⓰ activities
❸ invitation	❿ member	⓱ mentioned
❹ coalition	⓫ enhance	⓲ devoted
❺ illegal	⓬ illegal	⓳ assistance
❻ volunteers	⓭ influence	⓴ convenience
❼ solution	⓮ continuous	

提示： 請寫一封邀請學者至一門大學課堂上分享演說的邀請信件。第一
段請說明邀請學者演說的緣由及課程性質，第二段說明演說時
間、期望的主題，並請講者回覆意願。

Dear Ms. Lawrence,

I hope this email find you 1 _____.

On 2 _____ of the senior class in the English Department,
Hoping University, I would like to 3 _____ you to speak to about
your recent book <Pop Culture and Language>. You are a 4 _____
writer and researcher in the field of social linguistics and semantics. Your
masterpieces 5 _____ the language variation in different 6 _____
scenarios, and how 'humor' works in formal negotiations are 7 _____
in the designated reading material for the 8 _____ "Language and
Culture." Several of our classmates have heard you speak, and they were
9 _____ by your eloquence. So, we would like to invite you over to
give a seminar 10 _____ sometime in the spring semester this year.

勞倫斯女士，您好

展信愉快。

謹代表和平大學英語系三年級的同學，在此邀請您主講介紹您最近的
新書<流行文化和語言>。您在社會語言學及語意學方面是一位著名的作家
及研究者。您有關於不同溝通情境下語言變化、以及「幽默」在正式協商
場合如何運作的傑出文章，是我們「語言與文化」課程的指定閱讀教材。
有些同學有聽過您的演說，對您的口才相當印象深刻。所以我們希望在今
年春季的學期邀請您來給予一個演說。

We 11 _____ every Wednesday morning, 9 – 11 am, and we
hope that one of the Wednesdays will fit into your 12_____. The
themes 13 _____ how subculture on campus, 14 _____ social
network, and mass media 15 _____ the language have been the

focus of the course "Language and Culture" this 16_____. It would be our 17 _____ if you could offer a 18 _____ session of relevant themes. Please 19 _____ me about your thoughts on this 20_____. If you are interested in giving a talk, please call me to discuss the honorarium at your earliest 21_____.

Hoping for a 22 _____ reply, I am.

Sincerely yours,

Katarina Anderson

　　我們每週三上午9點至11點上課，希望您其中一個星期三會有空。這學期「語言與文化」課程主要在探討校園次文化、線上社群、以及大眾媒體對語言的影響。如果您能來發表一個相關主題的演說，我們會感到相當榮幸。請告知您對這個提議的想法。如果您有興趣發表一個演說，請儘早在您方便時打電話給我討論講費。

　　希望能得到您的正面回應。

　　凱特琳納‧安德森

◆ 填空引導式參考解答

❶ well	❾ impressed	⓱ honor
❷ behalf	❿ presentation	⓲ lecture
❸ invite	⓫ meet	⓳ inform
❹ renowned	⓬ schedule	⓴ proposal
❺ regarding	⓭ about	㉑ convenience
❻ communication	⓮ online	㉒ favorable
❼ included	⓯ influence	
❽ course	⓰ semester	

高階填空題

　　把文章的句型和結構都練熟了，已經有信心可以不用參考範文自己寫一篇了嗎？從這裡開始，你可以依照自己的狀況，套用模板句型練習寫作。請從以下的題目中選一個，現在就開始寫吧！

> **題目 ①：** Letter of promotion 寫一封信宣傳一個研討會，說明為何想介紹這個研討會給收信者，並且詢問參與的意願。

1. Letter of promotion

Dear Jeff Bezos,

I hope _____
_____.

Regarding the issue that you raised in the previous mail, _____
_____. Over the
years, several management studies have showed that _____
_____
_____. As _____
_____, you might need to
consider several critical questions, such as _____
_____, and _____
_____ It is my belief that _____
_____.

　　It is my pleasure to inform you that _____
_____
_____. Participants can learn how to
_____, how to _____
_____, how to _____
____, and how to _____
__. We offer _____
_____. You can reserve a place for yourself by _____
____ at your earliest convenience.

　　Hoping for a positive response, I am.
　　Sincerely yours,
　　Thomas Wegener

1. Letter of Promotion

Dear Jeff Bezos,

I hope this email reaches you in good health and spirit.

Regarding the issue that you raised in the previous mail, I understand that you are eager to improve the efficiency of business operation. Over the years, several management studies have showed that the single most important characteristic of an entrepreneur is the ability to manage time. As a leader, a supervisor, and a facilitator for your employees, you might need to consider several critical questions, such as how you can meet deadlines, and how you can determine a monthly, quarterly, or annual goal for the company. It is my belief that a good entrepreneur should keep improving himself/herself in this aspect.

It is my pleasure to inform you that the Lucky City Entrepreneurship Coalition will host a two-day workshop on time management skills. Participants can learn how to set priorities, how to organize your time with special tools, how to deal with unnecessary politics at the workplace, and how to eliminate inefficient staff of group projects. We offer special registration fee to all members of our association. You can reserve a place for yourself under a minute by signing a signing the enclosed postage-paid reply card of by calling 800-520-1717 to register at your earliest convenience.

Hoping for a positive response, I am.

Sincerely yours,

Thomas Wegener

2. Letter of Recommendation

Dear Mr. Wilson,

_____.

In response to _____, I'd like to __

_____. I am writing to recommend _____

_____. She is _____,

and she _____

__. She also _____

_____.

I have personally interacted with _____, and she is

_____. So, I am pleased to

recommend her as _____. I have also _____

_____. I would like to invite you

to _____.

Please inform me _____. If you are

interested in this idea, _____

_____.

Looking forward to a favorable reply, I am.

Best regards,
Henry Edwin

2. Letter of Recommendation

Dear Mr. Wilson,

I hope this email finds you well.

In response to the proposal in your last email, I'd like to express my appreciation for your idea about publishing a book of anecdotal records. I am writing to recommend a young but talented blogger, Emily Dickenson. She is a teacher at a private elementary school, and she keeps a record of the funny episodes of the interaction between she and the students. She also records some interesting daily conversations with the parents with creative annotations or illustrations.

I have personally interacted with Ms. Dickenson, and she is as easygoing as she appears in her writing. So, I am pleased to recommend her as the author of our next book. I have also confirmed about her willingness to publish her manuscript, and she agreed to collaborate with us. I would like to invite you to an informal meeting for discussing more details about the matter.

Please inform me about your thought on this proposal. If you are interested in this idea, we can move forward to signing a boot contract with Ms. Dickenson.

Looking forward to a favorable reply, I am.

Best regards,

Henry Edwin

Part 2 | 私人邀約

 思路第一站

一、正式英文書信的形式

下面提供正式英文書信的形式範例，其中①至⑦的標號，請看下面的列點解釋說明。

> 1. 寫信者地住址（address）
>   寫信的日期（Date）
>
> 2. 開頭敬詞（Salutation / Greeting）
> 3. 寫信的本文（Body）＿＿＿＿＿＿＿＿＿＿＿
>   ＿
>   ＿＿＿＿＿＿＿＿＿＿＿＿＿＿＿＿＿＿＿＿＿
>   ＿＿＿＿＿＿＿＿＿＿＿＿＿＿＿＿＿＿＿＿＿
>   ＿＿＿＿＿＿＿＿＿＿＿＿＿＿＿＿＿＿＿＿＿
>   ＿＿＿＿＿＿＿＿＿＿＿＿＿＿＿＿＿＿＿＿＿
>
> 4. 結尾語（Closing）
>
> 5. 結尾敬詞
> 6. 署名（Signature）
>
> 7. 附筆（P.S）

---

①所占的空間一般為二行（住址一行，日期一行）。若住址太長，則寫成二行，然後第三行寫日期。

②占一行空間。注意：敬辭後要使用逗號「,」。

③書信本文文視需要可長可短。

④與⑦可以寫，也可以不寫，乃視實際情況來決定。

⑤結尾敬辭占一行空間。注意：結尾敬辭後要使用逗號「,」。

⑥署名占一行空間，且名字要寫在結尾敬辭的正下方。

二、敬辭的寫法

敬辭就是在英文信本文開始上方要寫的「稱呼語」，如My dear sister, Dear Mr...等。寫法視寄信者和收信者雙方的熟識狀態而定，但最常見的還是以「Dear XXX,」開頭，如「Dear friend,」、「Dear Jones,」、「Dear Johnson,」、「Dear Madam,」。

三、結尾語

本文寫完後，可在最後加上簡短的問候語，如中文的「祝闔家安康」、「敬祈回音」等。注意英文結尾語的書寫方式，結尾語後面不使用句點「.」，而使用逗號「,」。主要有3種寫法：

1. 以With開始

- With my best wishes to your family, （代我向您家人問好）
- With our kind regards, （祝闔家安康）

2. 以命令句開始

- Please give / send my kindest compliments to sb., （請代我向某人問候）
- Take care, （保重）

3. 以-ing現在分詞開始

- Expecting to hear from you as soon as possible, （期待您早日回信）
- Hoping that you'll get well soon, （希望您早日康復）

四、結尾敬辭的寫法

中文信在署名的下方，通常結尾敬辭會寫「頓首」或「敬上」，而英文亦有類似的用語，如Yours truly, / Sincerely yours,。然而依照寄信者和收信者的關係不同，寫法也稍有相異之處。寄信者和收信者大致上會出現以下3種關係：

1. 家人或親戚

寫信給兄弟、姊妹、父母、叔嬸等，一般用Affectionately作為結尾敬辭即可，但是也可在前面或後面加Yours等字，亦可把affectionately的ly去掉，後接關係的稱呼。用法列點如下：

- Affectionately Yours, / Yours affectionately,

- Your affectionate son / daughter / nephew / niece,

- Yours very affectionately, / Yours ever most affectionately,

- Your loving son (or daughter), / Your affectionate brother (or sister),

2. 朋友

寫信給比較親近的朋友，不管男生或女生，一般會使用：

- Yours always, / Yours ever,

- Always yours, / Ever yours,

如果寫信對象是較不親近的友人，可以使用下列的用語：

- Yours sincerely (/ truly), / Your sincere friend,

- Sincerely (/ Truly) yours,

3. 親友之外的其他人

寫信對象是親友之外的人，結尾敬辭使用：

- Yours faithfully, / Faithfully yours,

- Yours very faithfully,

如果對象是長輩或老師，則可用：

- Yours respectfully, / Respectfully yours,

【註】以上3種關係所使用的結尾敬辭，亦可以加上I am / I have the honor to be (or remain) / I remain / Believe me to be 等作為開頭。例如：

- I am yours sincerely,

- I remain yours ever,

- Believe me to be yours affectionately,

模板攻略步驟藍圖：電子郵件E-mail

　　電腦網路時代的來臨，傳統耗時的書信方式（snail-mail）幾乎都要被快捷便利的「電子郵件」（electronic mail）全部取代。傳統郵件發送的過程繁複：擬好文本→裝入信封→寫好住址和郵遞區號（zip code）→將信投入郵筒。而信寄出之後，還要擔心郵件會不會在寄送中途失蹤，又得耗時好幾天才能等到回信。而E-Mail電子郵件，藉由通訊網路的方便，將訊息傳送給對方，往往只需彈指之間一點一下滑鼠按下寄送鍵便可達成，其標榜的「即時性」、「私密性」以及「低成本」特性，更符合現代人惜時如金（Time Is Money）的性格。

• E-Mail 的基本格式：

　　下面提供E-Mail書信的形式範例，其中①至⑩的標號，請看下面的列點解釋說明。

① ▶ From:	aim0202@kmail.com	
② ▶ Mail to:	james222@umail.net	
③ ▶ Cc:		
④ ▶ Bcc:		
⑤ Subject:	Congratulations!	

Dear James,⑥
⑦
I've just heard the wonderful news about the birth of your daughter.
Congratulations!

What's her name? She must be a beautiful baby. If I have time next month,
I'll pay you a visit. Say hello to Joyce and the baby for me. I wish your family
the happiest in the world. (^_^) ⑧

Sincerely, ⑨

Mia ⑩

P.S. Send me a photo of the baby, will you?

① From 是「發信者名稱」。這裡的aim0202@kmail.com是發信人的E-Mail信箱。從發信人的E-Mail中也可以探出一些端倪：

- aim0202@kmail.com＝使用者名號十at十網域名稱。aim0202是使用者名號(handle name)，@是英文字「at」，kmail.com是網域名稱（domain name）。

② Mail to 是「寄給……」，也就表示「收信人」。

③ Cc是「副本收件人」（Carbon Copy）。Cc的功能就是，當我們發信給A時，若是也想將同一封信發給 B、C、D，這時你只須在寄給A的電子郵件中Cc的欄位，輸入B、C、D的E-Mail信箱發送出去，除了A之外，B、C、D三人也會同時收到這封信。

④ Bcc 是「密件副本」（Blind Carbon Cop）。在這一欄中輸入的電子郵件信箱，將不會被其他收件者看到。所以如果寄信時，不想讓A知道同封信還有寄給B，則可以選擇將B的信箱資訊打在這裡。

⑤ Subject 是「信件主題」。信件主題要清楚，但也要掌握字數。不要把Subject的欄位當作本文使用，盡量寫得簡短而明白。例如要祝賀朋友生小寶寶，你就可以使用Congratulations!來作信件主題。

⑥ 在本文之前，對寄信者表示禮貌的「開頭敬辭」，通常都是用「Dear XXX,」開頭，像這封信的「Dear James,」，注意在人名後面要加上逗點「,」。

⑦ 這裡開始撰寫信件內容，也就是信件的「本文」。寫E-mail時必須注意「網路禮節」（netiquette）如「文章字體不全以大寫書寫」、「為文須精簡」、「不用攻擊或輕視字眼」等。

⑧ 寫信時會使用如表情的符號稱作「符號臉譜」（Smiley）。在E-mail中使用表示寄信者的情緒。例如：::>_<::（哭泣）、^_^（微笑）、*^_^*（臉紅）、>_Q（調皮）、:)（微笑）等。

⑨ 信件完成後，在結尾的地方會加上「結尾敬辭」。通常結尾敬辭根據郵件性質會有不同的寫法。若是「一般的電子郵件」，可以這樣寫：

- Sincerely yours, / Sincerely,

  若是「私人性質的電子郵件」，則可以這樣寫：

- With best regards, / Best regards, / Regards,

- With best wishes, / Best wishes,

- Yours, / As ever, / Cheers,

⑩ 署名。在結尾敬辭之後，寫上自己的名字，代表由誰寄出這封信件。若是第一次寫信，寫出全名比較禮貌，也可以在全名後面加上能表示性別的敬稱（Mr. / Ms.），方便收件者分辨寄件者是男生或女生。若是寫信給熟識的親朋好友，通常可以只留名字，因為彼此認識，所以不會造成收件者的誤會或是有不禮貌之虞。

 **單字裝入袋**

因為撰寫書信有一定的格式，所以即便收件者不同，呈現的方式大同小異，也會用到相同或類似的開頭敬辭、文章的開頭、開展、收尾與結尾敬辭。以下分別列出開頭／結尾敬辭、文章開頭、開展、收尾的重要句型。試著先把它們記熟，只要學會這些句子，你就已經掌握書信的大致寫法，之後碰到書信題型時，就能自然寫出一封正確的書信囉！

◆ 書信開頭敬辭

❶	親愛的先生或女士：	Dear Sir or Madam,
❷	親愛的博士／先生／女士／小姐／太太：	Dear Dr. / Mr. / Mrs. / Miss / Ms. _____,（Ms.用來稱呼不知已婚或未婚之女士）
❸	親愛的_____：	Dear _____,（空白內填入收信者職稱如 Sales Department Manager）

◆ 書信文章開頭句型

❶	我希望你一切安好	I hope this letter finds you well.
❷	我希望你一切都好	I hope you are doing well.
❸	我希望你在享受這好天氣	I hope you are enjoying this fine weather.
❹	我很開心聽到……	I was delighted to hear that...
❺	我很開心知道……	I was very happy to learn that...
❻	我很激動知道……	I was thrilled to find out that...
❼	我很高興聽到……	I was glad to hear that...
❽	如果你願意……我會很高興	I'd (I would) be grateful if you could...
❾	如果你願意……我會很感激	I would appreciate it if you could...

◆ 書信文章開展單字或片語

❶	譬如說	For instance,
❷	除此之外	In addition,
❸	此外；並且	Moreover,
❹	同樣地	Also,
❺	相同地	Similarly,
❻	儘管	Although,
❼	反而	Instead,
❽	然而	Nevertheless,
❾	但是	But,
❿	如此；從而	Thus,
⓫	因而；所以	Therefore,
⓬	結果	Consequently,
⓭	結果；所以	As a result,
⓮	於是	Accordingly,
⓯	以這個理由	For this reason,
⓰	同樣地	By the same token,
⓱	而且	And,
⓲	第一	First,
⓳	首先	In the first place,
⓴	第二	Secondly,
㉑	下一個	Next,
㉒	之後	After,
㉓	最後	Finally,
㉔	抱著這個觀點	With this in mind,
㉕	依次	In turn,
㉖	總之	Anyway,

◆ 書信文章收尾句型

❶	最後我……	In closing / Finally, I...
❷	簡短來說	In short,
❸	總結來說	To sum up,
❹	就整體來看	On the whole,
❺	總的說來	By and large,
❻	從任何事情來說	In any event,
❼	希望能盡快聽到你的消息	Hope to hear from you soon.
❽	再次向您致謝	Once again, many thanks.
❾	期待下次和您見面	I look forward to seeing you.
❿	期待能聽到您的消息	I look forward to hearing from you.
⓫	我期待下次與您的會面	I look forward to meeting you.

◆ 書信結尾敬辭—正式電子郵件

❶	感激地	With gratitude,
❷	溫暖的關懷	Warm regards,
❸	誠摯地	Cordially,
❹	祝你好運	With all good wishes,
❺	（恭敬地）敬上	Respectfully,
❻	（恭敬地）敬上	Respectfully yours,
❼	親切的關懷	Kind regards,
❽	（真誠地）敬上	Yours truly,
❾	（最由衷地）敬上	Most sincerely,
❿	（由衷地）敬上	Sincerely yours,
⓫	謝謝	Thank you,
⓬	謝謝你的體貼	Thank you for your consideration,

◆ 書信結尾敬辭—私人電子郵件

❶	非常愛你的……	Lots of love,
❷	非常感謝	Many thanks,
❸	願愛與和平以及快樂	Peace, Love & Happiness,
❹	虔誠地	Prayerfully,
❺	和平與祝福	Peace and Blessings,
❻	保重	Take care,
❼	好好保重	Take good care,
❽	別太辛苦	Take it easy,
❾	之後再連絡	Talk to you later,
❿	祝你一切順利	Thinking the best for you,
⓫	期待下次相會	Till we meet again,
⓬	下次再見	Until next time,
⓭	獻上我最溫暖的問候	Warmest greetings to all,
⓮	最溫暖的關懷	Warmest Regards,
⓯	願你一切順利	Wishing you all the best of everything,
⓰	願你順利	Wishing you the best,
⓱	由衷地	With kind affection,
⓲	個人由衷地	With kindest personal regards,
⓳	熱烈地	With warmth,
⓴	願祝你好運	With all good wishes,
㉑	敬愛的	With love,
㉒	你一直是我掛念的人	You're in my thoughts,
㉓	（真誠地）敬上	Yours truly,
㉔	（忠實地）敬上	Yours faithfully,
㉕	（最由衷地）敬上	Yours most sincerely,
㉖	（恭敬地）敬上	Yours respectfully,
㉗	敬上	Yours,

 **模擬小示範**

　　學會上面的「模板必備武器─書信撰寫句型」之後，現在來實際看看這些句型套在書信中的用法吧！下列提供兩篇書信，一封是一般書信，一封是電子郵件。

Dear Dad and Mom,

I hope this letter finds you well. It's been a month since I have come to America. I miss you so much that I wish I had wings to fly to your side. How's everyone in the family?

I have made a lot of friends here, and they are really good people. They come from different countries, therefore, **I have a chance to better understand different cultures.** As a result, **I have developed an international view.**

By and large, **I'm doing great here, so don't worry about me**. I'm looking forward to seeing you **during summer vacation.** Please take good care yourselves!

Lots of Love,
Gina

親愛的爸媽：

　　我希望你們一切安好。我到美國已經一個月了。我好想念你們，多希望自己有雙翅膀可以飛到你們身邊。家裡其他人都還好嗎？

　　我在這裡認識了很多朋友，他們都是很好的人。他們來自不同國家，所以**我也有機會認識不同的文化**。因此**我也發展了國際觀**。

　　總的來說，**我在這裡都好，所以不要擔心我**。我很期待**暑假時**跟你們見面。要好好照顧自己喔！

非常愛你們的
吉娜

▶ From:	Tommy1234@gmail.com
▶ Mail to:	ChiaChiaLin@net.com.tw
▶ Cc:	
▶ Bcc:	
Subject:	The meeting next Monday

Dear Miss Lin,

I was glad to hear that **the E Project has been approved**! First, **it's really our pleasure to work with your company.** Second, **I'm really looking forward to working with you again since last time we get along with each other pretty well.**

Finally, **I'd like to arrange the first meeting for the new Project.** Do you have time next Monday around 10 o'clock? Please reply to me when it's convenient for you. Thank you very much!

Respectfully yours,
Tommy

▶ From:	Tommy1234@gmail.com
▶ Mail to:	ChiaChiaLin@net.com.tw
▶ Cc:	
▶ Bcc:	
Subject:	下週一的會議

親愛的林小姐您好：

我很高興聽到**E方案審核通過了！**首先，**與貴公司合作真的是我們的榮幸。**第二，**我也很期待能再次與您共事，因為上次我們彼此合作愉快。**

最後，**我想要安排新方案的首次會議**。您下週一早上10點有空嗎？請您抽空跟我確認，非常感謝！

Tommy敬上

 更上一層樓

下列提供兩題書信寫作範文，每一題皆會給予寫作提示與寫作注意事項。請參考提示，看看別的同學是如何寫出一篇正確流利的書信吧！

【84年甄試書信寫作範例】

提示：高中生王治平收到美國筆友George的來信，告訴治平他要隨父母到台灣來住兩年左右，並問治平：「Can you give me some advice and suggestions so that I know what I should do and what I should not do when I am in Taiwan?」現在請你以治平的身分，擬一封適當的信給George，歡迎他來台灣，並針對他的問題，提出一些具體的建議。

July 7, 1999

Dear George,

I am glad to hear that you and your parents are going to move to Taiwan. Living here is very convenient. It will be easy for you, as a native speaker of English, to find a job teaching English because learning English has become necessary for every student in Taiwan. **However**, you should learn Chinese as well so that you can communicate easily with the people around you.

In addition, if you want to live in a big city such as Taipei or Kaohsiung, I suggest that you should make the best of the local transportation system because the traffic is comparatively heavy in these two cities. **Therefore**, buying a car may not be a good idea. **Anyway**, welcome to this beautiful island. I believe that you will feel welcome and relaxed as soon as you land on our paradise island.

Your friend,

Chih-ping

1999年7月7號

親愛的喬治：

　　我很高興聽到你和你的父母即將要搬到台灣。台灣的生活相當便利。身為一個英文為母語的人，你可以很容易在這裡找到一份教英文的工作，因為台灣的學生都必須要學習英文。**然而**，你也必須要學習中文，你才能輕鬆和週遭的人溝通。

　　除此之外，如果你想要住在像台北或高雄那樣的大城市，我建議你可以好好利用大眾運輸系統，因為這兩座城市相較下擁有繁忙的交通，**所以**買車似乎不是個好主意。**總之**，歡迎你來到這座美麗的寶島。我相信一抵達這座天堂寶島，你就會馬上感受到親切與放鬆。

你的朋友

治平

★注意本篇書信的開頭和結尾敬辭，分別是Dear George,和Your friend,。另外書信內文以 I am glad to hear that 開始，中間敘述的段落，有使用到 However,、In addition,、Therefore,、Anyway, 等連接詞來連結句子。全篇使用了正確的書信撰寫格式。

實戰克漏字

◆ 填充翻譯式引導作文

　　實際套用過書信句型，也看過範例，了解如何寫出一篇流暢的書信，現在練習自己寫寫看吧！只要注意基本的書信格式，例如開頭敬辭、結尾敬辭，並且利用文章開頭、開展和結尾常用到的單字片語或句型，把書信內容好好分段架構，保證你能寫出一篇清楚正確的書信喔！以下提供三篇書信讓你進行填空練習，請根據題目，在仔細參考每篇提示後，開始寫信吧！

題目 ①： A Letter to my Mom

提示： 你是不是有些話想對父母、師長、朋友或同學說，但又覺得不方便當面說出來？請寫一封信給他或她，說出你想對他或她說的話。感謝對方過去的幫忙，或是為了某件事向他或她道歉均可。

Dear Mom,

　　First, I would like to say "1 ＿＿＿＿＿＿＿＿" to you. I shouldn't have 2 ＿＿＿＿＿＿＿ to you a few days ago when you scolded me because I have failed in the exam. My heart was 3 ＿＿＿＿＿＿＿ when I saw the tears in your eyes. 4 ＿＿＿＿＿＿＿ did I mean to make you sad or angry. Please listen to my sincere apology, and I 5 ＿＿＿＿＿＿＿ you that I would never ever do that again. I 6 ＿＿＿＿＿＿＿ to God! But will you please listen to what I want to say? I know you and Dad 7 ＿＿＿＿＿＿＿ a lot from me, and I will do everything I could to meet your 8 ＿＿＿＿＿＿＿. However, I also need time for 9 ＿＿＿＿＿＿＿ and a little space to cultivate my 10 ＿＿＿＿＿＿＿. When I see things 11 ＿＿＿＿＿＿＿ from you, it does not mean that I don't love you. When I take a break from my heavy 12 ＿＿＿＿＿＿＿ to play online games or read 13 ＿＿＿＿＿＿＿, it does not mean I am a bad boy.

　　Please have 14 ＿＿＿＿＿＿＿ in your son. In the journey of my life, I will never take the wrong path or do anything to 15 ＿＿＿＿＿＿＿ you.

Love you,

Your son

親愛的媽媽：

　　首先我向妳說「對不起」。前幾天妳因為我考試考得不好而訓我時，我不應該頂嘴。當我看到妳雙眼泛著淚光時，我心都碎了。我絕不是有意要惹妳傷心或生氣。請接受我誠心地道歉，我保證以後絕不再做那樣的事，真的！但是請妳也聽聽我的心聲好嗎？我知道妳和爸對我期望很大，而且我也會盡力去達成你們的期望。然而，我也需要休閒時間以及一點空間讓我去培養我的嗜好。當我對事情看法與妳不同時，並不代表我不愛妳。當我從沉重的課業中抽出一點時間玩線上遊戲或看漫畫時，並不代表我是壞小孩。

　　請妳對自己的兒子要有信心，在我人生的旅途中，我絕不會走入歧途或是做出任何使妳蒙羞的事。

愛妳的兒子

• 填空引導式參考解答

❶ sorry	❻ swear	⓫ differently
❷ talked back	❼ expect	⓬ schoolwork
❸ broken	❽ expectations	⓭ comic books
❹ By no means	❾ recreation	⓮ confidence
❺ promise	❿ hobbies	⓯ embarrass

提示：請描述你購買某一產品所遇到的問題及你所期望的解決方式。

Dear Sir or Madam,

   I bought a SAMS ML-91210 inkjet 1 _____ at SOHO Department store on September 1st this year. 2 _____, your printer hasn't worked 3 _____ advertised. First, the paper always 4 _____. I have used 5 _____ inkjet paper, but the paper still gets jammed often. Moreover, when it prints, there is a strange sound 6 _____ from the printer, which is very annoying and sounds like a 7 _____. Last but 8 _____, your ink is expensive. Your 9 _____ say that your printers can save the most ink, but this is not true.

   The printer has a one-year 10 _____ period. 11 _____ to solve these problems, I would like to 12 _____ the printer and get a 13 _____. I'm looking forward to receiving your 14 _____. Please call me 15 _____ phone at 07-0806449.

                                                              Yours,

                                                    your customer, John May

敬啟者：

　　我今年9月1日在SOHO百貨公司購買了一台SAMS ML-91210噴墨印表機。很遺憾地，你們的印表機並不如廣告上所寫的那麼好用。首先，它常常卡紙。我用的是高品質的噴墨列印紙，不過還是常卡紙。再者，印表機列印時會發出奇怪的聲音，聽起來真的很煩人，就像火災警報器的聲音。最後，你們的墨水很貴。你們的廣告宣稱你們的印表機最省墨水，事實卻不是如此。

　　這台印表機有一年的保固期，為了解決這些問題，我打算把貨退還並要求退錢。期望能得到你們的回覆。請來電與我聯繫：07-0806449。

顧客約翰・梅 敬上

・填空引導式參考解答

❶ printer	❻ coming	⓫ In order
❷ Unfortunately	❼ fire alarm	⓬ return
❸ as well as	❽ not least	⓭ refund
❹ jams	❾ advertisements	⓮ reply
❺ high-quality	❿ warranty	⓯ by

高階填空題

◆ 自由發揮

現在開始試著自己寫出一篇完整的書信吧！這裡就不再有中文可以參考，而是要你根據所提供的題目與提示，運用前面所學的書信常用單字片語和句型練習，寫出一篇切合題意、格式正確的書信。現在就開始寫下面這兩題吧！完成書信後，你還可以參考後面的「自由發揮的參考解答範本」，看看同樣的題目還能如何發揮喔！

題目 ①：Annual Meeting of the Financial Department

提示：你（名字為Rebecca）要寫一封電子郵件，提醒部屬Lisa年度大會的開會時間與注意事項。請注意：寄信者與收件者的電子郵件網址和信件主旨已提供，不需要另外撰寫。

▶ From:	rebeccam@co.com
▶ Mail to:	lisaw@co.com.
Subject:	Annual Meeting of the Financial Department

Dear ＿＿＿＿＿＿,

The annual meeting of our department ＿＿＿＿＿＿＿＿＿＿＿＿＿＿＿＿.

The meeting will start ＿＿＿＿＿＿＿＿＿＿＿＿＿＿＿＿＿＿＿.

Please ＿＿＿＿＿＿＿＿＿＿＿＿＿＿＿＿＿＿＿＿＿＿＿.

In addition, ＿＿＿＿＿＿＿＿＿＿＿＿＿＿＿＿＿＿＿＿＿,

so ＿＿＿＿＿＿＿＿＿＿＿＿＿＿＿＿＿＿＿＿＿.

To sum up, ＿＿＿＿＿＿＿＿＿＿＿＿＿＿＿＿＿＿＿.

Thank you for your help!

＿＿＿＿＿＿,

Rebecca

Dear Lisa,

The annual meeting of our department is going to be held this Friday afternoon. The meeting will start from 2 o'clock and is expected to finish by 4. Please arrange your busy schedule to make sure you can attend this important meeting.

In addition, please help print 10 copies of the annual report and pass them out before the meeting, so every colleague can get a copy of it.

To sum up, please remember to print the annual report and attend the meeting on time. Thank you for your help!

Kind regards,

Rebecca

Chapter

5

書信聲明文

提示：妳（名字為Jane）從日本寫信給死黨Anna，告訴Anna妳最近在日本過得如何。雖然是寫給好朋友的書信，語氣上會比較輕鬆，不過書信該有的開頭敬辭、結尾敬辭還是不要忘記加進信件中。

Dear Anna,

    I hope you are doing well. It's my second month in Japan, _____
_____ And I have to tell you: _____
_____
_____
_____.

    Although my classmates are all nice and friendly, _____
_____. _____
_____
_____ Nevertheless,

      _____
_____.

    In short, I'm doing OK. _____
_____
_____. Hope to hear
from you soon. _____, _____,

Jane

262

• 自由發揮的參考解答範本：

Dear Anna,

I hope you are doing well. It's my second month in Japan, I think I'm getting used to the people and culture here. And I have to tell you: the food here is excellent! I think I can't never have enough of ramen and curry rice. They are really delicious.

Although my classmates are all nice and friendly, I have a hard time keeping up with studies. Learning Japanese is a whole new experience for me. I haven't got a chance to learn another language except for English, and Japanese is a totally different system of language. Nevertheless, I'll still try my best and study as hard as I could.

In short, I'm doing OK. I'll keep you updated on my latest news, so don't worry about me. Hope to hear from you soon.

Peace, Love & Happiness,

your BFF,

Jane

Part 3 | 官方聲明

思路第一站

官方聲明類似公告通知，使用的時機包括政策變更、舉行會議、新工作夥伴加入、新辦公室落成、價格或租金調動、催繳帳款等場合。撰寫這類聲明的時候，需要包括誰、什麼、何時、何地、為什麼等細節。另外，除了離婚和宣布死訊之外，應盡量使用愉悅的語氣傳達宣布的事項。

🖊 公告架構 ① ：引言（introduction）

• 進入主題，說明主要公告事項

公告的開頭可以直接說明主要宣布的內容。例如：Important notice of change in terms: Effective January 1, 2020, your credit card agreement will be amended as follows.（條款變更重要通知：您的信用卡約定條款將會有以下變更，自2020年1月1日起生效。）

如果是會議通知，會直接說明時間、地點、和目的。例如：A meeting of Benign Community Council will be held at October 15th at 7 p.m. in the Victory Bank boardroom to elect board members and officers for the coming year.（優良社區協會會議將於十月十五日晚上七點在勝利銀行會議室舉行，已選出下一年的理事會成員及理監事。）

這樣一來，讀者可以在閱讀引言之後就清楚掌握作者所想要傳達的中心主旨，準備好閱讀後面要說明的細節。

公告架構 ②：信件主體（main body）

• 公告事項細節

說明主要公告的事項之後，繼續說明變更事項的細節。例如：Please be advised that your payment due date has been changed to the tenth day of each month.（請留意，您的付款期限已改為每個月的第十六天。）

如果是召開會議的公告內容，也可能說明會議進行的流程等其他細節。

例如：The candidates who volunteer to improve the welfare of local people will share their thoughts before the board of directors election.（自願義務改善本地人福祉的候選人將會在監理事選舉之前分享他們的想法。）

公告架構 ③：結語（closing）

• 請公告對象注意的事項或其他相關訊息。

公告結尾可提供其他相關訊息，或說明希望公告對象注意的改變。例如：Enclosed is the new version of credit card agreement; the amended terms have been highlighted for you.（附檔為新版本的信用卡合約；修改過的條文已為您特別標示出來。）

在會議相關的公告中，可能會加上與會者需要注意的事項。例如：Local residents are welcomed to participate in the meeting. Online registration is required. Advance registration deadline is October 5th.（歡迎本地居民參與這次會議。需要在線上登記。登記的期限是十月五日。）

 **單字裝入袋**

撰寫正式通知的時候，可以依照溝通事項的不同，選用下列的單字：

◆ 表示「宣告」的相關動詞

❶	宣布	announce
❷	通知	notice/ inform
❸	提到	mention
❹	揭露	reveal
❺	示意	signal
❻	介紹	introduce
❼	報告	report
❽	建議	advise
❾	要求	request
❿	決定	settle
⓫	提議	propose
⓬	極力主張	urge
⓭	分享	share
⓮	慶祝	celebrate

◆ 公告相關的形容詞

❶	開心的	happy / pleased / delighted
❷	榮幸	honorable
❸	驕傲	proud
❹	失望	disappointed

◆ 公告相關的名詞

❶	宣告	announcement
❷	資訊	information
❸	政策	policy
❹	報告	report
❺	附件	attachment
❻	指示	instruction
❼	程序	procedure
❽	請求	request
❾	截止日	deadline
❿	列表	listing
⓫	進度	progress
⓬	狀態	status
⓭	回饋意見	feedback
⓮	通知	notice
⓯	總結	summary
⓰	指導原則	guideline
⓱	概要	outline
⓲	提醒	reminder

◆ 催收款項聲明相關單字

❶	債務	debt
❷	未支付的	outstanding
❸	逾期的	overdue

❹	餘額	balance
❺	催收	collect
❻	負債	liability
❼	逾期的	past-due
❽	有關的	concerned
❾	誤解的	misunderstanding
❿	未付的	unpaid
⓫	使成為必須	necessitate
⓬	優良信譽	creditworthiness
⓭	未付款	nonpayment
⓮	償清	repayment

◆ 與聲明相關的單字

❶	協議	agreement
❷	條件	condition
❸	談判	negotiation
❹	交易	transaction
❺	安排	arrangement
❻	義務	obligation
❼	條款	provision
❽	許可	consent
❾	決議	settlement
❿	規定	stipulation
⓫	授權	warrant

⑫	條款	clause
⑬	保證	guarantee
⑭	簽名同意	underwrite

 **句型萬用包**

　　開始下筆寫作前，總要想好一篇作文要如何開頭、承接、結尾。快來把以下的句型套色的部份當作模板，然後在黑色畫底線的部份依照自己的狀況放入適合的單字（想不出填什麼的話，也可以可參考前面「實用單字」的部份找尋靈感）。這樣就能輕鬆完成考場必備的超實用金句、一口氣加好幾分！

• 第一部分：文章開頭先背這些句型！

❶ （某單位）（表示開心／遺憾等形容詞）宣布（公告的事項）。

Broadband Civil Engineering, Inc., is joyful to announce the opening of offices in Taipei and Taichung City.

---

❷ 在此通知（公告的主題）。

An official notice is hereby given that Master City Bank has been relocated to 120 Majestic Avenue, Daan District, Taipei City.

A public announcement is hereby given that merger of Vigilant Renewable Energy, Co. Ltd. and Golden Power Corporation takes effect on January 1st.

---

❸ （某單位）愉快地宣布（公告的事項）。

Mrs. Rachael Whites takes pleasure in announcing the engagement of her daughter Mandy to Edward Sweitzer.

It is with great pleasure that Taylor' outfit shop announces that it has moved to its new location, which is right next to Mega City in Xinyi District City, Taipei.

---

❹ （某單位）想宣布以下事項（公告的事項）。

The administrative office would like to announce the following guidelines for the fire drill on March 30, 2020.

The management committee of the building would like to announce the following principles for building maintenance.

• 第二部分：文章開展再記這些句型！

❶（新規定）將會於（指定的時間）生效。

The new regulations and stipulations will take effect on April 10, 2020.

The new policy of property tax deduction will be implemented on May 10, 2020.

---

❷ 請見以下資訊以了解（公告相關的事項）。

See below for the new procedure for travel reimbursements. / See below for the outline projected work through the end of the year.

---

❸（某單位）說明（公告相關事項）程序變更。

The human resource department would clarify recent changes in procedure of the maternity leave application. / The accounting office would clarify recent changes in procedure of reimbursing the expenses on the business trip.

• 第三部分：文章收尾就用這些句型！

❶（某單位）應履行（公告相關的規定）。

All employees should comply with the amended stipulation in the agreement. / Owners of Mastercard should comply with the new stipulations in the agreement.

---

❷（公告對象）都應該（預期有的作為）。

All residents are expected to follow the revised condominium maintenance guidelines. / All citizens are welcomed to join the public concert at the auditorium of the city hall.

 模擬小示範

連接超實用的單字和好用的必備模板句型，就能拼出一篇完整的文章囉！

Announcement of Relocation of Store
商店喬遷公告

We are pleased to announce that **the store of Pink Lady Outfit will be relocated from Tokyo to Hokuto City in Yamanashi Prefecture as of December 1, 2020.** Over the past few years, we were so crowded in the old location that our customers sometimes have to stand shoulder to shoulder or squeeze through the aisles. After we move to the new store, it would be easier for shoppers to browse through the items and find the ideal outfit in their mind. The convenient parking and amenities like children ball pit and lounge area of our new store will being our customers the more relaxing shopping experience.

Enclosed is a map showing the new location, along with one-time 20 percent discount coupon. All our regular customers are welcomed to visit us while the paint is still fresh!

商店喬遷公告

我們很高興通知您**粉紅佳人服飾店將於2020年12月1日從東京搬遷到山梨縣北斗市。**過去幾年來，我們舊址店面是如此擁擠，以致於顧客可能要站得離彼此很近或者勉強用擠的走過通道。在我們搬到新的店面之後，購物者可以比較輕鬆地瀏覽商品並且找的他們心目中的理想服裝。我們新店面停車方便，也有小孩球池以及休息區，讓我們的顧客可以有更加放鬆的購物經驗。

附檔中是我們店面新地址的地圖，還有一個可以使用一次的八折優惠券。歡迎我們的常客趁著一切新鮮的時候來店消費。

Announcement of Annual Assembly
會議公告

An official notice is hereby given **that the annual assembly of Marketing Department in AC & G Automobile Co., Ltd. will be held on May 5th, 2020 at Conference room 2 in the 7th floor of our headquarter building.**

The attached outline covers the projected work through the end of the year. The outline was specified in accordance with the resolution of the latest board meeting. We will review progress on the first of each month and adjust the work and timelines accordingly. Our department plays a significant role in this company and we need the interlocking pieces to fit comfortably. Also, your attendance will be taken as a factor for the merit evaluation system.

Please review the scheduled work and let me know your opinion, particularly of the feasibility of project goals and deadlines.

年度大會通知

　僅此通知**AC&G 汽車公司行銷部門年度大會將會在2020年5月5日於總部大樓七樓的第二會議室**舉行。

　　附檔的大綱涵蓋直到年底前的工作概要。這份大綱是根據最近一次董事會議的決議所擬定的。我們會在每月1日檢視進度並且調整工作與時程。我們的部門在公司扮演重要的角色，我們需要互相聯繫才能自在地配合。此外，您於此會議的出席會被納入考核因素中。

　　請參閱排定的工作項目並且告知您的意見，特別是關於案件進行以及完成期限的可行性。

 更上一層樓

　　學會使用模板句型寫出一篇漂亮的文章後，還可以怎麼在一些小地方讓文章錦上添花呢？

1. Announcement of New Service

Perfect Financial Services Inc. would like to announce that **we are certified as the professional institution to offer the following services**:

1 A complete review and analysis of our clients' financial structure and condition.

2.The preparation of written investment objectives outlining preferable investments. portfolio foals, risk limits, and diversification possibilities.

3.The establishment of preferred depository or certificate agreements with banks or saving and loans.

4.Providing monthly portfolio status reports with sufficient detail for accounting and recording purposes.

The Perfect Financial Service Inc. will submit quarterly statements for service. Our fees will be billed in advance. Fees can be reviewed and adjusted annually on the anniversary date determined collaboratively by Perfect Financial Service Inc. and the client. Our qualification for as the service providers takes effect on January 1st, 2020.

新服務的公告

完美金融服務公司在此宣佈<u>我們成為一個合格機構，可提供下列服務：</u>

1. 針對客戶的財務結構與狀況提供完整的審查和分析。

2. 準備書面投資計畫，簡述事宜的投資對象、投資目標、風險限額、及分散風險的可能性。

3. 安排適合的儲蓄機構、銀行證券或儲蓄信貸。

4. 提供每月投資報告，內含可供會計與記帳使用之充分細節。

完美金融服務公司將會每季提供服務報表。我們會提前寄發帳單。完美金融服務公司會和客戶一起，每年在雙方共同指定的日期審閱及調整服務費率。我們提供這些服務的資格自2020年1月1日起生效。

★這篇文章具備了公告的基礎架構，在開頭和結尾應用到常用的句型，對讀者來說簡明易懂。

2. Announcement of Business Merger

Dear customer,

Paragon Electronics and Ace Computer are jointly announcing that **we are officially operating as one corporation titled as Petragon, Co., Ltd.**

Over the past years, many of you have expressed support for this combination, and we appreciate your confidence in our ability in coordination of hardware and software. We pledge our commitment to enabling your success and delivering the benefit we expect from this merger.

Our combination creates the most comprehensive offering of on-demand and on-promise situations available today, giving customers choice in how they procure, develop, implement, and deploy the hardware and software resources for business application.

Our regular customers are encouraged to **interact with us through the online forum of Petragon, Co. Ltd.** Please visit our official website for detailed information about the innovation after the combination, how the user groups are merged, and consumer service.

Thank you for your continued support.

Sincerely,

Jason Wu

President, Paragon Electronics

公司合併公告

敬愛的顧客，

　　模範電子和王牌電腦共同宣布**我們會將會正式合併為和碩運作**。

　　過去幾年來，許多貴客戶對這次整併表達支持，我們感謝貴客戶的對我們整合硬體與軟體能力的支持。我們會竭盡所能確保貴客戶能夠因為這次合併而獲得最大的利益。

　　我們的整併創造出最全面的服務來協助辦公室情境中的即時需求，同時提供顧客更多選擇，符合採購、發展、安裝、及部署硬體與硬體資源於商業應用上的更多選擇。

　　歡迎**老顧客透過和碩有限公司的線上討論區和我們互動**。請上我們的官網了解更多合併後創新措施、用戶群組合併方式、以及客戶服務的細節。

　　　　　　　　　　　　謝謝您持續的支持。

　　　　　　　　　　　模範電子總裁 吳傑森 敬上

★公告開門見山地說明主旨，也就是公司合併。公告內容表達對讀者（公司客戶）的感謝，並且交代了如何查詢公司合併後會有的變化。

實戰克漏字

◆ 填充翻譯式引導作文

翻譯能翻得好的人，絕對也能寫出順暢的英文作文！直接開始下筆還沒有把握的話，先從把中文翻譯成英文開始做起吧！每篇文章都有中文可以參考，請照著中文填入單字片語，這樣就可以很快熟悉文章的結構、瞭解到句型如何實際運用在文章裡了。套上顏色的地方，都有套用前面的模板句型喔！

題目 ①：An announcement of Vaccination

提示：寫一段官方聲明，提醒地方民眾接種流感疫苗。

Influenza Vaccination made mandatory during peak season

A 1 _____ announcement is 2 _____ given that vaccination of flu will be made mandatory for children 3 _____six and elderly people who are 65 and older during the peak season of flu.

Previously, influenza vaccines were 4 _____ voluntarily. The vaccine is known for 5 _____ people from four different flu 6 _____, including an influenza A (H1N1) virus, another influenza A (H3N2) virus, and two influenza B viruses. Vaccinating the 7 _____ can protect them 8 _____ infection for about two years. On the other hand, flu shots can 9 _____ babies and children 6 months to 9 years old 10 _____ the flu season.

流感高峰期必須接種流感疫苗

僅此公告，流感盛行期間，6歲以下的孩童和65歲以上的老年人都必須要接種流感疫苗。

先前，人們可以依照個人意願接種流感疫苗。此種疫苗可以防止人們感染四種不同的流感病毒，包括一種A型流感(H3N2)病毒、另一種A型流感疫苗(H3N2)病毒、以及兩種B型流感病毒。老年人接種疫苗可以保護他們兩

年左右不受感染。另一方面，流感疫苗可以保護六個月的寶寶到九歲的孩童於流感盛行季節抵抗病毒。

To 11 _____ the flu outbreak, the 12 _____ government of Golden City has made taking flu 13 _____ mandatory for residents who are 14 _____ to infection of flu 15 _____. People who are registered as Golden City residents are eligible to take the 16 _____ influenza vaccination. The policy takes effect on November 20, 2020. All 17 _____ who fulfill the above-mentioned 18 _____ are expected to 19 _____ the influenza vaccination at the 20 _____ clinics or community health centers.

為了預防流感爆發，黃金市政府宣布容易感染流感病毒的族群都必須要接種疫苗。戶籍設在黃金市的居民都以資格可以接種政府補助的流感疫苗。這個政策在2020年11月20日生效。符合上述條件的居民應該要在指定的診所或者社區健康中心接種流感疫苗。

• 填空引導式參考解答

❶ public	❾ protect	⓱ residents
❷ hereby	❿ through	⓲ conditions
❸ under	⓫ prevent	⓳ receive
❹ taken	⓬ municipal	⓴ designatede
❺ protect	⓭ shots	
❻ viruses	⓮ vulnerable	
❼ elderly	⓯ viruses	
❽ against	⓰ subsidized	

提示： 請寫一封表揚優良護士的頒獎公告，文中註明得獎者、表揚的時間地點、並邀請同仁參加。

To: All hospital staff

It is with great 1 _____ to announce that nurse Nicole Kidman has been 2 _____ as the year's recipient of the Nurse of the Year Award. This 3 _____ is given annually to a 4 _____ that demonstrate exceptional 5 _____ and devotion to the duty while 6 _____ the health care profession. It's a prestigious 7 _____ that serves to recognize the best of the best within our ranks.

Ms. Kidman is a 10-year 8 _____ of our hospital, having been taking care of hundreds of 9 _____ during her tenure here. She is a certified 10 _____ practitioner, and she is also qualified for dealing with medical 11 _____ affairs. Nurse Kidman has 12 _____ an Associate's degree in Medical Practice, and she is currently working on her Master's degree on Medical Science from Nobel University. She also teaches health care lessons to 13 _____ school children in our district.

致全體員工

在此很高興宣布本院護士尼可‧基曼女士獲選為本年度最佳護士獎得主。這個獎項每年會頒發給在執行健康照護業務時有出眾的耐心以及投入的護理人員。這是我們這一個行業的最高榮譽。

基曼女士是在我們的醫院工作10年的資深護士，已經照顧過數百名的病患。她是一位合格的護理人員，她也有資格可以處理醫療行政業務。護士基曼女士有醫療照護的副學士學位，而她目前在諾貝爾大學攻讀醫療科學的碩士學位。她也有在我們的行政區教小學生有關健康照護的課程。

In choosing the 14 _____, several things are considered, including years of service, leadership, and 15 _____. What set Ms. Kidman from other 16 _____ was her ability to deal with stressful situations, along with the fact that he has served as a 17 _____ for several novice nurses over the past few months.

Mayor Benedict Cumberbatch will formally 18 _____ this award to Ms. Kidman at a 19 _____ held at City Hall on October 10th at 7 p.m. I hope you will make plans to attend this banquet in order to show your 20 _____ for one of our own. In the meantime, you are 21 _____ to extend your personal 22 _____ whenever you see her.

Sincerely,

Robert Downey

Hospital President

在選擇受獎者時，有幾項條件會那納入考慮，包含服務年資、領導能力、以及人格特質。基曼女士與其他候選人不同之處在於她處理高壓情境的能力，而且她在過去幾個月裡，擔任過幾位新任護士的職場導師。

市長班尼迪克‧康柏拜區將會在10月10日晚上七點於市政廳的晚宴上正式將此獎項頒發給基曼女士。我希望各位可以計畫去參加這個晚宴，表達對我們自己人的支持。同時，也鼓勵各位在遇到基曼女士時可以對她表達祝賀之意。

院長 勞勃‧道尼 敬上

• 填空引導式參考解答

❶	pleasure	❾	patients	⓱	mentor
❷	chosen	❿	medical	⓲	present
❸	award	⓫	administration	⓳	banquet
❹	nurse	⓬	obtained	⓴	support
❺	patience	⓭	elementary	㉑	encouraged
❻	practicing	⓮	recipient	㉒	congratulations
❼	honor	⓯	character		
❽	veteran	⓰	candidates		

 **高階填空題**

把文章的句型和結構都練熟了，已經有信心可以不用參考範文自己寫一篇了嗎？從這裡開始，你可以依照自己的狀況，套用模板句型練習寫作。請從以下的題目中選一個，現在就開始寫吧！

> **題目 ①：**請寫一份新任執行長接任的公告內容包含宣布公司即將任用新的顧問，介紹新任顧問。

1. We are pleased to introduce_____, who has recently joined us as a Consultant for _____.

Sunder Pichai earned his degree from _____ _____ and is _____ __. He holds a _____ _____, and an _____ _____, where he was named _____ _____, respectively. Prior to joining _____ _____, Pichai worked in _____. He brought with his over 10 years of _____ _____ experience.

Pichai will be responsible for_____ _____ _____.

We are confident that Mr. Pichai will fulfill his role to the best of his ability and to _____ _____.

• 自由發揮的參考解答範本：

1. Announcement of new Executive

We are pleased to introduce Sunder Pichai, who has recently joined us as a Consultant for Petragon Electronics.

Sunder Pichai earned his degree from Indian Institution of Technology Kharagpur in metallurgical engineering and is a distinguished alumnus from that institution. He holds a Master of Science from Stanford University in material science and engineering, and an MBA from the Wharton School of the University of Pennsylvania, where he was named a Siebel Scholar and a Palmer Schoolar, respectively. Prior to joining the electronics sector, Pichai worked in the Computer Science industry. He brought with his over 10 years of hardware and software management experience.

Pichai will be responsible for liaising with our clients and providing them with the best strategies to maximize the efficiency in hardware and software management.

We are confident that Mr. Pichai will fulfill his role to the best of his ability and to maintain our standard of proficiency in business.

> **題目②**：New product Lunch Announcement 請寫一個宣佈新產品發行的公告，介紹新產品。

Dear _____,

　　We are excited to announce _____.
It's an app that can _____.

　　In the last few months, we have been tirelessly working to improve out service and we believe that the _____ can help _____ to _____.

　　So, what is _____ about?

　　When you register for _____, you will _____. Then, the system will _____ _____. Then, you can use the App to _____ _____. The feature of _____ is that _____. This serves as _____ _____.

　　You can download our app directly from the App Store and Google Play. The first 50_____ who register for the App can enjoy _____.

　　Sincerely,

　　_____

2. New Product Lunch Announcement

Dear English Enthusiast,

We are excited to announce the release of our new App, Chatty Bird. It's an app that can connect you to our native speaker teachers for practicing English conversation.

In the last few months, we have been tirelessly working to improve our service and we believe that the Chatty Bird can help enthusiastic English learners like you enjoy the experience of learning conversational skills and being exposed to authentic English language input.

So, what is Chatty Bird about?

When you register for Chatty Bird, you will take a grading test. Then, the system will lead you to the page that list of conversation classes that cover different themes according to your proficiency level. Then, you can use the App to learn English through the dialogue with the qualified teachers. The feature of Chatty Bird is that the teacher can display the new words or new concepts to the learners by writing down the phrases on a specially designed whiteboard that is connected to the screen. This serves as the visual aids for the learners.

You can download our app directly from the App Store and Google Play. The first 50 students who register for the App can enjoy 10 free classes.

Sincerely,

Sesame Language Institute

Chapter

5

書信聲明文

Note

原來如此 系列 E223

深度解密！完勝英文寫作的十二種關鍵分類精華技法！

超精準學習分類，以12大情境教你正確建立寫作脈絡邏輯！

作　　　者	李宇凡◎著
顧　　　問	曾文旭
社　　　長	王毓芳
編輯統籌	耿文國、黃璽宇
主　　　編	吳靜宜、姜怡安
執行主編	李念茨
執行編輯	吳佳芬
美術編輯	王桂芳、張嘉容
封面設計	阿作
法律顧問	北辰著作權事務所　蕭雄淋律師、幸秋妙律師

初　　　版	2020年04月
出　　　版	捷徑文化出版事業有限公司
電　　　話	（02）2752-5618
傳　　　真	（02）2752-5619

定　　　價	新台幣320元／港幣107元
產品內容	1書

總 經 銷	采舍國際有限公司
地　　　址	235 新北市中和區中山路二段366巷10號3樓
電　　　話	（02）8245-8786
傳　　　真	（02）8245-8718

港澳地區總經銷	和平圖書有限公司
地　　　址	香港柴灣嘉業街12號百樂門大廈17樓
電　　　話	（852）2804-6687
傳　　　真	（852）2804-6409

▶本書部分圖片由 Shutterstock、freepik 圖庫提供。

捷徑 Book站

現在就上臉書（FACEBOOK）「捷徑BOOK站」並按讚加入粉絲團，
就可享每月不定期新書資訊和粉絲專享小禮物喔！

http://www.facebook.com/royalroadbooks
讀者來函：royalroadbooks@gmail.com

國家圖書館出版品預行編目資料

深度解密！完勝英文寫作的十二種關鍵分類精華
技法！／李宇凡著. -- 初版. -- 臺北市：捷徑文化,
2020.04
　面；　公分
　ISBN 978-986-5507-17-6(平裝)
　1. 英語　2. 作文　3. 寫作法
805.17　　　　　　　　　　　　　　109001420